ANGEL IN RED

Christopher Nicole titles available from
Severn House Large Print

Cold Country, Hot Sun
A Fearful Thing
The Falls of Death
The Followers
The Voyage
Ransom Island

ANGEL IN RED

Christopher Nicole

Severn House Large Print
London & New York

This first large print edition published 2009
in Great Britain and the USA by
SEVERN HOUSE PUBLISHERS LTD of
9-15 High Street, Sutton, Surrey, SM1 1DF.
First world regular print edition published 2006 by
Severn House Publishers Ltd., London and New York.

British Library Cataloguing in Publication Data

Nicole, Christopher
  Angel in red. - Large print ed.
  1. Fehrbach, Anna (Fictitious character) - Fiction 2. World
  War, 1939-1945 - Secret service - Germany - Fiction
  3. Suspense fiction 4. Large type books
  I. Title
  823.9'14[F]

ISBN-13: 978-0-7278-7754-3

Printed and bound in Great Britain by
MPG Books Ltd, Bodmin, Cornwall.

'Oh, wherefore come ye forth in triumph from the north,
          from the north,
With your hands, and your feet, and your
          raiment all red?'

Lord Macaulay

Contents

Prologue

Visiting the Countess always induced in me mixed feelings of apprehension and anticipation. It was difficult not to be apprehensive of a woman who had rubbed shoulders with many of the most famous, and infamous, people of her time; who had cut her way through them and lived to tell the tale, while nearly all of them were dead. She had told me that her survival had been due largely to her speed of thought and decision, comparable perhaps to that of a great batsman at cricket, who has the ability to determine the length and direction of the ball, and thus the stroke to be played, a split second faster than ordinary mortals.

At the same time it was impossible not to anticipate being in the intimate presence of a woman known for her numerous love affairs who, when well into her eighties, retained sufficient evidence of her former beauty to quicken the blood. I had searched for this woman, or any trace of her, for some forty years. I had always believed that she was still alive, and at last I had found her and been granted an interview. That had been the most thrilling experience of my life. And now I had been invited back again!

The villa was several hundred feet up the mountain known as Montgo, overlooking the Jalon

Valley on the Spanish Costa Blanca. The narrow road twisted its way up the hillside until one reached the villa's wrought-iron gates. A wire fence extended to either side, and indeed round the entire property. There was no evidence of any serious deterrent to intruders besides the locked gates, but as the Countess had illustrated to me on my previous visit, she was not only capable of protecting herself, but was also prepared to go out in a blaze of glory, taking as many of her surviving enemies with her as she could. She had always been prepared to do that. I got out of the car and rang the bell.

'Si?' asked the familiar voice of the Spanish maid.

I preferred to stick to English, which I knew she understood. 'It is Mr Nicole, Encarna.'

'Ah! Señor Nicole! The Countess is expecting you.'

The electrically controlled gates swung open and I drove up the hill to park behind the house. Encarna was waiting for me. She was a plumply pretty young woman. I had no idea if she knew anything of her mistress's background.

'The Countess is on the naya,' she said, and led me through the house to the glass double doors that led on to the veranda.

Anna Fehrbach sat in her favourite cane armchair looking down at the swimming pool below, one hand resting on the glass-topped table beside her. Even sitting her height was obvious. She remained slim – perhaps too slim for her age – but the swell of her loose shirt hinted that little had changed since the days when she had turned

10

heads in every drawing room in Europe. Her bone structure was perfection, providing her face with the most flawless features, even if the suntanned flesh was perhaps a little thin. She had long since cut the magnificent straight golden hair I had admired in her early photographs, and now wore it just below her ears; it was quite white.

Her exposed earrings were tiny gold bars dangling from a gold setting, and she wore a single ring on the third finger of her right hand; the size of the ruby solitaire suggested that it could well pay for the entire villa. A solitary indication of her essentially innocent Catholic girlhood was the gold crucifix on a chain round her neck. I could not stop myself from looking to see if I could spot the automatic pistol she apparently always kept handy and could produce with such startling rapidity. But to me it was invisible.

'Mr Nicole. I have decided to call you Christopher, since you have returned to see me again.' Her voice, low but still resonant, retained just a hint of the Irish brogue she had inherited from her mother.

'After what you told me the last time, no human power could have kept me away,' I replied.

'Then you must call me Anna. Sit down. Encarna!'

Encarna hurried forward with the tray on which rested an ice bucket containing an open bottle of Bollinger and two flutes. Anna now raised hers.

'Here is to ... story-telling. So, now you know one of my secrets, or perhaps two. Have you told anyone what I said the last time?'

11

'I have it on my computer, ready for publication when you give your permission. I shall, of course, submit it to you first for your approval.'

'Thank you. And what do you think of Anna Fehrbach, Countess von Widerstand, the Honourable Mrs Ballantine Bordman? What a mouthful. And that was all before I was twenty!'

'As I said when last we met, Anna, the biggest regret of my life is that I wasn't around to meet you then.'

She gave one of her entrancing smiles. 'But then you would not be sitting here now. It is always better to be alive than dead.'

'Do you glory in the number of people you have killed? You have confessed to seven ... ah...'

'Murders?' she asked gently. 'And those too were by the time I had celebrated my twentieth birthday. But only two were actually murders. Or, as my employers would have it, "executions". The other five were in self-defence. As were most of the others,' she added reminiscently.

'Were there very many others?'

Another smile. 'That is what you are here to find out, isn't it? But is that all you wish to know of me?'

'I wish to know everything about you. I know you were forced to do what you did. Will you tell me about your family, and about the hold Himmler and Heydrich had on you?'

Now the smile faded. 'It was a very sad period of my life. Where would you like me to begin?'

'After you escaped England, in May 1940, you returned to Germany as a double agent. Were you welcomed?'

'Oh, indeed, thanks to the British press trumpeting about the beautiful German spy who had escaped capture. My Nazi masters were very pleased with me.'

'And they allowed you to see your parents.'

'After a while. Heydrich decided to take a month to debrief me.' Her mouth twisted. 'You may take that literally if you wish.'

'That must have made it difficult for MI6 to contact you.'

'It did.'

'And then Russia,' I mused. 'Is it true that you are the only person ever to escape the Lubianka? How did you manage that?'

Anna Fehrbach smiled.

One

Memories

The Mercedes Tourer proceeded slowly through the trees. The road was hardly more than a track and very uneven. Tall pines clustered to either side and turned the bright June morning gloomy. Captain Wilhelm Evers glanced at the woman seated beside him. He was a slim young man, handsome in the black uniform of the SS and, unusually for an officer in that elite corps, he was nervous. When the woman returned his glance, he gulped anxiously.

He had been told that Anna Fehrbach was not yet twenty-one. Certainly her face, shaded by a huge picture hat with its blue ribbon fluttering in the faint breeze, suggested the most utter innocence. But, from what he had been told, her beauty alone would have affected any man. Her slightly aquiline features were flawlessly carved and enhanced by the shroud of her long, straight, pale-golden hair. She was several inches taller than himself, and the calf-length blue dress she was wearing indicated that her figure would almost certainly match her beautiful face.

15

She looked utterly calm, even relaxed, her blue eyes hidden behind her dark glasses. But, according to Colonel Glauber, she was the most treasured agent of the SD – the *Sicherheitsdienst*, the most secret of the German secret services. And today he was to be her minder. He licked his lips. 'You do understand, Fraulein, that there are certain things you may not say?'

'I understand.' Her voice was low, soft, caressing.

'And I am to allow you only half an hour in there.'

'Half an hour. After two years. It is not very long.'

'The visit has been arranged at *your* request, Fraulein. Not theirs. It is for your reassurance. We have arrived.'

Before them stood a pair of large wooden gates. To each side an equally high barbed-wire fence extended out of sight. There could be no doubt that they were entering a prison. A guardhouse stood immediately within the gates and from this two uniformed men now emerged.

'Herr Captain!' shouted one of the men. 'This is a restricted area.'

Evers took a folded sheet of stiff paper from his breast pocket. 'The order is signed by General Heydrich.' He passed it through the bars.

The sergeant read it and then saluted. 'Heil Hitler!' He signalled to the private, who opened the gates. Evers got back into the car and drove through. By this time the two soldiers had noticed his companion, and now three more men emerged from the hut to stare at the young woman. Perhaps, Anna thought, they are hoping I am a new inmate, with the promise of future unimaginable pleasures. She smiled at them, and the car drove on.

Within seconds the tall gates and barbed-wire fence were out of sight as they rounded a bend. Several rustic buildings with thatched roofs came into view. The setting was idyllic, save for the armed guards standing outside the largest of the buildings – and the two Alsatian dogs that now advanced, fur bristling and teeth bared.

An officer emerged from the building. 'Do not get out,' he called. 'I will have the dogs chained.'

Anna Fehrbach ignored him, released her door catch, and stepped down.

'My God, no!' Evers shouted.

The dogs emitted low growls and ran at her. Anna stood absolutely still and, taking off her glasses, stared at them. They halted within a few feet of her, returning her stare for a few seconds before sitting down, clearly uncertain as to what to do next.

'Holy shit!' the officer exclaimed, coming up beside her. 'They are trained to kill!'

'So am I,' Anna said, as softly as ever.

The officer looked at Evers. 'Fraulein Fehrbach is here by order of the SD,' Evers

17

explained.

'To...' The officer now looked at Anna, and swallowed.

'To see my parents, Herr Major,' Anna said. 'And my sister.'

'Ah.' The major nodded. 'Of course. Please come inside, Fraulein.'

Anna walked past him to the open door. The two dogs padded along behind her. The three guards stood to attention, clearly petrified. Anna heard the major giving instructions and a moment later he joined her.

'In here, Fraulein,' he invited, opening an inner door.

'I am to see them alone,' Anna reminded him.

He looked at Evers who had followed them into the office. 'General Heydrich has agreed to this?'

Evers nodded. 'The Fraulein understands where her duty lies.'

The door was opened and Anna stepped into what seemed like a large games room. There were straight chairs arranged around the walls and a ping-pong table in the centre of the floor. Her practised eye immediately picked out wall fittings that might contain microphones or hidden cameras. The door behind her closed. She took off her hat and walked slowly across the room, her high heels clicking on the wood. She faced another door, which now opened to allow two women to enter the room.

'Annaliese?' cried the older of the pair,

18

taking a couple of steps forward. 'Is it really you?'

Anna placed her hat and glasses on the table. 'Mama!'

They hugged each other tightly for a long time, and then Jane Fehrbach held her daughter at arms' length.

'How well you look, Anna.' She spoke English, her mother tongue, as she had always spoken English to her daughters.

'And you, Mama,' Anna replied in turn, although she had no doubt that at least one of the listening Germans would be able to understand English, and she knew that she could neither risk any confidences nor change her pre-determined plan.

Anna's reply was not as truthful as she would have liked. No one could have had any doubt that they were mother and daughter. Jane Fehrbach was in her early fifties. She was tall, with the same golden hair as her daughter, hers worn short and now streaked with grey, and the same chiselled features, but these were lined with stress and worry. Her figure was somewhat fuller, but she moved gracefully enough.

Many people had been astonished when in 1919 Jane Haggerty, correspondent for a top English newspaper, after being sent on assignment to Vienna, had elected to remain there and marry a Viennese journalist. As far as Anna knew, it had been a genuine love match, resulting in her appearance a year later. She had been raised in a liberal background which had, inevitably, taught her to oppose Fascism and the dictators it spawned. Johann Fehrbach had been constantly in trouble with the Dollfuss government, but the real crisis had arisen when, following the dictator's assassination and the relatively relaxed rule of Schusnigg, Hitler had decided to quell further opposition by making Austria part of the Reich.

Anna now recalled the day, just over two years ago, when the Wehrmacht had triumphantly marched into Vienna. Johann and his entire family had been arrested. Anna had not known at the time why she had been separated from her parents and sister. She had been handed over to the SS because, with her beauty and intelligence, she was obviously too valuable to be merely brutalised and then thrown aside.

From the start it had been made clear that if she worked with and for her captors then her family would remain unharmed, albeit in confinement. Should she decide to defy them, she was left in no doubt that her parents would die in a concentration camp while she would be sent to a brothel. And so she had submitted to them, learning how to seduce men when commanded to do so – and to kill them when commanded to do so. Her quick thinking and sharp concentration, regardless of the possible consequences, had made her what she was today: the most valuable agent in the SD.

That she hated them and all they stood for

20

– for their treatment of her as much as for what they had required her to do – was her secret. That she was fighting them in her own quiet way was shared with half a dozen men, but was an even more deadly secret. None of which could possibly be revealed even to her mother, even if she did not know that their conversation was being taped. And so now, jolting herself out of her reverie, she peered at the tormented face in front of her.

'You *are* all right, aren't you, Mama?'

'We are in a prison. But we have a cottage of our own, and your father is given certain writing tasks.' Jane's mouth twisted. 'It is simply that he must write what he is told to write, and that we are not allowed to leave this place.'

'But you are adequately fed? And you are not ill treated?'

'No.'

Anna turned to the girl beside her. Katherine was eighteen and was in many ways a younger version of her sister, but the slight coarseness of her features, and the thickness of her body, indicated that she would never match Anna for looks. Now she in turn came forward for an embrace.

'And Papa?' Anna asked.

Jane sighed, and sat down. 'He would not come. He believes what the guards tell us, that you are working for the Nazis.' She gazed at Anna. 'Will you reassure me so that I can reassure him? He is very distressed.'

Anna returned her mother's gaze for some

seconds. Then she drew a deep breath. 'I am doing what I have to do, Mama, for all of our sakes.'

Slowly a frown gathered between Jane's eyes. She looked Anna up and down, as if for the first time, taking in the obviously expensive frock, the silk stockings, the court shoes, and the many items of valuable jewellery. 'My God! Your father is right. You have become a German whore!'

Even before the interview had been arranged, Anna had realized this was the easiest, and safest, conclusion for her mother to draw, and so had dressed the part. 'As I said, Mama, I do what I have to do to survive. We all need to survive.'

'You unutterable wretch!' Jane stood up. 'I despise you.'

Would you rather be dead? Anna thought. But that was not something she could risk saying to the listening Germans. 'I am sorry, Mama. It will all come right one day, I promise.'

'Not for you,' Jane snapped. 'Not for any of us.' She went to the door, opened it and left the room.

The sisters looked at each other. 'Do you feel the same way?' Anna asked.

'It ... it's all so confusing,' Katherine said. 'Major Luther tells me that if I cooperate I could leave this place. He says that I could become like you.' Her eyes were enormous.

'Would you like to become like me?' Anna asked.

'That dress, that ring ... Would I have things

22

like that to wear?'

'Perhaps.'

'And would I have to sleep with men?'

'Perhaps,' Anna repeated. 'But it can be a difficult life, and it would destroy Mama and Papa. It would be better for you to remain here for the time being.'

'But for how long?' Katherine almost wailed.

'I do not think it will be for very long,' Anna said. 'The war is virtually over. Then things will be different. Be patient and keep your health. Now you had better go.'

'Will I see you again?'

'I am sure of it. One day.'

'An uncooperative woman, your mother,' Captain Evers remarked as the car made its way back along the track to the highway. 'It makes one wonder why such a long journey was necessary for such a brief and unsatisfactory interview.'

'It was necessary to me,' Anna said quietly. 'Where are we going now?'

'To the airport. There is a plane waiting to take you back to Berlin.'

He was looking at her, she knew, but she continued to stare straight ahead. The visit had not lightened her mood, but had she really expected anything better? She knew she would be forgiven everything if her mother knew her true situation. But despite her optimistic words of farewell, she had to wonder if that would ever happen. For eighteen months she had been the Honourable Mrs Ballantine Bordman, to the satisfaction of both her husband and her German masters, thanks to Bordman's position as an under-secretary at the Foreign Office, and his gullible weakness for sharing his professional secrets with the wife he had adored. But she had fled England – and her husband – in the first week of May, when the Allies and Germany had been poised for battle. Both sides had been confident of victory; now, only five weeks later, the Allies were utterly defeated. So where did that leave her, and by extension, her parents? Her value to the Reich lay in her ability to bewitch men as much as to carry out her orders with ruthless efficiency. Were the war to end in an overwhelming German victory, where would her value then lie? There would then surely be no one to seduce and no one to assassinate. Heydrich would have no more use for her, and she knew him well enough to know that he would discard her like a piece of unwanted paper. Her family would undoubtedly follow. As for Clive Bartley, the man for whose love she had agreed to work for the English, while she felt that he personally would do everything he could to extricate her, he was in turn at the mercy of his superiors in MI6. Nor could she ever openly accept his help without destroying her parents. When last they had been together he had been full of confident promises, because soon the British Government would control events in Europe. But as it seemed Germany was not going to be defeated...

'On the other hand,' Evers ventured, interrupting her train of thought, 'I do not suppose there is any great urgency. Would you like to spend a night in Warsaw, Fraulein?' He hurried on, terrified by his own audacity. 'The city has been rather knocked about, but it is still a beautiful place. And there is at least one good hotel still standing.'

He waited, anxiously, until Anna at last turned her head. 'I can think of nothing I would like less, Herr Captain. So please take me to the airport and speak a little less.'

His flush deepened. 'You are a very arrogant woman, Fraulein. I have heard that you do not like men. I can provide a woman, if you wish.'

'Then do so, Herr Captain. For yourself. You are correctly informed. I do not like most men, but that is probably because I have met so few men worth liking.'

The door was opened by a secretary. 'Fraulein Fehrbach, Herr Colonel.'

'Anna!' Colonel Glauber rose from behind his desk and hurried forward.

Before he could reach her, Anna came to attention and saluted, arm outflung. 'Heil Hitler!'

'Ah. Heil Hitler. Come and sit down. You are satisfied?'

Anna sat before his desk and crossed her knees. 'I am satisfied, Herr Colonel, that my parents and my sister are alive and appear to

25

be in good health.'

'Well then...' Glauber's manner was habitually genial; this went with his somewhat overweight figure, bulging against his uniform, and his round red features. Anna knew he was capable of paroxysms of violent rage, but he had seldom inflicted them on her, and she was in a mood to prick him a little.

'But they are depressed and unhappy.'

'Well, they opposed the Reich. They should be in a concentration camp. They *would* be in a concentration camp but for you, my dear girl. However, it will not be for much longer.'

'Can I really believe that, Herr Colonel?'

'You can. The war is over.'

Anna sat straight. 'Sir?'

'France surrendered yesterday.'

'My God!' If this was the news she had been anticipating, it was also the news she had most feared. 'And the British?'

'They are still making bellicose and absurd statements of defiance, or at least that lunatic Churchill is. But as we have destroyed more than half of their air force – and all of their army, to all intents and purposes – this can only be a temporary phase. The Fuehrer is about to make a speech pointing out their situation and calling upon them to accept a negotiated peace. He is the most reasonable of men, you know.'

Anna drew a deep breath. 'Then I am redundant, Herr Colonel.'

Glauber chuckled. 'As regards the British, you were redundant the moment you boarded that ship out of Southampton.' Anna felt a sudden, physical pain in her chest. 'But do you suppose a girl like you could ever be truly redundant? I remember the first time I saw you in Vienna two years ago. A seventeen-year-old schoolgirl sitting on a chair in the middle of that cell. What were you thinking of at that moment, Anna?'

'I was wondering how soon I would be raped or tortured or shot, Herr Colonel.'

'What terrible thoughts for a young girl to think. But do you know Hallbrun – you remember Hallbrun?'

'He arrested me, and my family.'

'Yes,' Glauber agreed. 'But did you know the lout actually offered you to me as a mistress?'

Anna's head jerked.

Glauber smiled. 'And I thought to myself, such beauty, such intelligence, such sheer charisma – in a seventeen-year-old girl! What will she be like when she is a woman? And you suppose you could be redundant? We may have defeated the Western Allies, but that does not mean that the task of Nazi Germany is completed. I told you two years ago what that task was, did I not?'

'To combat Soviet Russia,' she said hesitantly.

'And to *destroy* it,' Glauber insisted. 'I don't suppose you include Russian among your many accomplishments?'

'No, sir.'

'Next week you will begin a course. I wish

27

you to be fluent in the language in one month. Can you do this?'

'If I am doing nothing else, Herr Colonel.'

'That will be your principal concern. However, I do not suppose you had a great many opportunities for training in London. And then there was that business of falling down the stairs. You spent several weeks in hospital, did you not?'

Anna kept her face immobile; she still felt the occasional twinge where Hannah Gehrig's bullet had slammed into her ribs. There was, in fact, still a blue mark on her flesh, which meant she had to be careful about who she let see her exposed body. Heydrich had certainly been curious but she had told him it was a birthmark. 'Yes, Herr Colonel.'

'And when last did you have to undertake executive action?' Glauber asked jovially. 'That unhappy woman, Mayers, was it not?'

How little you know, Anna thought. 'Am I required to execute a Russian, Herr Colonel?' Her voice could be like the cooing of a dove.

'One would hope not. But you never know. I also want you to spend a week with Doctor Cleiner. You will do this first.'

Oh, Lord, Anna thought. The week she had spent in that training camp had been the most horrendous of her life. 'I am perfectly fit, sir, and I have forgotten none of my skills.'

'No one can ever be too highly trained, Anna, not even you. But you do not like the idea of going back to the doctor? He was very fond of you.'

'I know. He will wish to strip me naked and paw me about.' And see the blue mark, she thought.

'The perks of being a doctor. I envy him. You will go to the training camp tomorrow. A car will pick you up at ten. After your spell at the camp, you will undertake concentrated lessons in Russian language, manners, mores and history. That is your programme for the next five weeks. Then you will be given your instructions.' He beamed at her. 'I want you to know – and always be sure – that I, and all of us in the SD, are proud of you. Proud to have you working with us. Now go home, have a good night's rest, and be prepared to start work tomorrow.'

Anna took a taxi to the apartment block situated in a street just off the Unter den Linden. Berlin sparkled in the summer sunshine. It was, in fact, one of the best summers in living memory, and the Berliners, always eager to enjoy sunshine, had been drinking beer at the pavement cafes. But this year, having achieved the most outstanding military success in their nation's history – the more euphoric for being so largely unexpected – there were nothing but smiles to be seen. Indeed, as the news of the French surrender had only recently been released, today there were cheers and dancing on the pavements, giving lie to the fact that there was a war on. But apparently the war was over. Anna was in limbo. From everything she had ever read or heard, Russia was not an attractive prospect. True, what she had been told was largely Nazi propaganda. But the British attitude, including that of Clive Bartley, had not been so very different. Oh, Clive! How she wanted to be in touch with him. But her orders, given her on the night she had fled England, had been to wait. He would get to her. But could she afford to wait, now that she was about to receive new orders from the SD?

When she had left England, she had been given a set of written instructions, to be memorised and then destroyed. They had been simple enough, but the essential words remained burning in her brain: Antoinette's Boutique. Antoinette's Boutique. Did she dare? She had been so occupied with Heydrich over the preceding month, and with the anticipation of seeing her family again after so long, but now...

She leaned forward and tapped on the glass. The driver slid it aside. 'Do you know of a dress shop called Antoinette's Boutique?'

'Oh yes, Fraulein. It has quite a reputation, amongst the...' He looked in the rear-view mirror and judged that Anna had to be an aristocrat. 'It is very expensive. Run by an Italian gentleman.' Now his tone was disparaging.

'Is it far?'

'Three blocks, Fraulein.'

'Take me there.'

He chose his moment and turned across the stream of traffic without further comment.

* * *

As the taxi stopped, Anna realized that his remarks had been entirely appropriate: the only word for Antoinette's Boutique was extravagant, from the richly dressed mannequins in the window to the garishly large letters over the glass swing doors.

'Wait for me,' she said before crossing the pavement and entering the large, airy display room.

A well-dressed woman hurried forward. 'Fraulein? May we be of assistance?'

The emporium might be Italian-owned, but this woman was definitely German.

'I am the Countess von Widerstand,' Anna announced. 'I am seeking an outfit for a party, and I was told by my friend Belinda that this would be a good place to look.'

The woman showed no response to either name. 'I am sure we will have what you require, Countess. If we do not, we shall create it for you.'

Anna had been surveying the visible stock. 'You have your own dressmakers?'

'Certainly, Countess.'

'What I am looking for,' Anna said, having ascertained just what was *not* present, 'is a calf-length, pale-blue sheath, with a scarlet hem and belt.'

The woman clearly had to make an effort not to wrinkle her nose at such appalling taste.

'With scarlet shoes,' Anna added.

'Yes, Countess. I am sure we will be able to

manage that. Unfortunately, two of our seamstresses are off sick, so it may take a week or two.'

'That will be acceptable. The party is in a fortnight. But I must have a fitting by the end of next week. I shall be out of town until then, anyway.'

'Of course, Countess. There should be ... ah...'

Anna opened her handbag and sorted out a hundred marks. 'Will that be sufficient?'

'Of course, Countess. If you will just step inside so that we may take your measurements. And we will require a telephone number.'

Anna took a card from her bag and followed her into one of the fitting rooms.

Later, Anna entered the lobby of her apartment building.

'Good afternoon, Fraulein,' said the concierge. Like most men he was always pleased to see his most glamorous tenant. 'Did you have a good trip?'

'Yes, thank you.' Anna smiled at him and went across to the elevator. Her apartment was on the sixth floor. Every time she entered this apartment she had a sense of disbelief. Her parents' home in Vienna had been comfortably middle class; there had been no money for elegance or excessive luxury. When she had been swept into the clutches of the Gestapo training school she had assumed that even such comforts as she had known would be lost forever. Now she lived in this absolutely sumptuous place, with its soft carpets, deep-upholstered furniture, valuable prints on the walls and a bedroom and bathroom of the very latest and most expensive fashion.

Birgit emerged from the kitchen. Although older than Anna, she was a young, vivacious woman, dark-haired and slender, excitedly enthusiastic at working for who she supposed to be a member of the aristocracy. Anna liked her at least partly because, unlike her previous maids, she was not a superior member of the SD, sent to monitor her every movement and every thought. Did the fact that she had been allowed to find her own maid since returning from England mean that her employers now accepted her as one of them? She had to doubt that.

'Oh, Countess, I did not expect you back until tomorrow.'

'There was nothing to stay for,' Anna said. 'But I am going away again tomorrow for a week.' She looked at her watch; it was just coming up to five. 'So I would like the evening to start now. I will have a glass of champagne, dinner at seven, and then I will go to bed.'

'Yes, Countess.'

Anna undressed and peered at herself in the full-length mirror. There was no ignoring the blue mark some four inches below her right breast. She could remember that afternoon as if it were yesterday, even if at the time she had rapidly fainted from shock and loss of blood. But in those few minutes she had broken Hannah Gehrig's neck, and in doing so all but destroyed her cover. She would have been lost but for Clive. MI6 had acted with a speed and precision not even equalled by the SD disposal squads. The British had let it become known that Frau Gehrig had been uncovered as a German spy, but had managed to flee the country before she could be arrested. The SD were still mystified by her disappearance – still, in fact, expected her to turn up some day, perhaps soon. But that was no longer her concern, except that her story might now have to be revised, and utterly convincingly.

Anna lay in bed that night and stared at the darkened ceiling. In the early days of her career as a spy and seductress – and executioner when required – her then minder, Elsa Mayers, had put her to bed every night with a sleeping pill. Since her marriage to the Honourable Ballantine Bordman she had abandoned the sedatives. Life had not really been any less traumatic, but the knowledge that Clive Bartley was in the shadows behind her had been totally reassuring. Of course she'd also had to endure the attentions of Bally. To him she had been like a toy; he had been unable to keep his hands off her. His constant pawing, his constant desire for sex, had done nothing to better her low opinion of men in general.

She knew there were some people who

believed her to be a closet lesbian. Others, mainly her employers, thought that she was simply devoid of any emotion, erotic or otherwise. This pleased them. They liked the way she went about her duties with cold and calculated ruthlessness. They had no idea of the mental anguish she suffered every time a job was completed – the screaming, mind-consuming desire to get out, the utter despair at the knowledge that she could never do that without sacrificing her parents and sister.

She had, not for the first time, an urgent desire to go to church. She had not confessed for more than two years, since the day before the German invasion of Austria in 1938. But how could she confess now? *Forgive me, Father, for I have sinned. Tell me of these sins, my child. I have killed men and women, over and over and over again. Forgive me, Father, for I have sinned. How have you sinned, my child? I have betrayed people who thought they were my friends, I have betrayed my country, I have betrayed my religion, I have betrayed myself. Forgive me, Father, for I have sinned. How have you sinned, my child? I have lived a lie, I am living a lie, I will go on living a lie for the foreseeable future.*

Only Clive stood between her and perdition. He was the rock to which she must cling, surrounded as she was by a maelstrom of political, emotional and distressing situations. Did she love him? If she did not, it was because she knew she could not allow herself to love anyone while living in these circum-

stances. Besides, she could not be sure if he –
for all his obvious desire for her when they
were alone together – loved her, or wished to
do so. She was a prize, who had dropped
unexpectedly into his arms, and into the arms
of his superiors, a lethal weapon thrust into
the heart of Nazi Germany to be used, twisted, as they thought best for the Allied cause.
She wondered when the first twist would be
made and what it would entail.

And now she was required to return to the
clutches of the man who, of all the dislikeable
men with whom she had been forced to
associate over the past two years, was the
most loathsome.

'May I say, Countess, that it is a great privilege to meet you and to know that we shall be
working together.'

Another nervous young captain was now
sitting beside her in the back of a car. His
name was Gutemann, and like Evers he kept
casting her surreptitious glances, half admiring and half anticipatory, although today she
wore a somewhat severe dress. She was on
her way to work. He was some years younger
than Evers was, and not as good looking. He
seemed anxious at once to please her and to
avoid being overwhelmed by her.

'I am sure that it will be a privilege for me
as well, Herr Captain,' she agreed.

They were out of Berlin and following the
road she remembered so well.

'Then, as we are to be, shall I say, intimate,

shall we not be more friendly? My name is Gunther.'

'Gunther Gutemann,' Anna mused. 'I do not think your parents liked you, Herr Captain. I also do not think that our intimacy should extend beyond, shall *I* say, office hours. We have not yet reached the office, have we?'

He flushed, with a mixture of embarrassment and anger. 'They told me that you were an unnatural creature,' he remarked. 'So beautiful, but so cold.'

'Well,' she said, 'would you not agree that I am engaged in an unnatural pursuit?'

He digested this for some moments, then ventured, 'And if you were instructed by our superiors to have sex with me, would you still be as cold as ice?'

'By no means. I am a professional. I would make you the happiest man in the world.'

'Then...'

'Equally,' she added, 'if immediately afterwards I was instructed by our superiors to kill you, I would do so without hesitation. But it would be as quick and painless as possible.' At last she looked at him and smiled. 'As I said, I am a professional.'

He moved across the seat, as far away from her as possible.

The camp seemed exactly as she had left it two years before; it could have been yesterday. She was not even sure that it wasn't the same sergeant at the desk of the female barracks.

'Fraulein Fehrbach, it is good to see you again. Doctor Cleiner wished to see you the moment you arrived.'

'I shall just place my valise in my quarters,' Anna said.

'I will do that for you, Fraulein.'

'Thank you. Are there any other ladies in residence?'

'There are two, Fraulein. They will be overwhelmed to meet you. But Doctor Cleiner comes first.'

'Of course.' Anna went to the outer door, where Gutemann had waited for her. He fell into step beside her as she walked along the gravelled path towards the doctor's offices.

'I see you know your way about this place,' he suggested.

'Why, yes. Did you not know that?'

Once again he fell silent. But she had a fairly good idea of what he was thinking – how much he would like to have this arrogant bitch in his power for even a few minutes. She found that amusing. She was in the mood, as she had been since that terrible meeting with her mother, to indulge her dislike for the entire human race.

Their walk took them past the parade grounds, filled with sweating, panting recruits being introduced to the weapons they would use in combat. All were under the imperious eyes of their drill sergeants but none could resist the temptation to look at the beautiful young woman in their midst.

Anna reached the command house, went up the short flight of steps, and tapped on the door.

'Enter.'

She opened the door into an outer office where a hard-faced woman sat behind a desk and a typewriter. 'Ah!' the woman said, 'you will be Fehrbach. The doctor is waiting for you.'

Anna crossed the room to the inner door. She knew Gutemann was immediately behind her. She stopped and turned. 'I am sure the doctor will wish to see me alone.'

He gazed at her uncertainly, but she opened the door, stepped through, and closed it behind her before he could react.

'Anna!' Doctor Cleiner hurried round his huge desk and took her in his arms for a bear hug. He was overweight, bald, wore horn-rimmed glasses on a pudgy nose, and sweated. It was several seconds before he released her, his fingers running up and down her spine as if he was looking for a dislocated disc. Then he stepped back, now holding her arms, allowing his hands to slide down her short sleeves and then her forearms to hold her hands. 'It is so good to see you again. And looking so well. Do you know, I would swear that you have not changed a bit in the last two years.'

'Neither have you, Herr Doctor.'

'Ha ha! And I am to make sure that you are as fit, mentally and physically, as when last we met. That is good.'

Cleiner returned behind his desk, sat down and picked up the sheet of paper lying there. 'You are to undergo the complete course, as if you were a novice. But this time I am sure you will find it very easy. And I am sure there are some aspects in which you no longer need instruction. You have enjoyed the experience of being a married woman, have you not?'

There was no other chair in the room, so Anna remained standing before the desk. 'As you say, Herr Doctor.'

'Did you enjoy it, Anna?'

'I was doing a job of work, Herr Doctor.' She wanted to change the subject. 'I understand you have two trainees in residence.'

'Ah, yes. They came in this morning. They are very excited at the prospect of working with you.'

'So, it seems, is Captain Gutemann. Is he necessary?'

'Well, you know he is. But you also know he is not allowed to touch you – or any of the others – unless so commanded by me.' He looked at his watch. 'It is an hour until lunch. There is time for me to give you a physical examination. Undress.'

'I do assure you, Herr Doctor, that I am as fit as, or perhaps even fitter than, I was two years ago.'

'And even more modest? I cannot believe that, Anna, as you are a married woman.'

'I *was* a married woman, Herr Doctor.'

'You still are, my dear girl. Your husband may be suing for divorce, but these things take time. You are likely to remain married for another year.' He chuckled. 'Unless, of course, you were to fall into the hands of the British, when they would terminate matters by hanging you. You are still an English citizen, are you not?'

'You say the most encouraging things, Herr Doctor.'

'But it is not our intention to let that happen. Now come along, Anna. I wish to look at you. I do enjoy looking at you.'

Anna sighed. She had formed a plan as to how to deal with the coming crisis; it was a matter of whether or not he would believe her – and how soon he would divulge what she told him to her superiors. She took off her bandanna, shook out her hair and removed her dress.

'Lay it on that table,' he suggested.

This she did, carefully spreading the material so as to avoid crushing it. Then, with her back to him, she took off her cami-knickers.

'Everything,' he said.

Anna sighed again, although she had known he would require this. She stepped out of her shoes, released her suspender belt and, bending over, rolled down her stockings. She heard him come across the room, and a moment later his hands closed on her buttocks. Instantly she straightened. 'Are you examining me, Herr Doctor?' she asked innocently.

'Why, yes. Turn around.' Anna did so and he looked her up and down. 'As you say, perfection. There can be no more delightful vision than a beautiful naked woman. Even if he discovered you were a spy, that man Bordman must have been out of his mind to divorce you. But do you know, Anna, after what I have read in your file, I almost expected to find a pistol strapped somewhere.'

'I do not need a pistol, Herr Doctor. You taught me not to need a pistol.'

'I did indeed. Although you may remember that I also taught you how to use one. Tell me, how many people have you killed since you shot that fellow here in this camp?'

'At your command, Herr Doctor,' Anna reminded him. 'As for how many others, is it not in my file?'

'Two are listed. Elsa Mayers and Gottfried Friedemann. Both are recorded as enemies of the Reich; one was killed with a bullet, the other with a single blow to the carotid. I taught you that blow, Anna. I am proud of that.'

'May I get dressed, Herr Doctor?'

'Oh, no. I have not yet examined you.'

She waited while he peered at her, keeping her breathing under control. The moment of truth was approaching. Needless to say, he found it necessary to finger her breasts before slowly moving down her ribcage and suddenly bending forward. 'What is this?'

'A bruise, Herr Doctor.'

Cleiner looked more closely, taking off his spectacles as his nose almost touched her flesh. 'I never thought you would lie to me,

Anna. I never thought you would dare. You may have become a valuable member of the SD, but in this camp I retain the power of life and death over any one of my pupils.'

'Herr Doctor...'

Cleiner touched the blue mark with his finger. 'This was a bullet wound.' He straightened. 'There is no record in your file of you having been shot. Why is this?'

Anna licked her lips. 'It was a private matter, Herr Doctor.'

'How can being shot be a private matter?'

'Because it had nothing to do with my mission. My husband shot me.'

'As I suggested, he must have been mad. Why did he shoot you?'

'He thought he had found out that I was having an affair.'

'I see. When did this happen?'

'In August last year.'

Cleiner sat down at his desk to look at her file, replacing his spectacles. 'It says here that in August last year you fell down a flight of stairs and broke several ribs. You were in hospital for over a month.'

'That was the story given to the press, Herr Doctor. Bordman was an important man. We were prominent in London society. If it had come out that he had shot me, the scandal would have been tremendous.'

'I see. So, tell me, had you had an affair?'

'Certainly not.'

'Because you basically do not like men. Or sex.'

43

'That is correct, Herr Doctor.'

'That must have been very frustrating for him. Had I been your husband, I would probably have shot you without the excuse of adultery. Tell me why this incident was never reported to your superiors?'

'As I said, sir, it had nothing to do with my assignment. I did not report it because it would have unnecessarily complicated things.'

'But you went on living with Bordman for another nine months.'

'When he realized his mistake, he was utterly contrite. Besides, I still had my work to do. Being the Honourable Mrs Ballantine Bordman was the very core of my work as an agent. The information I was able to gather in that position was invaluable.'

'And he had nothing to do with the eventual betrayal which caused you to flee England?'

'No,' Anna insisted.

'Well, you understand that I must enter this in your file. It is possible that General Heydrich may wish you to explain it further. Now get yourself dressed and join your fellow pupils.'

Gutemann was waiting for her outside. 'I trust all went well, Fraulein?'

'Why, yes, Herr Captain. Did you suppose it would not? I can find my own way back to the barracks.'

She stepped past him and walked along the

path. She carried her bandanna in her hand and let her hair float behind her. Her heart was pounding. Cleiner had been simple because, like so many of her adversaries, he suffered from the handicap of being more than a little in love with her, but she did not feel that Reinhard Heydrich was capable of being in love with anyone – save perhaps Reinhard Heydrich. But having adopted that cover story she now had to stick with it.

The problem was that the date of her 'accident' was recorded as 25 August 1939. This was the same date as Hannah Gehrig was recorded as having disappeared, just as it was also the day before news had been released of the Nazi–Soviet Pact, which had created the favourable conditions for this war to be started in the first place. She knew that Gehrig had been ordered to flee England, as *she* had not taken out British citizenship, and would almost certainly have been arrested when the news broke. That she had successfully escaped had always been accepted. That her charge and accomplice had fallen down a flight of stairs, while no doubt in an agitated state of mind, had also been accepted. But that that accomplice should have been shot by her husband on the same day that Gehrig had disappeared was perhaps moving into the realms of extreme coincidence.

At the barracks she smiled at the sergeant, went along the corridor and opened the door to the dormitory, which had not changed in two years. There was the same row of neatly made beds along one wall, the same lockers beside each bed, the same shower and toilet facilities at the far end, and the same high, barred windows.

There were also two young women sitting on adjacent beds, engaged in animated conversation, both of whom sprang to their feet as she entered. She smiled at them in turn. 'I am Anna,' she said.

'Anna Fehrbach!' gasped one of the girls; they were both younger than she.

Anna frowned. 'You know my name?'

'We were told it at training school,' the other girl said. 'Do well, they told us, and you could be another Anna Fehrbach.'

Anna looked from one to the other. 'Well then, I think you should introduce yourselves.'

'I am Lena Postitz,' said the first girl. She was a short, dark-haired young woman, with small, somewhat tight features.

'Lena,' Anna said, and turned to the other girl. She was taller, also dark-haired, but with much stronger, handsome features. There was something vaguely familiar about her. 'And you?'

'I am Marlene Gehrig,' the girl replied.

Two

The Boutique

For a moment Anna could not think.

'My mother told me of you,' Marlene Gehrig said. 'She was very proud of you. She often told me that you were the best agent she knew.' She smiled. 'I think she wanted me to be like you. And then she became your Controller.' The features puckered. 'But I have not seen her for nearly a year. Can you tell me where she is now?'

Anna had been making some very rapid calculations. As this girl's name was also Gehrig, Hannah had clearly not married the father. That she had spared the time to get pregnant by any man was a surprise in itself. Having been forced to live with her for several months, Anna had had no doubt that she was a lesbian, and not of the closet variety. As she knew that the SD recruited at least as many volunteers as those they conscripted, the fact that Hannah should have offered her daughter to the services of the Reich was not the least improbable: she had been the most dedicated of Nazis.

'I'm afraid I have no idea where your

mother is now,' she said with her usual convincing innocence. Save, she thought, that I am pretty sure she is somewhere in hell.

'But ... was she not in England with you?'

'Of course. But she received orders to leave England the day it became certain there was going to be a war. This she did. Is she not here in Germany?'

'She never came home,' Marlene said sombrely. 'Nothing has been heard since she left England. What can have happened to her?'

'Oh, my dear girl,' Anna said. 'She was a most capable officer in the SD. I am sure she must be somewhere.'

To her great relief a bugle call rang through the camp. 'Lunch! It is not something you wish to miss.'

As Anna remembered, while they ate in the communal mess hall, the three girls were segregated from the men, and while they attracted interested glances, no one dared speak to them. The large room was entirely overlooked by several NCOs, and all conversation was necessarily in hushed whispers.

'What is going to happen to us?' Lena asked.

'You will begin by learning about men,' Anna told her. 'How to seduce them, and how to allow yourself to be seduced by them.'

'Gosh!' Lena exclaimed. 'Do they ... well...?'

'Oh, yes. You have to touch them, and they have to touch you.'

'But...'

Anna smiled at her. 'You will have to make them very happy.' She gazed at the girl. 'You know what I mean?'

'Oh, good Lord! I have never, well, seen a man. Well, I have, of course, but never, well...'

'Had sex with one? Neither had I, when I first came here,' Anna assured her. 'You will get used to it. You may even enjoy it. It helps if you do.'

'And you enjoyed it?' Marlene spoke for the first time.

Anna met her gaze, sensing hostility that could not be more than instinctive. 'No. I did not enjoy it.'

'But you passed out with honour?'

'Honour? There is no such thing in our profession.'

There was little further conversation over the meal. Lena was lost in a private world; whether it was a world of dreams or nightmares Anna could not be sure. Marlene stared at her between mouthfuls. Anna would have given a great deal to know what was going on inside that brain – what things her mother might have told her.

Well, she thought, we are only going to spend this week together, and then hopefully we may never meet again. And as only she and a handful of British MI6 agents knew the truth of what had happened, any dislike Marlene felt for her must be instinctive, and would remain so. Then she frowned. There were five others in the know: Belinda

Hoskin, Clive Bartley's fashion editor mistress; Bowen, Ballantine's valet; and Ballantine himself, who had walked in on the scene, plus the police inspector and his sergeant who had been summoned. Clive had assured her they had all been sworn to secrecy, and she had to believe that. But the very presence of this rather intense young woman made her uneasy.

She was relieved when the bell went to end the meal.

Anna was even more relieved to find that she was not required to attend the initial classes. She had always found it distasteful to fondle a man and even more to be fondled by him, unless his name happened to be Clive Bartley. Gutemann instead took her off to the gymnasium for a severe workout.

She was also required to attend the hospital for an X-ray of her ribs. Cleiner joined her here. 'It was a long time ago,' she reminded him. 'I am perfectly all right.'

'We must be absolutely sure,' he insisted, and without warning drove his fingers into the scar. Anna gave a squeal and sat up. 'There. You see?'

Anna glared at him. 'I would have reacted the same, Herr Doctor, had you done that on my other side.'

'But I have never seen you react like that. I thought for a moment you were going to hit me.'

'If I had hit you, Herr Doctor, the course

would be over. Unless you have a replacement waiting.'

He chuckled. 'You are a treasure. One day you and I must get together.'

Over my dead body, Anna thought. But she would prefer it to be his.

Needless to say, the other girls were in a twitter in the barracks that evening. Or at least Lena was. Marlene continued to say little and stare at Anna.

'She worships you,' Lena whispered when Marlene went to the bathroom.

'I do not believe that,' Anna said, brushing her hair. 'She is just finding it a bit overwhelming. That is not surprising. I know I was completely overwhelmed on my first day here. Don't tell me you are not affected?'

'Oooh! He was so big. Are all men that big?'

'Thankfully, no,' Anna said, remembering her husband.

'What does it feel like to have a man inside you?'

'It can feel very nice, if it's the right man. Unfortunately, we do not select our partners. Have you never had a boyfriend?'

'Well, I was in the Youth, you know. We had some fun when camping in the woods.'

'But you're still a virgin. Or you wouldn't be here.'

'Well, yes. But isn't it strange, that they want only virgins, when they are training us to seduce men?'

Anna shrugged. 'It is part of their determination to be in total control. You will lose your virginity when it is considered best for the Reich. Not for you.'

'You speak so badly of the Reich. Yet you work for them. They say there is no more dedicated female agent in the service.'

Anna's mouth twisted. 'I do what has to be done. That is the only way to survive.'

By this time Marlene had returned and had overheard the end of the conversation. 'My mother told me you do not like sex at all, either with men or with women. She said that you first came to her attention when you nearly killed a girl who made advances to you at the training school.'

'I broke her arm in two places,' Anna said quietly, wondering just what else Hannah had confided to her daughter. That was something she certainly needed to find out.

'What do we have to do tomorrow?' Lena asked, anxious to defuse the incipient conflict.

'Tomorrow,' Anna said, 'you will be taught how to hurt a man.'

For this lesson Anna was required to remain with the girls. Cleiner beamed at them. 'Yesterday was amusing, was it not?'

Lena and Marlene stared at him, uncertain what response he was seeking.

'What did you enjoy more – playing with him or having him play with you? Come along now.'

Lena licked her lips. 'Playing with him,

Herr Doctor.'

'You would like to have one of your very own, eh? Perhaps even if it was not attached to a body. Ha! And you, Marlene?'

'I did not like him at all, Herr Doctor.' She drew a sharp breath, as if wondering if she had said the wrong thing, and cast a quick glance at Anna, seeking support.

Cleiner gave one of his chuckles. 'Oh, Anna would agree with you. But she has the ability, which you must learn, to make any man feel she desires him more than anything else in the world. This is the secret of her success. As it must become your secret as well. Do you not agree, Anna?'

'As you say, Herr Doctor.'

'But at the same time you must always remember that the man you are told to deal with will be an enemy of the Reich, and therefore an enemy of you. And thus there will be occasions when you must be, shall I say, *rid* of him, perhaps immediately. This means that while learning to love the man, you must also learn how to destroy him, when required.' He smiled at Anna. 'Anna is an expert at this.'

Anna's feelings of discontent were growing all the time. She did not like being depicted as a monster when it was men like Cleiner who had created that monster, just as it was a man like Clive Bartley who had reminded her of both her humanity and her femininity. But the act had to be maintained, whatever her own simmering anger at her position, until exactly the right moment. So she merely smiled.

Cleiner rang the bell on his desk, and immediately the two guards opened the door to admit a man who had been standing outside, also with a guard. A push had him stumbling into the room, trying to maintain his balance; his hands were cuffed behind his back. He seemed just like the man Anna had been given to work on two years before – of medium height but burly, unshaven, and shabbily dressed in shirt and pants and rope-soled shoes. Having got his balance back he blinked at the doctor and then at the three young women, who were as usual wearing only singlets and shorts.

'This is Boris,' Cleiner announced. 'He is a Polish Jew and speaks no German. So he will not interrupt our conversation, eh? Ha ha.'

The girls looked petrified; Anna presumed that the man they had been introduced to the previous day had been young and reasonably attractive. This man was not.

The guard pushed Boris forward to stand in the open space beside the desks at which the girls were seated.

'Now,' Cleiner said. 'This fellow is at least twice the weight of any of you, and I can assure you he is very strong. But there is no man who can withstand an educated and determined attack. The question is to get in your delivery before he gets in his. Now, Lena, supposing you had to completely disable this man, what would you do?'

Lena again licked her lips and glanced at Anna, who remained impassive as usual. 'Well,' she said, 'I suppose I should kick him there.' She pointed at Boris's crotch.

'Anna?' Cleiner asked.

'That would hurt him but not disable him,' Anna said quietly. 'Assuming he did not catch your leg before you could reach him. It would certainly make him very angry.'

'Exactly. When you hit it must be to disable, if only for a few seconds. You go for the pressure points, from which emanate the vital functions of the human body.' He went up to Boris and began touching him with his wand. 'Here. And here. And here. A blow to any one of these places will at least momentarily paralyse his ability to function. Of course, in most cases – certainly with a man like Boris – he will recover quickly enough, so the destruction must be completed during the short time he is incapacitated. Then, for example, if he is down, you may stamp on his neck, or on his genitals. But you must be absolutely certain that he is unable to use his hands, as if he manages to catch hold of you it could turn out very badly. So come along, Marlene. We will start with you.' He stood behind Boris. 'These are the kidneys. A properly delivered blow here will cause the most severe agony. Hit him. Remember that it must be with all the strength you can command.'

Marlene also looked at Anna for a moment, then got up and stepped behind the man and swung her arm. Anna knew that the girl would already have learned the rudiments of unarmed combat and the correct way to deliver a blow, but she did not seem to have any great effect upon Boris. Clearly he was hurt. He grunted and staggered but did not fall, while he looked from one to the other of the people around him with aggrieved eyes.

'No, no!' Cleiner said. 'That was no good at all. You must hit with your full strength. You must get every ounce of your weight into the blow.'

Marlene was massaging her arm and breathing heavily, while Boris, having somewhat recovered, looked around himself in angry bewilderment.

'Anna,' Cleiner said, 'show them how it should be done.'

Anna sighed, but she had known it would come to this. She stood up and took a couple of deep breaths. When something had to be done, it had to be done to the exclusion of everything else. Every thought, every emotion, every hope, every fear, every memory, and any pity had to be entirely excluded. She stepped forward behind Boris and in the same movement swung her arm, delivering all her weight into the edge of her palm. Boris uttered a shriek, fell to his knees, and then over on to his side, moaning and writhing.

'Gosh!' Lena gasped.

Marlene stared at the stricken man.

Cleiner smiled. 'There, you see? I do not expect you to be as good as Anna right away, but you must become so. Get him up,' he told the guards.

It took two of them to set Boris on his feet and he remained unsteady while panting, but the pain was wearing off.

'He may well have suffered permanent damage,' Cleiner pointed out. 'Anna has killed with that right hand. Not with a kidney punch, of course. But there are certain places where a properly delivered blow can be fatal. Illustrate, Anna.'

Anna turned her head sharply.

'Oh,' Cleiner said, 'he is of no more use to us now. Show these young ladies how you disposed of Fraulein Mayers, Anna. I know that General Heydrich was most impressed.'

Anna realized that this was the opportunity she had been waiting for. It was a very high-risk strategy, but if it reduced the later risk of condemnation by Heydrich it would be worth it. 'I did not kill Fraulein Mayers in cold blood, Herr Doctor,' she said in a low voice.

'Come now, Anna. Your blood is always cold, is it not?' He turned to the girls. 'The blow is delivered here.' He touched where Boris's neck joined his shoulder. 'Under there is the carotid artery. It conveys the blood to the brain, and as I am sure you know, when the brain is robbed of blood it cannot function. For how long it cannot function depends on how long the artery is closed, but a blow of sufficient strength will stop the blood flow long enough for death to follow. Anna!'

Anna looked at him, then at the two girls,

then acted with tremendous speed, hitting Boris at the indicated place, but pulling the blow at the last moment. It was still completely effective. Boris went down without a sound.

'There, you see? It is really very simple. Take him out.'

The two soldiers stooped to grasp Boris's body, and one looked up. 'You wish him brought back, Herr Doctor?'

'What are we supposed to do with a corpse?' Cleiner enquired.

'But he is alive, Herr Doctor.'

'What?' Cleiner stooped and took Boris's pulse. Then he looked up at Anna. 'What happened?'

'You wished a demonstration of what could be accomplished with that blow, Herr Doctor. I have given that demonstration. You know I could have killed him had I wished, but I did not see the necessity for it.'

Cleiner slowly stood up. His face was red. 'Come into my office,' he snapped.

Anna glanced at the two girls, who were even more petrified than before. Then she followed the doctor from the room.

Anna sat on her bed, for the moment alone. She could not prevent herself being frightened; she remembered too well that session in the SD's torture chamber. It was not so much the caning or even the electrodes being thrust into her body that got to her, but the utter humiliation of being at the mercy of so many unpleasant human beings, one of whom had been Hannah Gehrig. She wondered if Hannah had told her daughter about that incident, and had a sudden disturbing thought: was Marlene Hannah's only daughter?

How simple it would have been to avoid this new crisis by simply killing that man. Could his death, which was certain to happen in this camp anyway, be of the least importance beside the other seven people she had on her conscience? Even her dear Clive Bartley would probably have advised her to do as Cleiner commanded and avoid the confrontation. But I am not a monster, she told herself savagely. So now I must face the consequences. And what she had done had been a deliberate stratagem; it was too late to change her plans now.

The door opened and the two girls came in. 'Anna!' Lena cried. 'What has happened to you?'

'Nothing has happened to me.' *Yet*, she thought.

'But when you did not come back...'

'The doctor seemed to be very angry,' Marlene suggested.

'Oh, he is always very angry about something or other. Listen, I do not know what is going to happen to me, or whether I will be here for the rest of the course. But if you wish to survive, do not fail him. He will ask you to shoot at a living target. Do so, and kill, and live.'

★ ★ ★

Despite everything, she knew she had an ace up her sleeve. When she had returned from England, a master spy fleeing one step ahead of the British police, General Heydrich had welcomed her with open arms. Although he had lost a beautifully placed agent, the publicity given to her escape – and to her activities in England, a ploy devised by Clive to save her reputation with the Nazis – had been such valuable propaganda as to be sufficient compensation. It was as if he had seen her as a woman, rather than a *thing*, for the first time.

She had in fact been afraid that he was going to appropriate her entirely as his mistress. But they had only slept together a few times. To Reinhard Heydrich sex, even with a beautiful and compliant woman, was secondary to his desire for power, for the manipulation of other human beings.

Clive was not aware of that relationship as it had only occurred after her return from England, and he had not been in contact with her since. She thought it possible that he would have liked the situation to continue. Heydrich was as potent a source of secret information as anyone in Germany, save perhaps Hitler himself. But she had been happy not to be called upon over the past few weeks. Of all the men she had ever met she hated her commanding officer the most. But now she had to carry out the seduction of her life.

'General Heydrich is waiting for you,' the

secretary said.

She did not get up from her desk to open the doors. Anna drew a deep breath, opened the doors herself and stood to attention, staring at the huge painting of Adolf Hitler that hung on the wall behind the desk. 'Heil Hitler!'

She was wearing one of her most flattering, form-hugging dresses, in pale green, with sufficient décolletage to be interesting, high heels, and her principal jewellery, but had left her head bare, her silky hair a golden mat below her shoulders. This was make or break.

'Heil Hitler.' Reinhard Heydrich was a tall, slim, very blond man, his pale colouring exaggerated by his black uniform. His features should have been handsome, but were spoiled by an utter coldness that particularly seemed to affect his mouth and eyes. And she had slept with this man, who held her life in the palm of his hand. 'Close the doors.' His voice was as lacking in warmth as his gaze, although she did not doubt that he liked what he now saw.

Anna closed the doors and advanced to his desk. To her relief there was no one else in the large room, and very little furniture; Heydrich liked to be surrounded by space. There was however a chair before the desk. She sat down and waited, as usual in these circumstances, forcing herself to breathe normally, and to look at his face and nowhere else.

Heydrich flicked the papers on his desk. 'Sometimes I despair of you, Anna. This

61

report is quite damning. You know the rules under which you – we – must operate: instant and unquestioning obedience to any command given by a superior officer.'

'Instant and unreasoning obedience to any command given me in the name of the Reich or in the furtherance of the Nazi Party, Herr General. Surely not to gratify the desires of a lecher.'

'Did he ... interfere with you?'

'In the pretended process of giving me a physical examination, sir. When I first attended the camp two years ago there was no physical examination. It was accepted that if I had been selected for special training as an agent for the SD, I was by definition both physically and mentally fit. On this occasion, after I think I can say two years of some success in the field, the first thing he did was command me to strip, so that he could look at me. He was quite open about this.'

She paused, not having been able to control her breathing as she would have liked. Heydrich studied her. 'I agree that was uncalled for, although you must admit, Anna, you are a temptation to any man. That is why we employ you. And it appears that this uncalled-for examination turned up something of interest. Why did you tell me the mark was a birthmark instead of reporting this incident with your husband?'

Anna had known this was coming. 'I was too embarrassed, sir. And when Bordman shot me, Herr General, I fainted from loss of blood. I was in an intensive-care ward for several days, and then, as you know, had to remain in hospital some weeks longer. I had no means of communicating with any of our people until Celestina came to see me. By then the police and the government, in their determination to avoid a scandal which would involve Lord Bordman's son and heir, had put out the story of my having fallen down the stairs. It seemed pointless to tell the truth at that stage, especially as it might have jeopardized my mission. I am sorry, but it was a decision I had to take on my own.'

'And you did not feel you could tell Celestina? She was your superior officer.'

'I am sorry, Herr General. I could not bring myself entirely to trust her when first we met.'

'I take your point. Poor Celestina. She died for the Reich.'

'I know,' Anna said sadly. *She died when I put two bullets into her chest.*

'But there is also the matter of your public disobedience of the doctor's orders.'

'Again I am sorry, Herr General. I believe you know that if you commanded me to kill someone, anyone, for the protection of the Reich, I would do so without hesitation. But I think that for me to start killing people for the amusement of others would have a derogatory influence upon both my ability and my powers of decision. Killing can never be a sport, Herr General.'

Again Heydrich considered her for several minutes. 'Your intellectual powers are considerable. I think, when your value as a field agent has ended, we should train you as a departmental lawyer. You would probably become a judge. But hopefully that is still some distance in the future. Very good, Anna. No more will be said of this. You know that on Monday you are to commence a crash course in Russian. I do not expect even you to become fluent in a month. But you must be able to understand what is being said around you.'

'I think I can manage that, Herr General. Am I being sent to Russia?'

'You will become Personal Assistant to Herr Meissenbach, who is currently Chief Secretary to the Governor General of Czechoslovakia, but who will shortly be taking up a new post as Chief Secretary at the Moscow Embassy. You will accompany him and I have no doubt you will rapidly become an important part of the social scene.' He gave a brief smile. 'I am informed that there *is* a social scene, even in Moscow, amongst the commissars and the diplomatic corps at any rate.'

'And you think they will divulge important information to a member of the German Embassy?'

'Probably not. But you have a target.' He opened a drawer, took out a photograph and held it out.

Anna studied it. The man was in his forties, she estimated. As it was head and shoulders only, she could not deduce his height, but he was clearly well built. His features were heavy but by no means ugly, and he had lively eyes. His thick black hair was brushed straight back from his high forehead. He wore what appeared to be a military tunic, but with no trace of insignia or medal ribbons.

'What do you think of him?' Heydrich asked.

'He looks quite pleasant.'

'Let us hope he is. You are to become his mistress.'

Anna raised her head sharply. 'Sir?'

'I think he will prove a far superior lover to Bordman. He has a great reputation for virility.'

Oh Lord, Anna thought. 'And he is an important man?'

'Very. His name is Ewfim Chalyapov, and he is one of Marshal Stalin's closest associates. A sort of trouble-shooter. As such he has access to the innermost workings of Stalin's mind. Your business will be to gain access to *his* mind, and what he knows.'

'But are the Russians not our friends, Herr General?'

'I never thought of you as naïve, Anna. The Russians are above all our enemies. We needed their alliance, or at least their acceptance of our wish for peace between our two nations, to give us a free hand in the west. Now that we have won the war, we must look east. The Bear cannot have expected us to win so quickly and so completely. He now finds himself facing a Europe that is united under the Swastika. He will undoubtedly be disturbed by this development. We need to know *how* disturbed, and if he has any plans for doing anything about it.'

Anna could not resist the temptation. 'Is England now a part of this united Europe?'

'England is no longer of any importance. It will either have been invaded and forced to surrender or have made peace by the end of this year.'

'And you think that this man Chalyapov will go for me?'

Heydrich smiled. 'My dear Anna, you are too modest. We have done our homework on Herr Chalyapov. He is unmarried, but goes for women rather than men. He changes his mistress roughly once a year. He likes them young, well built, intelligent, and blonde. Do you think he will not regard you as a gift from the gods? He also likes them to be able to match his virility, and I at least can vouch for that. In fact, I would like to test you again for myself. We will go down to my country house in Bavaria for this weekend. Does that please you?'

Shit, Anna thought; she had hoped for a couple of days at home just in case Antoinette's Boutique wished to get in touch with her. 'That would please me very much, Herr General. There is just one point: under what name will I be going to Moscow? Surely the Russians have heard of the infamous Mrs Bordman, the German spy?'

'They may have heard of you in that capacity, Anna. They may even have obtained

66

a photograph of Mrs Bordman. But I doubt it will be a very good one. In any event you are going as the Countess von Widerstand. They may be Bolsheviks and claim to be classless, but they remain fascinated by titles.'

'And you think this man will pick me up and then cast me down again. Within a year?'

'Do I detect a touch of feminine pride? I have no doubt that he will "pick you up", as you put it. How you handle that is up to you, but perhaps you could be a little hard to get, in the beginning. Above all be patient. Be at your vibrant best when in his company, but he must make the first move. There must be no risk of his suspecting that you are anything more than an innocent, if perhaps amoral, young woman. As to whether he will throw you out after a year or so, I would say that also will be up to you. But if by then you have milked him for all the information you can, would that not be the perfect solution? Then you would return to Berlin in a huff and no one would be any the wiser. I will have additional instructions for you before you leave. For the time being concentrate on your Russian. My car will pick you up tomorrow afternoon at five.'

'I look forward to it, Herr General. May I ask a question?'

'Certainly.'

'How much does Herr Meissenbach know of me?'

'Good point. Obviously, in view of the publicity we have given to your escape from

England, he knows that you have been a spy, and may still be. But he knows nothing of your' – he smiled – 'special skills or accomplishments. To him you will be Anna, Countess von Widerstand, a very lovely and compliant young woman, who works for the SD. It would be better if you did nothing to enlighten him as to your secrets. Unless, of course' – he smiled again – 'it should become a matter of life and death.'

'But will he know I am going to Moscow to seduce this man Chalyapov? I mean, I have to have some reason for being there at all.'

'Herr Meissenbach is to know nothing of your mission. He will be told only that he has to find some employment for you during office hours, but that he is not to interfere with or restrict your social activities.'

'But if I am officially in his employ, isn't it possible he may disapprove of my taking up with a Russian commissar? What happens if he attempts to prevent this?'

'You will remind him that your social life is no concern of his.'

'And if he wishes to dismiss me? Or at least report me to the Ambassador?'

'The Ambassador can do nothing without the approval of the SD. And he will be told to keep his hands off. Does that satisfy you?'

'If it satisfies you, Herr General, it satisfies me. I look forward to tomorrow afternoon.'

'What do you think of the Gehrig girl?' Heydrich asked, running his fingers up and down

Anna's spine.

She had actually nodded off, enjoying the warm sunlight on her naked body. In a life as filled with tension as hers, she had had to cultivate the ability to empty her mind and relax whenever possible, and this was certainly the most delightfully relaxing of places, at least in the summer, with the distant snow caps of the Alps providing such a scenic background. But it had been less easy to relax than usual, not only because being with Heydrich was a stressful business, but because she had so much on her mind.

It was now coming up to two months since she had fled England, and there had not been a word from Clive; there had been no message waiting for her from the Boutique. She kept telling herself it was pointless to expect it so soon, but if she was being sent off to Moscow, MI6 simply had to be informed immediately.

And now, just as she had managed to drift away, this damned man had brought her back into her problems with a bump. 'I did not know you knew of her,' she said.

'Didn't you? I thought Hannah was a close friend of yours. I know she was forced to punish you for that breach of discipline last year, but she was only doing her duty.'

'I understand that, Herr General. And I do not hold it against her.' One should never hold grudges against people when one has broken their necks.

'And you were very close when you served

together in London, were you not? She never mentioned her family to you?'

'No, sir. She was always very conscious of her superior rank.'

'Well, answer my question about the girl.'

'She seemed very enthusiastic,' Anna ventured. 'And she certainly knew a lot about me.'

'You resent this?'

Anna rolled over and allowed him to have a go at her breasts and stomach; there was no harm in causing his mind to wander. 'I did not resent it, Herr General. But it is an uneasy position to be in, meeting someone who knows so much about you, while you never knew she existed.'

'That is a good point. She is a problem.'

'Sir? She did not fail the course?'

Heydrich sat up. 'As you say, she was very enthusiastic, very eager. But she was just not up to it. Do you know, she emptied three magazines against her target in the final lesson, and did not succeed in killing him?'

Anna sat up in turn, memory flooding back to two years before, when the helpless condemned prisoner had been forced to run across the firing range so that they could prove their proficiency with the pistol. Her fellow pupil, Karen, had been unable to shoot him, for which lapse she had been condemned to an SS brothel. That Anna had obeyed her orders with deadly proficiency had earned her the position she now held. But Marlene ... 'She has not been degraded?'

'Cleiner wished to do so, certainly. But the fact is that the girl really tried. She hit the target several times, but could not do so fatally. And being Hannah Gehrig's daughter ... Well, he referred the matter to me.'

'And what was your decision, Herr General?'

'I have not yet made a decision. It is difficult, you see. Once a girl has been accepted for the training camp and has been subject to our training methods, she cannot be returned to what might be called a normal civilian life. Women do talk to each other and seem to have a compulsion to share their experiences and seek a sympathetic ear. But as I say, to condemn Hannah's daughter to a military brothel, or worse, is really not something I wish to contemplate.'

Anna was surprised. She had no idea he possessed that much humanity. 'I would not like to see her degraded either, Herr General, but I cannot offer an answer to the problem.'

'You can provide the answer, Anna.'

Anna turned her head.

'You are going to Moscow as PA to Herr Meissenbach, which is an important and senior position. No one could question your possessing a PA of your own.'

Anna gulped.

'That way she would be employed within the SD, understanding the secrecy that is required, and you would be able both to guide her and teach her, and at the same time assess her. If she failed you, you would inform me and her position would be terminated. While under your guidance it is entirely probable she may turn out to be a valuable servant of the Reich. Just like yourself. I think that would be an ideal solution to our problem. Don't you?'

'Yes, Herr General. Has she received complete training?'

'What do you mean?'

'After I had completed my initial training, Herr General, you may remember that I spent a month under the tutelage of Frau Mayers, being schooled not only in the Party philosophy, but also in how to behave and dress in the highest circles, and how to hold my liquor. Only when Frau Mayers was satisfied did I attend Doctor Cleiner's course.'

'Ah. Marlene Gehrig needs no schooling in the Party philosophy. She is, after all, Hannah's daughter. But she has not been educated in the social graces. You will attend to that. It may amuse you.'

I am sure it will, Anna thought. 'And will she speak Russian?'

'She will attend your course with you. You will be friends.'

Anna reflected that having disobeyed so many orders given her by her German superiors, one more was unlikely to make much difference.

What a foul-up, Anna thought as she got into a taxi at the station.

She really had no time for Marlene Gehrig,

but she *had* killed the girl's mother. So did that mean she owed the girl anything? She might like to feel that she was not a monster, but she was entirely alone in an ocean filled with sharks, not one of whom would hesitate for a moment to take a bite out of her if they felt it necessary.

The temptation to stop at the boutique and see if there was anything for her was overwhelming. She needed a shoulder to cry on. But again she reminded herself that she had been instructed to wait for them to contact her. So she let the taxi drive by.

'Oh, Countess!' Birgit's greeting was as enthusiastic as ever. 'Did you have a pleasant weekend?'

'I was sharing a bed,' Anna told her, and left her to make what she could of the reply.

She went into the bedroom and began undressing. Then she discovered that Birgit was hovering in the doorway. 'Herr Toler called. He wished to know if you would be joining the class tomorrow?'

'And you told him yes, I hope.'

'Yes, Countess. And the secretary of a man called Herr Meissenbach called. She made him sound terribly grand.'

'I suppose he is terribly grand,' Anna agreed as she began running a bath.

'She said that Herr Meissenbach wished to take you out to dinner.'

So soon? Anna thought. And she had not been ordered to seduce *him*.

'I told her I could not agree a date until you

returned, and she said she would call back.'

'Excellent.' Anna added bath foam and sank into the suds. 'I must try to be out then, too. Anything else?'

'Yes, Countess. The Antoinette's Boutique telephoned. They said the gown you ordered is ready for a fitting, and wished you to come in at your convenience.'

Bath water scattered as Anna leapt from the tub.

Three

Incident in Prague

Anna telephoned the boutique, but it was closed. She had had to wait until nine the next morning. Toler's Russian class began at nine, but he would have to wait too.

'Countess von Widerstand,' the woman said. 'When would suit you?'

'As soon as possible. I look forward to seeing the dress.'

'Ah, yes. Would eleven o'clock be satisfactory?'

'Eleven o'clock. Yes. That would be quite convenient.' She replaced the receiver and immediately telephoned the SS school to inform the tutor that something important had cropped up and she would not be able to attend class until after lunch. He sounded somewhat disgruntled, but had to accept the decision of so important an agent.

'Will you be in for lunch, Countess?' Birgit asked.

'Probably not.' Anna picked up her hand-bag, went to the door, and the telephone jangled. 'I'll take it,' she said as Birgit hurried into the hall. She was surprised at how anxious she was; if this was the boutique calling back ... 'Yes?'

'Would I be speaking with the Countess von Widerstand?' the man asked.

Anna drew a deep breath. 'This is she.'

'Countess! I am so pleased to make your acquaintance, even at a distance. My name is Heinz Meissenbach. Perhaps you have heard of me?'

Released breath rushed through Anna's nostrils. 'Of course, Herr Meissenbach. I am told we are to work together. I am looking forward to that. Are you calling from Prague?'

Meissenbach also seemed to be taking deep breaths. 'No, no. I am in Berlin for only a few days, and I also am looking forward to our ... working relationship. I think it is necessary for us to get to know each other, if we are to adventure together.'

'I understood you – we – would not be going to Moscow until next month, Herr Meissenbach?'

'That is so, my dear lady. But it is essential that when we do go to Moscow, we are totally au fait with each other. I suggest we begin by having dinner tonight.'

'Tonight? Ah...' That was the very last thing she wanted.

'It is a convenient date for me,' Meissenbach said. 'My wife is joining me tomorrow.'

'Your wife,' Anna said thoughtfully. The situation was growing more fraught by the second. If in addition to seducing Chalyapov she was going to have to fight off the advances of this lout, she suspected it was going to be a rather busy year ahead. But she had to continue acting her role as an SD agent who, at least until the crunch, was totally obedient to her superiors. 'In that case, Herr Meissenbach, I shall be delighted.'

'Then I shall pick you up at seven.'

Anna thought that if the boutique had indeed prepared that absurd dress for her, she might well wear it.

'Ah, Countess, how nice to see you,' the woman said. Her tone was far warmer than on the occasion of their first meeting. 'Signor Bartoli is waiting for you.'

Anna followed her through a door at the rear of the showroom, and down a corridor into a surprisingly large room that contained several dummies and a variety of clothes and uncut cloth scattered about various trestle tables. There were also three sewing-machine tables, but currently no seamstresses. The only occupant was a small, dapper man, with a long nose and even longer hair. He was in his shirtsleeves, and appropriately had a tape measure draped around his neck. He looked Anna up and down appreciatively: she was wearing her best, with a picture hat.

'Countess von Widerstand! How nice to meet you.' His German was very heavily accented.

'My pleasure, Signor Bartoli. You have something for me?'

'Indeed. That will be all, thank you, Edda.'

The woman hesitated, as if reluctant to leave Anna alone with him. Then she left, closing the door.

Bartoli held up the blue dress with the red trim. 'One would almost suppose, Countess, that you are trying to fly some sort of flag.' His voice had dropped several octaves.

'I wanted to be quite sure I was brought to your attention, Signor.'

'You should not have come here at all, Anna. You do not mind if I call you Anna, I hope?'

'So what do I call you?' Anna asked.

'I think sir would be appropriate. I am your Controller in Germany.'

Anna sat down and crossed her knees; this war was growing longer by the minute. 'I do not even call my London Controller "sir".'

Bartoli regarded her for some moments. 'I was told you were a spirited young lady. You may call me Luigi.'

'Luigi,' Anna repeated without enthusiasm. 'So I am to place my life in your hands.'

'Is not mine in yours, Anna? Now come along. We cannot be here for too long. Undress.'

Anna gave him an old-fashioned look. If this was becoming the initial advance of every man with whom she came professionally into contact, it was also becoming rather tiresome.

Bartoli understood her expression. 'It is necessary, my dear girl, for me to be fitting you and measuring you should anyone walk in. It would be quite inappropriate for me to lock the door.'

Anna sighed, but she knew he was right. She removed her hat, got up and took off her dress.

'I think the petticoat as well, if you don't mind.'

Anna removed this garment also and instinctively stepped out of her shoes.

'No no. Keep the shoes. The dress must hang absolutely correctly.'

Anna replaced the shoes.

'You are exquisite, Fraulein. Has anyone ever told you that?'

'Everyone I meet,' Anna said.

'And it is Fraulein?'

'Here in Germany. It is Frau in England. You said we should not waste time.'

'Then will you stand here.' He indicated the position immediately in front of him, and took the tape measure from round his neck. 'Now, I am going to take your measurements again, just to be certain, you understand.' He stepped closer to her and began arranging the tape round the bodice of her cami-knickers, taking great care to place it exactly over the nipples. 'What is on your mind that makes you so impatient?'

'I have been here for eight weeks and have not been contacted. Have you instructions for me?'

He released the tape reluctantly and made a note on the pad on his desk. 'London has been waiting for you to settle down and to be given a position commensurate with your talents.' He chuckled. 'And your measurements.' He draped the tape round her waist. 'Are you so anxious to get back to work? As far as I have been able to ascertain, you have been enjoying yourself.'

'You mean you have been keeping me under surveillance?'

'We are in business together, Anna ... Your hips are perfection.' He released her to write the figures on his pad. 'And your legs. Are they perfection too?'

'It is for you to tell me.'

'But I am just getting to know you.'

'Before you do that, I need a confirming name,' Anna said.

'Ah, yes. Should you not have asked for that immediately?'

'I take my time, Luigi. So?'

'I was told Belinda would register.'

'Thank you. It does.'

'Tell me, Anna, if I had not had a name for you, or the name had not registered, what would you have done?'

'I would have broken your neck, Luigi.' Anna continued to speak as softly as ever. 'Then I would have opened the door and screamed that you were trying to rape me.'

'And you think the police would believe you?'

'I have nothing to do with the police. My German employers accept that I am inclined to react violently when insulted, and they would never let anything happen to me.'

'But I could betray you.'

'My dear Luigi, you would be dead.'

'Ah.' Luigi put down the tape measure.

'Now listen. I am about to take up a position as Personal Assistant to the First Secretary at the German Embassy in Moscow. I have been told this posting may be for a year. I have also been told I am to see what I can learn about current Russian attitudes towards the Reich, in view of the recent dramatic changes in the political situation. You should inform London of this immediately. If they have any instructions for me to follow in Russia, I have to receive them within the next three weeks. As they also have an Embassy in Moscow, it should be possible for them to contact me once I get there but it will have to be handled with the utmost discretion.'

Bartoli had been staring at her while she spoke. 'You speak so calmly. You act so calmly. Does nothing ever frighten or upset you?'

If you only knew, Anna thought. 'No, Signor Bartoli. I am made of ice. Were you not told?' She put on her slip and then her dress. 'I do not think I will have a fitting now. Complete the dress as it is, and then call me back. Remember, it must be within three weeks. Ciao.'

Having decided against being outrageous, Anna wore her favourite pale blue sheath evening gown, and was very glad to have done so: Meissenbach turned out to be far better than she had dared hope. He was taller than her, which was a pleasant change. His features, if rounded, were by no means soft, and his eyes were incisive. His hair was black with grey wings and he had a strong body. To top it all, his manner was an intriguing mixture of charm and hesitancy. She supposed this was a result of his diplomatic training. But she sensed, from his occasional directness, that there could be a layer of steel beneath.

'Countess!' He bent over her hand. 'I am enchanted. They told me you were an attractive woman, but that was clearly an understatement.'

'Thank you, Herr Meissenbach.'

'My car is waiting.'

He made no effort to touch her, even when assisting her into her cape, and although they sat beside each other in the back of the chauffeur-driven car, he scrupulously left a space between them. She felt herself warming to him, which had not been her intention.

The restaurant was upmarket. She had been here before with Heydrich, and Meissenbach was clearly impressed when the maitre d' greeted her obsequiously.

'So,' he said as they sipped their aperitifs after ordering, 'the Countess von Widerstand. Would you care to explain that to me, Fraulein?'

'You would have to ask General Himmler about that,' Anna said. Heydrich had told her to admit nothing of her background that was not already public knowledge.

'But you do have a real name?'

'Anna.'

'That is delightful. If I had been asked to choose a name for you I would have selected Anna. And I gather you have been living an exciting life?'

'It has been interesting. What should I call you, Herr Meissenbach?'

'When we are in public, it should be sir or Herr Meissenbach. When we are in private I should like you to call me Heinz.'

Anna nibbled her lobster salad. 'Are we going to be in private, sir?'

'We are in private now.'

Anna looked around the crowded dining room.

Meissenbach smiled. 'I should have said when we are off duty. Now, tell me why they are sending you to Moscow.'

'To be your PA, Heinz.'

He regarded her for several moments while they finished their first course and the meat was served. Then he raised his glass. 'I will drink to that. Do you have, shall I say, a man? A protector? Any young woman in this day and age needs a protector. Especially if she is as handsome as you.'

'You are absolutely right,' Anna agreed.

'Ah! I think we are going to have a very good relationship.'

'I sincerely hope so,' Anna said. 'I should tell you now that I do have a protector. His name is Reinhard Heydrich. Perhaps you know him?'

Meissenbach spilt some wine.

* * *

Anna sat up in bed to drink her coffee. 'This is not very strong.' She had not really noticed the previous morning, having had a slight head; Meissenbach had plied her with wine, but after her snub, he had not attempted to follow it up.

'We are nearly out, Countess,' Birgit protested.

'And you have not ordered more?'

'We are only allowed one kilogram a month, Countess. It has been rationed.'

'Good Lord! Well, no doubt they will have ample supplies of coffee in Moscow.'

'I am so excited, Countess.'

'So am I. Oh, what can that be?'

Birgit hurried from the bedroom to open the front door in response to the bell. Anna could not distinctly hear what was being said, but a few minutes later the maid returned carrying a bouquet of twelve red roses. 'Ooh, Countess! Aren't these lovely?'

Anna took the card. *I must see you again. Expect me at noon. Heinz.*

Anna looked at Birgit, who flushed; she had clearly read the note before bringing in the flowers. 'Put these in water and make sure the vase is conspicuous in the drawing room. You may have to entertain the gentleman for a little while before I get home.' Her morning session with the Russian tutor did not end until twelve.

She soaked in her bath and considered the situation. She was surprised. If he had been

84

going to follow up the evening she would have supposed he would have done it the day after. Now Meissenbach seemed to have recovered his nerve, but he had given no indication that this might happen when he had brought her home. He had, in fact, been in a great hurry to get away. He had not even kissed her hand.

But now he was coming on very strong. She actually thought he might be very congenial company. Obviously he wanted to get her into bed. It was a question of whether it was better to antagonize him now, or to go along with him and risk a much greater antagonism when she 'fell in love' with the Russian. But if she went along with him now, he might have exhausted his passion before the Russian business came to a head. But she still needed to be careful, at least until she discovered how Heydrich might view the situation.

Yet she hurried home from her lesson with pleasant anticipation, and there he was, sitting in an armchair drinking schnapps. He stood up, and this time kissed her hand. 'You have a most attentive maid.'

'I am sorry I am late.'

'You are taking Russian lessons. I know this.'

'It is rather boring.'

'But necessary. I understand. May I give you lunch?'

'I thought perhaps we would lunch here. Birgit is also a very good cook.'

'And afterwards?'

'We could talk, if you wished.'

'Talk?'

Anna gave a wry smile. 'There is not much else we can do at this moment. I am in a woman's situation.'

'Oh. Ah. But you would still like me to stay for lunch?'

'It does not affect my appetite, Heinz, or my appetite for entertaining attractive men.'

'You are delightful. Anna, I would like you to visit me in Prague. Will you do that? When this unfortunate situation has ended.' He gazed at her.

'Are you sure this is wise?' Anna asked.

Meissenbach flushed. 'I will confess something to you. I was so taken with you when we dined that I took the liberty of discussing the matter with General Heydrich yesterday. He assured me that while he is very fond of you, and regards himself as your protector, he lays no claim to your private life, except in so far as it might need that protection. He is sure I will take good care of you.'

The bastard, Anna thought, *he doesn't just regard me as a thing, he regards me as a whore.* But she was not going to be a total pushover. 'I am sure that greatly relieves you.'

'And you?'

Anna got up and refilled their glasses. 'If I come to Prague, will I have the pleasure of meeting Frau Meissenbach?'

'The weekend after next – which, incidentally, will be my last in Prague – she will be visiting her mother in Hanover.'

86

'Does she spend any time at all at home with you?'

Meissenbach smiled. 'We have an understanding.'

'But she is coming to Moscow with us?'

'Oh, indeed. And she will enjoy meeting you, I know, at the appropriate moment. There is nothing for you to be concerned about. So...'

'I think lunch is ready,' Anna said.

'I have a message from Anna,' Clive Bartley announced, standing in the office doorway.

Billy Baxter raised his head somewhat suspiciously, but then he was inclined to do everything suspiciously. The two men could not have offered a stronger contrast. Clive Bartley, if by no means handsome, was over six feet tall and built to match; his rather lank black hair tended to droop across features which were of the hatchet variety but could be relieved by his ready smile. He looked as if he was close to smiling now. Baxter, with his somewhat diminutive body, usually hunched over the papers he was reading, his thinning pale brown hair, his tobacco-stained tweed jacket and loosely knotted tie, suggested a down at heel retired academic. He could look gloomy even on a bright July morning, but this, Clive suspected, might be because of the news, which was not getting any better, even if, this far, the War had had very little effect on London's way of life.

Despite their character differences, each

man knew the other's worth. For all his appearance, Billy Baxter had possibly the most acute brain in MI6. This, and his willingness to accept the most difficult tasks, led to his having those tasks dumped on his desk with great regularity. Clive knew that he was not actually as cold-blooded as he sometimes appeared. He genuinely worried about the agents he had scattered all over Nazi-occupied Europe, genuinely grieved when one of them was picked up by the Gestapo to suffer a horrendous death. But that did not stop him immediately seeking a replacement.

Baxter, for his part, knew that Clive, for all his slightly raffish appearance and debonair attitude, was one of the most dedicated and, when necessary, deadly agents he possessed. But he also knew that Clive had gone overboard about the glamorous German spy he had managed to turn. Baxter was still not entirely convinced that Anna Fehrbach was to be trusted. Now he snorted. 'Are you saying she is bending the rules again?'

'She has sent it through the channel we gave her.'

'That channel was only to be used in response to a communication from us. I am not aware that we have sent any such communication.'

'Yes,' Clive said. 'And in my opinion that was a mistake. We have left this important agent in limbo for eight weeks. I don't blame her in the least for wondering what is going on.'

'Do we know what she has been doing in that time? What job she has been given which could be of value to us? The name of this game, as you well know, Clive, is patience. When she is posted somewhere important we will call on her for information. Until then—'

'She has been posted, Billy. That is why she needed to be in touch. She is going to Moscow as Personal Assistant to the Chief Secretary at the German Embassy.'

'Shit! Then we have lost her.'

'I don't think she would have hurried to give us that information if she wanted to be lost. Think of this, Billy. She is just about the most highly trained and dangerous operative the SD possess. I know we took a risk in sending her back, but she insisted on taking that risk for the sake of her family. And it would appear that her story has been totally accepted. That being so, would the SD send such a woman to Moscow just to be a PA?'

Baxter began to fill his pipe, a sure sign that he was thinking. 'She did not say why she was going?'

'Yes. She is to learn all she can about Russia's feelings towards Germany in view of the hegemony the Reich appears to have established over Europe.'

'That seems straightforward enough.'

'Billy, if we had Anna here in London under our sole jurisdiction, would we send her to Russia to tell us the Soviets feelings towards us? There has to be another reason. Perhaps she has not yet received specific instructions. But there has to be a reason, and it certainly isn't her proficiency as a typist.'

Baxter was busily dropping tobacco on his jacket and his desk. 'Who do we have in Moscow?'

'Commander Sprague. He is officially a naval attaché.'

'A good man?'

'Very. But Anna will not know him, or recognize him.'

Baxter struck a match and puffed. 'Can't he use the Belinda code?'

'I still think it would be risky. We should never forget Anna's little ways.'

Baxter leaned back in his chair. 'Are you saying...?'

'I am saying that if Anna got the impression she was at risk of exposure or betrayal, we would have to find a new naval attaché.'

'And you have actually slept with this creature.'

'As I have told you before, Billy, don't knock it if you have never known it.'

'What about Operation Tomorrow?'

'Done and dusted.'

'It's your baby.'

'Not any more. You know what the Czechs are like. They want our backing, they want our expertise, they want our weaponry. Then they want to be on their own. No interference. I don't even know their plans, save that it is scheduled for next weekend.'

'But you do know they're going after this

character Meissenbach instead of the Governor-General. Have they told you why?'

'Yes. It seems that Tropa is an amiable old goat. Meissenbach has been virtually running the country for the past year. He's the man who actually signed the death warrant for those two lads who pulled down the Swastika flag. Now it seems they have learned that he is about to complete his term of office and be transferred to other duties. They both want to make an example of him, and let the Nazis know they're still fighting.'

'And they realize there are liable to be some pretty fearsome repercussions?'

'They do, and they seem prepared to accept that. The point is that my part is done, and our prime agent needs looking after. Billy, think. Anna is going to Moscow. She could be going to commit murder; she could be going as a spy. You tell me why Germany, publicly holding hands with the Reds, would send their most lethal weapon into their midst. We have to find out what she is doing and whether or not it can be turned to our advantage. You can have me seconded to the Embassy as an attaché or something. Or I could go as a businessman. Just a visit, to make contact and arrange future liaisons.'

'And you would eagerly get between the sheets with the young lady.'

Clive flushed. 'Only if it could be done safely.'

'I don't think the word safely comes into it where Anna Fehrbach is concerned. But I agree it is necessary to contact her, and if you're hell-bent on committing suicide, so be it. What about Belinda? I am speaking of the lady, not the password.'

'She won't like it. She never likes it when I am sent away for any lengthy period. But she's got used to it.'

'I meant does she know about Anna?'

'Well of course she does. She was there when the woman Gehrig started shooting.'

'And Anna snapped Gehrig's neck. You never did tell me how Belinda reacted to that.'

'Well, she was shocked, of course.'

'Does she know that you and Anna had an affair?'

'Yes. She found out.'

'And forgave you?'

'Circumstances were unusual.'

'Oh, indeed. And does she have any idea what Anna does when she becomes agitated?'

'Well, it's difficult to watch a woman calmly break another woman's neck and not get the impression that she has her bad moods.'

'So how do you think she will react to your charging off after your glamorous viper again?'

'There is no need for her to know anything more than that I am being posted abroad for a few weeks.'

'Didn't you once tell me that you intended to marry her? Belinda, I mean.'

'I did, and I asked her, four years ago. She didn't like the idea of being an MI6 wife. She thought it was too close to being a widow. She is also not a hundred per cent domesticated, in the housewife sense.'

'I thought she was an excellent cook.'

'She is. Because she enjoys it. She does not enjoy, and has no interest in, such chores as washing a man's socks, or making his bed.'

Baxter stuck to the point. 'But four years ago was before any of us knew that Anna existed, and the world was a comparatively peaceful place. I think you should force the issue and marry her as soon as possible.'

'But then,' Clive pointed out, 'you would be asking me to commit adultery and deceive my wife.'

Baxter put down his pipe. 'You are an unmitigated scoundrel, Clive. You will receive your posting as soon as it can be arranged.'

'What's this?' Belinda Hoskin inquired in that deceptively quiet voice she used when displeased. A small, dark-haired woman with prettily sharp features, she presented the greatest possible contrast to Anna Fehrbach, not least in the intensity of her personality. Clive knew very well that Anna's personality was just as intense, but she kept it securely hidden behind that glacial exterior, even in moments of enormous stress.

Now he smiled as disarmingly as he could and held out the glass of scotch he had just poured. 'It's a suitcase, darling. I had no idea you were coming round tonight.'

'You mean you were planning a moonlight flit?'

He took her in his arms to kiss her, having to raise her from the floor to get her mouth level with his. But he knew she enjoyed this, especially as he had grasped her buttocks to hold her in position. 'I was going to tell you.'

She wriggled down his body, disengaged herself, took a sip of the drink, and carried it into the kitchen. It was her nature to take immediate control of every situation that presented itself, and even if she was in Clive's flat she intended to prepare dinner herself. Her system was perhaps necessary for the fashion editor of a leading London magazine. And he had no objection to her practising it around him; he knew she found him very frustrating because he was so often carried in an alternate direction by the requirements of his job. As he had told Baxter, although she claimed she was not into washing socks and preparing regular meals, he had no doubt that the real reason she had always declined to marry him was that lack of total control.

And recently she had been more adrift than usual. To walk in, as she had done the previous year, on her lover entertaining a stunningly beautiful woman in a compromising situation, had led to an immediate decision to deal with the situation. She had followed Anna Bordman back to her Mayfair apartment. She had never told him exactly what she had had in mind, or even what the two women had said to each other when she had gained access: she certainly had had no idea just who and what she was preparing to engage. But she had still been there when Anna's apparent 'servant' had appeared and sought to kill them both. Clive had never been sure which had upset Belinda more: the fact that she had looked death in the face, or that Anna had reacted with such consuming and lethal force.

If Anna had saved her life by that prompt action, Belinda had in turn saved Anna's life by immediately calling him to the rescue, while her rival lay on the floor, apparently bleeding to death. He supposed these things made a bond. In any event it had been necessary both to put Belinda as much into the picture as was required, and make her swear secrecy under the Official Secrets Act.

From that moment she had treated him with a new respect, and quite forgiven him for his brief fling. If she had always known he worked, and travelled, for MI6, this had been her first intimation of just how dangerous that work could be.

'So where are you going?' she asked now.

'Away for a couple of days. Company business.'

She started breaking eggs with more force than was actually necessary. 'That's a big suitcase, for a couple of days.'

'Well, it could be a couple of weeks. Shall I open a bottle of wine?'

'I hate you,' she announced. 'I loathe and

95

despise you. Do you have any of that Bollinger left?'

'Always happy to oblige, ma'am.'

He laid the table while she completed scrambling the eggs and making toast. They touched glasses as they sat facing each other. 'You're not going to get shot or something stupid, are you?'

'I shall be moving strictly amongst friends. Or at least neutrals.'

She brooded while drinking champagne. 'Do you think she got away?'

'Who?'

'Your inamorata. It's been all of two months.'

'Well, we didn't really expect her to telephone and say hello.'

'But she is working for us now, isn't she?'

'She worked for us, darling, to help us destroy that German spy ring here in London. So we sent her home. She wanted to go. She's done her bit as far as we're concerned.'

'And if the Nazis ever found out what she did?'

'That is not something to consider while eating scrambled eggs.'

Belinda shivered. Clive felt like doing the same.

'You may have next weekend off,' Anna said. 'I am going down to Prague.'

'Am I not to come with you?' Birgit asked.

'No. It is a private visit. Spend the days with your family; when we go to Moscow at the

96

end of the month you will be away from Berlin for perhaps a year.'

She dressed and went to her Russian class. She reckoned she was about as proficient as she was going to get in the limited time she'd been allowed. Obviously, even with spending an hour or so on homework every night, there was no possibility of her developing a Moscovite accent, but with her memory and her ear for words she had mastered the fundamentals of grammar and developed quite a vocabulary. She felt she was perfectly capable of carrying out the task of picking up what was being said around her. In any event, she had no doubt that Chalyapov would wish to speak German with her. However...

'There was another young lady supposed to join me for these lessons,' she remarked to Herr Toler after class.

He was an eager young man who wore a goatee beard and regarded her with longing eyes. He clearly enjoyed their one-to-one sessions, sitting beside her at the big desk, shoulders often touching as they parsed sentences and delved into what passed for Communist literature. 'Fraulein Gehrig. Yes, I have been expecting her, but she has not turned up as yet.'

'I see,' Anna said grimly. The wretched girl was going to be even more difficult than she had supposed. 'Well, let us hope she appears on Monday. I will see you then, Herr Toler.'

She took herself home to the apartment; she had not yet had any further communication from Antoinette's Boutique, and therefore intended to spend the afternoon in the gym.

Birgit rolled her eyes as she opened the door. 'There is someone here to see you, Countess.'

'Oh Lord!' She was not in the mood to fend off either amorous men or officious clerks. She opened the drawing-room door and gazed at Marlene Gehrig, who was on her feet and looking anxious.

'I have been told I am to go to Russia with you,' Marlene said in her husky voice.

Anna surveyed her. She wore a dress of no great style and low-heeled shoes. Her hair was in a bun and her face, although it could never be unattractive, wore an apprehensive expression. 'You were supposed to be here two weeks ago.'

'Well...' Marlene looked sulky. 'When that ghastly Doctor Cleiner dismissed me, he just told me to leave. I was taken to the SS female barracks and given a room, but as no one seemed to have any orders for me, I took a break.'

'One does not take a break unless specifically instructed to do so,' Anna pointed out. 'Where did you go?'

'Bonn.'

'What on earth did you have to do in Bonn?'

'I went to see my sister.'

Just what she had feared. The situation was becoming impossible. 'You have a sister living in Bonn.'

'Yes. Her husband works there.'

'I see. Tell me, how many other sisters do you have?'

'Only Elena. Then when I returned to Berlin, I was told I had to start taking Russian lessons. Do you know what is to happen to me?'

Anna supposed that one more Gehrig was tolerable. 'Yes,' she said. 'As you are coming with me to Russia you are required to speak Russian. You are supposed to have been learning the language for the past fortnight. Now you have just two more weeks. You will attend classes morning, afternoon and evening for those two weeks, commencing today.'

Marlene's lips were trembling. 'You're angry with me.'

'Well of course I'm angry with you. I should punish you.'

Tears rolled down Marlene's cheeks. 'Please don't be angry with me, Anna. I so want to work with you. I'll do anything you wish.'

'I have told you what I wish.' The girl looked so pitiable. Anna went to the sideboard and poured two glasses of schnapps, gave her one. 'Welcome. So you could not bring yourself to kill a living target?'

Marlene sat down, knees pressed together, holding the glass in both hands as she sipped. 'I tried. But my hand would not stop shaking.'

'Did you want to?'

'I don't know. I kept remembering what you

99

told me, that when a thing has to be done it has to be done. But then I also remembered that you refused to kill that man in the schoolroom.'

'As you have just reminded yourself, the essential aspect of being able to survive in our profession is to be able to do what has to be done when it has to be done. I have proved my ability to do this on several previous occasions. I do not enjoy killing people. So I saw no necessity to prove my ability again for Cleiner's amusement. You have not yet proved your ability – at anything. And I think you should know that I can be every bit as brutal as Cleiner, if I have to. You have been seconded to me by General Heydrich for the sake of your mother's memory. So I am now your commanding officer, and if I give you an order it must be obeyed instantly and without question. Our lives may depend on it.'

'But what exactly are we – am I – going to do?'

'We are going to spy for the Reich. I will do most of this, but I will require you to act as my back-up, as and when I need you, regardless of the consequences. Do you understand this?'

Marlene licked her lips and then swallowed the rest of her schnapps.

'So you will have lunch with me, and this afternoon you will come with me to the gym before going to your Russian class. I will inform Herr Toler that you are coming, and that you are required to work evenings as well for the next fortnight.'

'Am I going to the gym to shoot some-body?'

Anna smiled. 'To do whatever I tell you to do.'

Anna was aware of a most peculiar sensation. Although she knew that most people with whom she came into contact considered her to be a dominant personality, and she knew that she could be, she had spent her entire life thus far as a subordinate. Even when head girl in the Vienna convent, she had been strictly controlled by the nuns. Since being conscripted into the SD she had been entirely at the mercy of her superiors, and indeed had suffered a terrible punishment for trying to assert herself. This young woman's mother had been one of the punishers. She under-stood that she would never be free of the control of men like Reinhard Heydrich or Billy Baxter, although she often reflected with some satisfaction that if she played her cards right she could survive while one of them went to the wall at the end of the war.

But she remained totally vulnerable until that end came. And here she was being given total control of another woman for the first time in her life. To complicate the situation she also knew that this girl was a potential deadly enemy who might have to be destroy-ed if she ever gleaned the slightest inkling of how her mother had died.

But Marlene herself broached the subject

over lunch, again raising the question she had asked at their first meeting. 'Do you really have no idea of what could have happened to my mother?' she asked.

'I have not really had the time to think about it,' Anna confessed. 'As I told you, I only know that she was ordered to flee England because of the imminence of war. But shortly after she left I had an accident and was in hospital for several weeks. Then I was betrayed to the British and had to flee.' This was telescoping events but she did not think Marlene could possibly know that.

'But you fled back to Germany. Mother didn't. You don't think she could have been the one who betrayed you?'

'Is that something you really want to think about your mother?'

'Well, of course not. But has the thought never crossed your mind? After the way she just disappeared?'

Anna appeared to consider this. 'The first thing you want always to remember is that your mother is a dedicated Nazi and believer in the Third Reich. I do not believe it possible for her to have been a traitor. I'm afraid we must consider the possibility, perhaps the probability, that something went wrong with the escape route.'

'You mean she might have been captured by the British?'

'She cannot possibly have been taken alive or I would almost certainly have been arrested long before they actually got around to suspecting me. But when on assignment, we are all issued with cyanide capsules to be used in the last resort.'

Marlene stared at her with enormous eyes. 'You think...? Oh my God!'

'Your mother trained me,' Anna reminded her. 'So when I say that what has to be done has to be done, I am quoting her.'

'You admired her?'

I hated, loathed, and despised her, Anna thought. But she said, 'How could anyone not admire so strong and dedicated a character?'

Marlene burst into tears.

That did not encourage Anna to make her training any easier. If she still felt that the girl had to be a potential danger, she also felt that she might just need her, and over the next week she made her undertake an exhausting regime of both physical training and firearms practice in addition to her concentrated Russian lessons.

But this, as she knew, was but an aspect of her own uncertainty. However distasteful it had been to have to marry Ballantine Bordman and allow him the use of her body, it had been possible to approach the business with the single-mindedness that was her greatest strength. Even when Clive had entered her life to complicate matters, he had been both a back-up and the promise of an eventual haven. Now she felt utterly adrift. It was more than two months since she had left England, and not a word. She was committed to another love affair, no doubt as distasteful as the last. And now, to top it all, she had acquired Heinz Meissenbach. Her guilt and uncertainty was compounded by the fact that she was actually looking forward to her weekend in Prague. At the very least he seemed to be both an educated and a cultivated man. But she knew she was taking him on in anger at being ignored by London as much as anything.

And then on the Friday morning before she left for Prague, the telephone rang and Birgit appeared in the doorway. 'It is that boutique place, Countess.'

'Oh!' Anna knew colour had rushed into her cheeks. She brushed past the maid and grasped the phone. 'Yes?'

'Countess? Signor Bartoli here. I have made the alterations you wanted in that dress and it is ready for another fitting.'

'Oh!' Anna said again. The train left at four. 'I am going out of town for a few days, but I would like to take the dress with me if it is suitable. Shall I come in this morning?'

'Certainly, Countess. Shall we say ten?'

As if she did not have enough on her mind. But this had to be more important than anything else. She felt quite breathless.

Marlene turned up at nine to say goodbye. 'Do I continue training while you are away?'

Anna gave her a bright smile. 'You may take the weekend off, Marlene. Go somewhere and have a good time and I will see you on Monday evening.'

'A good time?'

'Don't you have any family left, apart from your sister?'

'No.'

Oh Lord, Anna thought, she's going to start crying again! 'You must have a boyfriend?'

'No. Do you have a boyfriend, Anna?'

'I think I am about to acquire one,' Anna said. 'What about friends? You must have some friends. What about the other SS girls in your barracks?'

'They have all heard of my mother and they seem afraid of me. And now they know that I'm working for you...'

Anna wondered if Heydrich had deliberately set this up to make her life more difficult. 'Well, you will have to go to a couple of movies or something. I will see you on Monday.'

She hurried her downstairs, watched her walk away along the street, and proceeded to call a taxi.

Bartoli beamed at her. 'Seeing you always makes the day brighter, Countess.'

Anna reflected that he had made a good recovery from the snubbing she had administered the last time they had met. 'As you always bring me back to reality, Signor Bartoli.'

He gave one of his gulps and ushered her into the fitting room, dismissing various females and closing the door. 'If you would be so kind...'

Anna removed her dress and petticoat and waited. The new dress was actually complete, and was even more garish than she remembered. But it fitted very well, although Bartoli found it necessary to bob about with pins and a piece of chalk. 'Yes,' he said, 'this will do very nicely.' His face was close to her breasts. 'When do you leave for Moscow?'

'A week today.'

'London is interested in anything you may be able to tell them about either current Nazi–Soviet relations, or current Soviet thinking. From what you said, this last is your prime objective, is it not?'

'Yes. You realize that I am being posted for what may be a year. I do not think I shall be allowed to return to Berlin during that time. After a year my information may be out of date.'

'You will be contacted in Moscow.'

'By someone discreet, I hope.'

'I understand so. Your contact will be known to you as you both are known to Belinda.'

Anna stared at him, feeling the blood rushing into her cheeks from her suddenly pounding heart. Could it be true?

Bartoli had been so close he might well have heard the quickened heartbeat. Now he stepped back and studied her. 'You are upset. Is the news reassuring, or alarming?'

It is both, Anna thought. To see Clive again! But they would have to be so terribly discreet. 'It is reassuring, Signor Bartoli. You may inform London that I understand the message and anticipate a profitable relationship with my contact.'

'Of course. And the dress?'

'I am sure it needs something else doing to it. If you can complete the work by next Friday, I would like to hear from you. If you cannot, I would burn it.'

'It is an expensive dress, Countess. My women have put in a lot of work on it.'

'So send the bill to my apartment. Ciao.'

The rest of the day passed in a dream. They had not only contacted her, but they were sending Clive!

But before then she had to accommodate Meissenbach. Almost she felt like telephoning to tell the secretary she had a stomach upset and would have to cancel their assignation. In fact both her mind and her body were in such an agitated state that that would not be such a lie. But she had to control herself.

It was a three-hour journey to Prague, and she shared the first-class compartment with two officers, who naturally wanted to flirt. She put them off by telling them she was going to spend the weekend with her uncle, who was Chief Secretary to the Governor-General. But it was all change in Dresden, and when she joined the Prague train they had disappeared. She was alone in her compartment, while people filed up and down the corridor, but the train had already pulled out of the station before anyone came in. She recognized him as a man who had actually passed her door three times while going to and fro looking for a seat. Now he raised his hat as he entered the compartment. 'Am I permitted, Fraulein?'

'Certainly, sir.'

He was an elderly gentleman, at least to her – certainly over fifty. His hair was grey, he wore horn-rimmed spectacles and a short beard. His three-piece suit was excellently cut, his shoes polished. He wore a gold watch chain across his ample stomach. His expression was benign. She put him down as a senior civil servant, a prosperous businessman or, most likely of all, a university professor. But incongruously, over his left arm was draped a topcoat, on a blazing-hot late July afternoon. Nor did he have any luggage. And her instincts warned her that he had actually been looking for her, and making sure that she was alone, before joining her.

But, whatever he was after, she was content to let him make the first move; it was in any event less than an hour to Prague. So, having given him a polite smile, she resumed looking out of her window.

He carefully placed his topcoat on the seat beside him and, having seated himself opposite her, he addressed her in an incomprehensible language.

'I am so sorry,' she said. 'I do not speak Bohemian.'

'That was Moravian,' he pointed out, reverting to German. 'You are not Czech?'

'I was born in Vienna, sir.'

'Ah. You are very young, and very attractive, to be travelling alone.'

Anna sighed. 'I am going to spend the weekend with my uncle. He is meeting the train.'

'Of course. He is with the...' He was clearly choosing his words with care. 'The German government?'

'I believe so,' Anna said carelessly.

He realized she was not going to answer any of his questions, at least in that direction, and lapsed into silence for the next fifteen minutes. Then he asked, 'You have been to Prague before?'

'This is my first visit.'

'Ah! It is the most beautiful city in Europe.'

'I am looking forward to seeing it,' Anna acknowledged. She had no extensive acquaintance with any European cities save Vienna, Berlin, London and, briefly, Rome during her flight from England. But she did not think she was being unduly patriotic when she still placed Vienna at the top of the list.

'It will be in sight when we top that hill. Did you know that, like Rome, Prague is built on seven hills? On either side of a river. There!' He pointed out of the window into the still-bright evening; it was just coming up to half past seven. 'The Vltava! Do you see all the bridges? And the spires? Prague is known as the city of a hundred spires, but actually there are many more than that.'

Anna smiled. He was so obviously a proudly patriotic Czech that she murmured, 'It is stupendous.'

The train was slowing. The man got up and picked up his topcoat with the same care as he had placed it. Anna also rose, smoothed her dress, straightened her hat, and lifted her small weekend valise down from the rack. Then, as he appeared to be waiting for her to lead the way, she opened the compartment door and stepped into the corridor, aware that he was immediately behind her. As they moved towards the exit, where several other people were already waiting, he suddenly held her arm, and she felt the steel ring of a gun muzzle being pressed into her ribs. 'I am truly sorry, Fraulein,' he said into her ear very softly. 'Just do as I wish, and I will endeavour not to hurt you.'

'What *do* you wish?' she asked without turning her head. She could not undertake immediate action because of the risk to the lives of the other passengers.

'Just to meet your "uncle". I am sure he is not alone.'

The train had stopped. The passengers disembarked one by one. Anna and her captor were last off, and there, some twenty feet away, stood Meissenbach alongside two other men, in plain clothes but with Gestapo virtually written all over them.

'Introduce me,' the man said, still holding her close.

The people who had disembarked in front of them had moved to either side, greeting

110

friends or relations, casting anxious glances at the clearly important trio who were waiting; presumably the Chief Secretary was known by sight to a good many people. The immediate vicinity was clear. 'I do not know your name,' Anna said.

'You may call me Herr Reiffel.'

'Herr Reiffel,' Anna said, and stepped to one side. As she did so, she dropped her valise and stamped down with the high heel of her shoe, at the same time swinging right round, delivering a back-handed blow with the edge of her hand to Reiffel's neck.

Four

A Necessary Tragedy

Reiffel fired, even as he gasped. The angle was not right for a killing blow, but he lost consciousness and fell to his knees. Anna, now standing over him, kicked him in the ribs and, as his body went flaccid, stooped to take the pistol from his hand.

There were several shots, and she stayed on her knees while she watched one of the Gestapo agents go down, and saw two men standing at the far end of the platform, both carrying pistols. They were surrounded by people, but she never doubted her skills. She levelled the automatic she had taken from Reiffel's hand and fired four times. Each of the two men received two bullets in the chest before they could determine that it was the woman firing at them. They both went down.

People were screaming and running in every direction, and the station was rapidly filling with both uniformed police and German soldiers. Anna looked down at the man at her knees. He was groaning and gasping for breath, his hands clutching his stomach. He was, as she had surmised, a Czech patriot. As, no doubt, were his two accomplices. So they were all basically on the same side. But she had destroyed them. Because she could not risk anyone ever learning the truth of her? Or in self-defence? Or had it been to save Meissenbach and her mission to Moscow? Or simply because she was so trained to kill she had reacted instinctively?

Meissenbach crouched to put his arm round her shoulders. 'Anna!' he said, gasping. 'My God, Anna! You saved my life. How...?'

Anna had already decided that the best way to avoid over-exposure was to revert to the innocent-girl act, if that were possible. 'Please, Heinz, take me away from here.'

'Of course, my darling.' His arm tightened and he raised her to her feet.

'Ahem!' said a uniformed officer standing in front of them. 'If you will permit me, Herr Meissenbach.' Very gently he removed the pistol from Anna's hand.

'This man...' Anna began.

'Oh, he will tell us what he was about, Fraulein,' the officer said. 'His accomplices are unfortunately dead. That was remarkable shooting.'

'I closed my eyes,' Anna murmured, 'and just kept firing.' The officer looked as if he wanted to scratch his head, but he resisted the urge. 'And that man,' Anna hurried on, looking at the fallen Gestapo agent. 'Is he...?'

There were several people round him as well. His partner looked up. 'He is hit, but he will survive. You saved our lives as well, Fraulein.'

'I just closed my eyes,' Anna protested again.

'I would like to have a word with you, Fraulein,' the officer requested.

'When the Countess has recovered,' Meissenbach said severely. 'Stand aside.'

The crowd parted and he picked up the valise and assisted Anna to the back of the platform, several of the policemen falling in around them. They emerged on to the street, which was also crowded with excited people. The car door was opened, and Anna collapsed on to the seat, Meissenbach beside her.

'Did I really kill two men?' she whispered.

'Yes,' he said, too thoughtfully, in her opinion.

'We were leaving the train and this man suddenly pushed his pistol into my back and told me to walk him past your guards. I knew he was planning something terrible. So I just, well...'

'Closed your eyes and went berserk,' Meissenbach suggested. 'But in a most professional way. Do you do this often?'

'Well of course I do not. I have never had a gun thrust into my back before.' Which was not absolutely true; she had dealt with the Gestapo agent attempting to arrest her in London in exactly the same way.

'And if this news gets around,' Meissenbach said, 'as it certainly will, I very much doubt that anyone will ever push a pistol into your back again. There is a great deal about you, young lady, that I feel I should know.'

114

'Is that not why I am here?'

'I was not thinking sexually.'

His tone suggested that he might have some difficulty in thinking of her sexually ever again. But that might not be a bad thing...

The car swung into the grounds of Prague's Hradcany Castle, where several men and women were waiting for them; obviously the police at the station had telephoned ahead. 'Are you all right, Herr Secretary?' someone asked.

'Yes,' Meissenbach replied. 'Thanks to the Countess von Widerstand.'

Anna gave them a shy smile. 'Do you think I could change my clothes?' she asked softly.

'Of course. Frieda, take the Countess to the apartment we prepared for her.' He looked at his watch. 'Eight o'clock. Will you join me for dinner at nine?'

'Yes. I would like that.'

She followed Frieda, who had taken charge of the valise. The woman was somewhat angular, her yellow hair secured in a tight bun, and had sombre features. She wore skirt and blouse and low-heeled shoes. 'I am sorry your arrival in Prague was so distressing, Countess.'

'So am I. Do things like this happen often?'

'I'm afraid the Reich is much hated here.' They had climbed a flight of stairs and proceeded along a wide corridor. Now she opened a door. 'But to attempt to assassinate the First Secretary ... well, that is outrageous.

There will be repercussions. Can I get you anything, Countess?'

'I should like a bath.'

'The bathroom is beyond that door. Shall I draw it for you?'

'Thank you, but I can manage.'

Frieda peered at her. 'Are you all right, Countess? Such an experience.'

'I will be all right,' Anna said bravely.

The woman did not look convinced, but she nodded and left the room. Anna ran the water; the bathroom was clearly shared with another bedroom, but she locked the intervening door. Then she undressed. *There will be repercussions*, she thought. How little that woman knew. But however much she regretted what she had had to do, she could have no doubt that it was the only thing she could have done while remaining Anna Fehrbach in the eyes of her German masters. How they would react was another matter.

She soaked in the bath and nearly nodded off; she was far more exhausted than she had realized, and now that the flow of adrenaline was starting to slow she felt absolutely drained.

'Anna?'

She sat up. Shit! She had not locked the outer door. 'I am in the bath. I will be out in a moment.' There was a short towelling gown hanging on the door. She wrapped herself in this, released her hair, and returned to the bedroom.

Meissenbach was standing at the window,

looking out. Now he turned to face her. 'Forgive me, Anna. I did not mean to intrude.'

'I did not realize you were so...'

'I have General Heydrich on the line.'

'So quickly?'

'The news of what happened was wired straight through to Berlin. He wishes to speak with you.'

Anna looked left and right.

'There is no telephone up here. You must come down.'

'Just give me a few moments to get dressed.'

'Anna, General Heydrich is on the line. Now.'

Anna sighed, and allowed herself to be escorted down the stairs and into an office, causing every head they passed to turn and look at her exposed legs and bare feet; they could tell that she was naked under the robe. She picked up the phone on the desk and held the receiver in the other hand. 'Herr General?'

'Anna! What has happened?'

'I had to shoot a man. Well, actually two men. To stop them killing Herr Meissenbach.'

'I was told a third man was involved.'

'Yes. But I didn't have to shoot him.'

'Anna, was not Meissenbach guarded? Were there no police on the platform? Did they not shoot anybody?'

'Well, no, Herr General. There were only three assassins.'

'And with all those policemen present as well as his guards, you were left to do the

117

shooting?'

'Well … I suppose I reacted the quickest.'

'As you always do. But Anna, we do not wish the Russians to get the idea that we are sending them a professional assassin. It might just put this fellow Chalyapov off.'

Anna looked over the phone at Meissenbach, who, while clearly enjoying the view, was also clearly listening: Heydrich had a penetrating voice.

'I will do my best to hush the business up,' the general went on. 'But as it happened in front of a few hundred people that may be difficult. However, I would be much obliged if you would refrain from shooting anybody else without orders from me. Now tell me this: I understand you left the train in the company of the third man, with a pistol held to your back. How did this happen?'

'He joined me in my compartment.'

'And?'

'Nothing. He made polite conversation. But there was something suspicious about him. I am sure he had been looking for me before joining me. And when the train stopped he pulled this gun and made me escort him towards Herr Meissenbach. I then realized his intention, and stopped him.'

'And his two accomplices. You say he was looking for you? How did he know who you were?'

'I do not know, sir.'

'Well, I wish you to find out. As of now you are in charge of the investigation as an officer

118

in the SD. I will inform the local Gestapo. But remember, no more shooting.'

Anna continued to look at Meissenbach, whose face was expressionless, but whose brain was clearly working very fast. 'And as regards anyone who might have been there, sir, and wishes to know more about it? Or me?'

'Whoever that may be, from the Governor-General down, refer him to me.'

The phone went dead.

Meissenbach was now looking decidedly apprehensive. 'I think you heard what he said,' Anna suggested.

'What do you want me to do?'

'I need to know everyone you told that I was coming. Everyone, please. I will go and dress and join you for dinner.'

Dinner was set in a small private room. A single waiter served champagne and was then dismissed; it was a cold table.

'You look enchanting,' Meissenbach said, bending over Anna's hand. 'You *are* enchanting. Will you...?'

Anna moved her finger to and fro. 'You heard the General, Heinz.' She served cold meat on to her plate, added salad and sat down.

Meissenbach did the same, sitting opposite her and pouring them each a glass of wine. 'But you are not coming to Moscow as my assistant.'

'Did you ever really suppose that I was?'

119

'And you are a professional assassin,' he said thoughtfully.

'I have been trained to kill,' Anna said carefully. 'When it is necessary to do so. It is not my prime function. But I am not prepared to continue this conversation in this direction. I am sorry, but as you have gathered, I am controlled by the head of the Secret Service.'

'I do understand, my dear Anna. But you must forgive me for wondering ... What is the purpose of your visit to Prague?'

'Why, Heinz, I came here to sleep with you. Is that not what you had in mind?'

Meissenbach drank some wine. 'Well, I did have that in mind.'

'But?'

'Well, let me put it this way. You are not exactly the young woman whom I thought I was ... How shall I put it?'

'Attempting to seduce? I suppose older men often misjudge the character of young women they attempt to pick up. Would you like me to return to Berlin?'

'Well, no, of course not. It's just that...'

Now that she had had a bath and a glass of wine, the adrenaline was racing through her arteries once again. 'Would you like *me* to seduce you, Heinz? A lot of men find this a good idea.'

'Did you make up that list?' Anna asked. The room was still dark, but there were chinks of light beyond the curtains.

Meissenbach rolled on to his side to nuzzle

her. 'Will you answer a question?'

'Another one? If it is not to do with my job.'

'Did you feel any passion at all? I almost thought you had an orgasm.'

'I did.'

'But you were thinking of other things.'

'When I am making love, Heinz, I am making love. Nothing else matters. Were you not satisfied?'

'I have never had an experience like that in my life.' He reached for her, rolling her on to her side to hold her against him. 'Will you do it again?'

Anna kissed him. 'Of course. But we must not be long; we have work to do.'

'And when you are working, you are working. Just as when you are killing someone, you are killing someone. I am beginning to understand certain things about you. But I doubt I could ever understand what is your driving force.'

Anna threw a leg across his and studied him. 'I think you probably could. But I am not going to tell you.' She felt beneath her. 'Let us love some more and then leave it for the day.'

He was like a very young man, at that moment, although she knew she was exhausting him and it took a long time. Then she lay on his chest and allowed her hair to trickle across his face. 'You are supreme,' he muttered, his hands caressing her buttocks. 'An absolute goddess.'

'You say the sweetest things.'

'I have fallen in love with you.'

She swung her legs off the bed and sat up. 'That would be very unwise of you, Heinz. It would also be very dangerous. You have me, for the next few months. Enjoy them. Love my body. But my mind is not a lovable place.'

She went into the bathroom, ran the water. He joined her a moment later. 'May I watch you?'

'There is room for two.' She sank into the foam. 'Then we must prepare that list. General Heydrich will expect to hear from us by lunchtime.'

He sat in the tub opposite her. 'There is no list. I told no one you were coming. The staff here only knew that I was expecting a guest for the weekend. They had no idea who the guest was.' He smiled at her. 'Neither did I.'

Anna soaked. 'But you sent me the tickets. Did you get the tickets and write the envelope yourself?'

'Well, no. My secretary did that.'

'Just as she also telephoned my apartment to set up our first date.'

'But she has been with me for the past year.'

'Which is probably at least eleven months too long,' Anna remarked. 'Will she come in today?'

'She does not come in on Saturdays, no. She will be in on Monday.'

'And that is forty-eight hours too late. You know where she lives?'

'Yes,' he muttered. 'You wish her picked up? Gabriella! I cannot believe it. What will you do to her?'

Anna got out of the bath and wrapped herself in a towel. 'Believe me, Heinz, I dislike the idea of doing anything to her. I would like to think she will be cooperative. But it would seem that she is a member of some resistance organization. She will have to be very cooperative if she is to save herself a lot of unpleasantness.'

Heinz also got out of the bath. 'But at the end of it...'

'She will either die or be sent to a concentration camp. I would say death is the preferable alternative. But she may think differently.'

'I am glad we did not have this conversation before ... well...'

Anna went into the bedroom and put on a flowered summer dress and high heels, added her ring and earrings and also her crucifix, then strapped on her watch. 'We do what we have to do to survive. I do, anyway. She must be picked up right away. But I wish her brought to me first.'

Anna was given a small office of her own, and was promptly visited by a little man in plain clothes who made her think of a ferret. 'I am Herr Feutlanger,' he announced importantly. 'Gestapo Commander in Prague.'

'Then do sit down,' Anna invited.

He did so, peering at her. '*You* are Anna Fehrbach?'

'I am afraid so.'

He stared at her dress and jewellery. 'You are not what I expected.'

'The story of my life,' Anna said sadly.

'I have been told that I am to treat you as a senior officer in the SD.' His tone suggested that he could not believe what he was saying.

'I am a senior officer in the SD.'

'But you are a young girl.'

'I began early. Is this a social call, or do you have something for me? I would like to know how the business is being handled.'

Feutlanger gazed at her for several seconds. 'It is reported in the press as an assassination attempt which was handled by Herr Meissenbach's bodyguards. I gather quite a few people saw you with a gun in your hand but it all happened so very quickly that no one can be certain who fired the shots. In any event, you will be kept anonymous. Those are my instructions from Berlin.'

'Thank you, that is very satisfactory. But I did not kill the third man.'

'That is what I wish to speak to you about. We would, under normal circumstances, expect to obtain vital information from this man, as regards his principals and other members of his group. Unfortunately, these are not normal circumstances.'

'What do you mean?'

'His neck is broken.'

'Surely not. I did not—'

'Hit him that hard? In that case, Fraulein, he is probably fortunate that his head is still on his shoulders. The fact remains that three vertebrae in his neck are shattered, he is breathing with great difficulty, and he cannot articulate at all. The doctor tells me he may regain some speech in the future, although he is likely to be paralysed from the neck down. However, the future is of no use to us.'

'I am sorry. I acted instinctively.' Feutlanger looked sceptical, so she continued. 'However, we have another lead, a woman called Gabriella Hosek.'

'You are speaking of Herr Meissenbach's secretary? We have no information that she is involved in any subversive activity.'

'Nevertheless, she is the only person, apart from Herr Meissenbach himself, who knew that I was coming to Prague. I do not mean that she knew anything about me, apart from my address, which presumably allowed me to be placed under surveillance, and my description given to the assassination squad so that I could be picked up and used as a shield for Reiffel to get close to Herr Meissenbach.'

'Which was unlucky for him,' Feutlanger observed. 'I had an uncle who worked in West Africa. One day he thrust his hand into a laundry basket to find something he thought he had left in the pocket of a dirty shirt, and pulled it out attached to a very large scorpion. He nearly died from the sting.'

Anna regarded him in turn for some seconds, then she said, 'You say the sweetest things. We must hope that Herr Reiffel is as fortunate as your uncle. Herr Meissenbach has sent some of his people to tell Fraulein

Hosek that she is needed. I will interview her when she is brought in, but perhaps you would like to be present.'

'If she has a radio or reads a newspaper, she will know what has happened, and has probably already left Prague.'

'In which case I expect you to find her and bring her to me. But I would like her to be in one piece and able to speak.'

Feutlanger nodded, and stood up. 'She will be found and brought to you. I will do this personally. But tell me, Fraulein, are there many women like you employed by the SD?'

'No,' Anna said. 'I am unique.'

Feutlanger closed the door, and she remained gazing at it for some seconds. Again she was aware of some most peculiar sensations. She supposed she could be developing a split personality. Her reactions to what had happened yesterday afternoon had been absolutely instantaneous. She had acted as a dedicated SD agent to the great gratification of her superiors, however much Heydrich might feel she had been overzealous.

But she was not a dedicated SD agent. She was working for MI6. And there was every possibility that the assassination attempt on Meissenbach had been set up by MI6. Why London should wish to eliminate Meissenbach, who did not appear to be a vital cog in the Nazi war machine, she could not imagine. The important point was that she had foiled the plot. There had, of course, been no reason whatsoever for London to inform her that there was a plot; they had no idea she had ever met Meissenbach, quite apart from the possibility that she might be setting off to spend this particular weekend with him. She had to wonder what Billy Baxter's reaction would be when the news of what had happened filtered back, as it certainly would.

And now she was committed to torturing some unfortunate female to find out, for the benefit of her Nazi superiors, just where, and from whom, the plot had emanated. Having herself suffered the sort of treatment she knew the Gestapo could inflict, the thought gave her goose-pimples.

There was a way to avoid that, but that was horrifyingly distasteful as well. On the other hand, whether or not Gabriella Hosek was a fellow MI6 employee, she could be quite sure that the woman would not be able to withstand the treatment, and would therefore reveal everything she knew, which might well jeopardize a much larger network than appeared on the surface.

Shit, shit, shit! she thought. She remembered her Shakespeare, how Richard III had been tormented by the shades of all the people he had sent to their deaths, innocent or guilty. Just how many shades would surround her when this was over?

Her head jerked as the door opened. But it was Meissenbach. 'We have lost her.'

'Obviously she heard or was informed. Feutlanger is after her.' Pray to God, she thought, she either uses her capsule or is killed trying to avoid arrest.

'So you also give orders to the Gestapo.'

She shrugged. 'Essentially they work for the SD, and I am the only SD representative in Prague at this moment.'

'So do you intend to spend the entire day sitting here? I had hoped we would be able to do things together. I mean,' he hastily added, 'like riding together, or going to the museum. Or the cathedral; it is only just up the hill.'

'I think I should stay here, Heinz, until at least lunchtime. We can go sightseeing this afternoon. Unless you think someone else may be waiting to take a pot shot at you?'

'You find all this amusing,' he suggested.

'It is interesting. I try to find all aspects of life interesting.'

'But it is always work before play.'

'Yes. It has to be.'

The telephone on the desk jangled and she picked up the receiver. 'Yes?'

'Who is this speaking?' a woman asked.

'Who do you wish to speak to?' Anna countered.

'Why, my husband of course, you silly girl.'

'Ah!' Anna said, and held out the telephone. 'Your wife.'

Meissenbach gulped as he took it. 'My dear!'

'Are you all right? I have just heard the news.'

'I am quite all right, my dear.'

'People were shooting at you, the radio

said.'

'But they all missed.'

'Good heavens!' Frau Meissenbach's voice was every bit as penetrating as Heydrich's. Anna couldn't decide whether she was pleased or sorry at the turn in events. 'I shall of course return immediately. Expect me for lunch.'

'Ah ...Yes, my dear. It is good of you to cut short your holiday.'

'You are my husband. My place is at your side in this hour of need. By the way, who answered the telephone? It did not sound like Fraulein Hosek.'

'It was one of the maids.'

'Well, she deserves a good caning. Her tone was quite brusque.'

'Ah. Yes, my dear.'

'Have a car meet me at the station.'

The telephone went dead and Meissenbach gazed at Anna. 'That seems rather to spoil your plans for the weekend,' she said. 'Unless you propose to attempt to carry out her suggestion?'

'My dear Anna, it is just her manner.'

'I was sure of it.'

'But, I suppose you should leave here before lunch.'

Anna smiled at him. 'I am not in a position to do that, sir. I have been ordered by General Heydrich to carry out an investigation into the attempted assassination of a German official. And, as I am sure you understand, I do not propose to disobey my master. If

129

Feutlanger is at all efficient, he will bring in Fraulein Hosek sometime today, so I should be able to leave either tonight or tomorrow morning. However, I agree that I should lunch alone. Perhaps you could have a sandwich and a glass of wine sent in to me?'

'Yes, yes, of course. Anna...'

'Nil desperandum! We shall be in Moscow together. But I do suggest you learn how to cope with your wife by then.' She smiled at him. 'I am sure you appreciate that it would be most unfortunate were she and I to, shall I say, come to blows.'

Left alone, Anna paced the room. The mood she had known in Berlin was back. She had again been catapulted into a position of supreme power, only this time she was not going to be able to sidestep it, to let events take their course. That course was already delineated. And it was attracting her, that was the terrifying thought. I am a monster, she told herself. I am not yet twenty-one, and I am a monster. Then she told herself, I am doing what has to be done. As long as I remember that, and do not use it for personal gratification, I surely can still, one day, become a human being again.

The telephone jangled. 'Feutlanger here, Fraulein. We have found the woman.'

Breath rushed through Anna's nostrils. 'Where is she?'

'She is here, in our downstairs department.'

'Is she badly hurt?'

'She is not hurt at all. Well, a few bruises.'

'Have you interrogated her?'

'Not as yet. I was under the impression that you wished to do that, personally.'

'Yes,' Anna said. 'I will be right down.'

She replaced the phone, remained sitting absolutely still for several minutes. She felt vaguely sick. There could be no doubt about what she had to do; even Gabriella Hosek would know she was being saved hours of agony and a horrible death. But that did not relieve her of the guilt. She had to kill in the coldest of blood. She had only ever done that twice before; all her other victims had been in immediate and dynamic response to a certain situation which could only be resolved by force. The two men she had executed had been on direct orders from her superiors. But if Clive could somehow be here, would he not command her to prevent this woman from revealing the names of her accomplices? She had to believe that. Hosek should have attended to the matter herself. But as she had not...

She opened her handbag and took out the cyanide capsule she always kept secreted in a special little pocket. Then she closed the handbag and slung it on her arm. The capsule she palmed inside her closed left hand, got up and went down the stairs.

She had reached the ground floor when she was suddenly joined by Meissenbach.

'Anna! I am told they have brought in

131

Gabriella.'

'Yes. I am going to see her now.'

'When you say "see"...'

'Yes, Heinz. I am going to ask her to give us the names of her associates in this plot.'

'Do you think she will tell you?'

Anna gazed at him. 'They always do.'

'You are a devil from hell.'

'I am a servant of the Reich, who has been taught to do her duty.'

He licked his lips. 'I should like to be present.'

'It gives you pleasure to see a woman tortured?'

'I wish to see you at work.'

Anna considered. But his presence might just provide the distraction she needed for Feutlanger and his people. She did not suppose a man so essentially uncertain in his relations with women would be unable at least to comment, if not actually interfere. 'If you wish,' she agreed. But she could not resist adding, 'And if you are sure your wife will not object.'

'She need not know of it.'

Anna shrugged and led him down the next flight of stairs as indicated by the Gestapo agent who was waiting for them. At the bottom there was a corridor and several closed doors. But one of these was guarded by another agent, who opened it for her.

'Fraulein!' Feutlanger beamed at her, then looked past her at Meissenbach. 'Herr Secretary?'

'Fraulein Hosek happens to be my secretary,' Meissenbach said.

'Yes, sir. Well...'

He stepped aside and Anna led Meissenbach into the room. Having been in a Gestapo interrogation chamber before, she was not affected by the rows of unpleasant-looking instruments on the walls, or hanging from the ceiling. But she was interested in the woman who was sitting in a straight chair before the desk, her hands cuffed behind her back. She wore a skirt and blouse, both somewhat dishevelled, and had lost her shoes. She was quite an attractive woman, with short fair hair and good features. Her eyes lit up as she saw her employer. 'Herr Meissenbach! Heinz!'

Meissenbach gave Anna an embarrassed glance. She waggled her eyebrows at him.

'Please help me,' Gabriella begged. 'These men...'

'Your people tried to kill me,' Meissenbach pointed out. 'And you were involved. Why did you do this, Gabriella?'

Gabriella bit her lip, and Feutlanger looked at Anna; it was his turn to raise his eyebrows.

'Yes,' Anna said. 'With respect, Herr Meissenbach, we are wasting time. Every moment is important if this woman's accomplices are not to get away.'

'Yes,' Meissenbach agreed. 'Yes. What will you do to her?'

'We will begin with a flogging. This often is all that is required, with a woman.'

133

'Absolutely,' Feutlanger said enthusiastically. 'Strip the bitch.'

'I will do it,' Anna said. The men all looked at her, and she smiled at them. 'I have my rights.'

Feutlanger and Meissenbach exchanged glances. As they did so Anna gave a little cough and put her hand to her mouth, slipping the capsule under her tongue. 'Excuse me,' she said and then bent over the woman. 'What a pretty blouse,' she said softly. 'It goes with your pretty face, Gabriella. Do you think your face will still be pretty when we have finished with you? I should like to kiss you.'

Gabriella stared at her in a mixture of horror and consternation, as Anna took her face between her hands and kissed her very firmly. Gabriella's lips parted, and Anna used her tongue to push the capsule into the woman's mouth. With her right hand she appeared to be stroking Gabriella's chin, but was actually holding her mouth closed, while with her left hand she stroked Gabriella's cheek, following the fingers with her lips to reach her ear. 'Bite,' she whispered. 'For God's sake, bite.'

She straightened and stepped back. 'Now then.' She dug her fingers into Gabriella's blouse and pulled, to tear the buttons open. 'I will need a knife for the underclothes,' she said.

'Fraulein!' shouted one of the agents. 'Fraulein!'

Anna again straightened and watched Gabriella's head droop.

'What the...?' Feutlanger pushed her out of the way, thrust his hand into Gabriella's hair to pull her head up and looked into the staring eyes.

'That is cyanide!' Anna cried, apparently distraught. 'My God, and I kissed her!' Her knees gave way and Meissenbach had to hold her up.

'How did this happen?' the Secretary demanded.

Anna was recovering. 'Was she not searched?'

'Of course she was searched,' Feutlanger snapped. But he was looking at his men for confirmation.

'Yes, Herr Feutlanger,' one of them said. 'I searched her myself.'

'You searched her mouth?' Anna demanded.

'Yes, Fraulein.'

'Well, you were obviously not very efficient. This is a shitting awful mess. She was our only lead.' She looked at Meissenbach. 'Will you kindly arrange for me to return to Berlin immediately? This whole sorry business must be reported to General Heydrich.'

'Fraulein,' Feutlanger protested.

'You will no doubt hear from General Heydrich in due course,' Anna told him, and left the room.

Although it was late Saturday afternoon before Anna regained Berlin, Heydrich was still

135

in his office. 'There's a pity,' he remarked. 'There can be no doubt it was a conspiracy. Now we shall never know who else was involved. I am not blaming you, Anna. I have no doubt that you have saved Meissenbach's neck. Do you think Feutlanger will get any further?'

Anna's nerves had settled down during the train journey, although her mind was still a mass of jumbled emotions. But her voice was as calmly composed as always. 'I very much doubt it, after the mess he and his men made over the Hosek arrest. What I would like to know is what the conspirators had in mind. Surely if they were going to murder anybody, it should have been General von Tropa, not his First Secretary.'

'Ah, but you see, von Tropa is an indecisive imbecile, and the Czechs know this. That they are kept in subjection is because of the ruthlessness of Heinz Meissenbach.'

Anna raised her eyebrows. 'Herr Meissenbach is ruthless?' She thought of the rather diffident Lothario who was apparently terrified of his wife.

'You did not know this, eh? Tell me, did you sleep with him?'

'Well...' Anna could feel her cheeks burning. 'He wanted to, and he is to be my boss. And he said you had given permission.'

'I did, but I assumed he would not seek to use the permission until after you had got to Moscow. You must have turned his head completely. Was his lovemaking gentle or brutal?'

'He actually found it difficult to get going at all. He had no idea, well...'

'That you could be more deadly than a black mamba? That too is a pity. As you remember, I did not want him to know so much about you. I will have to have a chat with him when he arrives on Monday. However, I would not like you to under-estimate him. He may have been temporarily overcome by your special skills, especially as he appears to have been entirely overcome by your looks, and he may also be somewhat afraid of his wife – she has the family money – but his record for quite savage behaviour towards those he regards as his enemies, or as enemies of the Reich, is unquestionable.'

'You told me that he would not be able to touch me – I mean in a disciplinary manner.'

'He has no powers to do so, certainly. But he is a man, as I have said, of rather deep in-stability. Just keep that in mind.'

'May I ask, Herr General, why you did not warn me of this when giving me this assignment? And would you have warned me of it now, but for that incident on the platform?'

Heydrich shrugged. 'What I do, or do not do, is not something I expect you to enquire into. Your job is to carry out your assignment and please me. However, I did not warn you because I did not suppose it would be neces-sary. You made it so. Now listen. General Himmler feels that it would be improper for us to leave Count von Schulenburg entirely in the dark, and that to do so may make your task more difficult than is necessary. The Count will not be informed of your exact mission, but he is being told that you are an SD agent who is carrying out a special and top-secret assignment.'

'Yes sir.'

'General Himmler also feels that, again to ease your position, it is necessary to put the head Gestapo agent in the Embassy into the picture. He will be told to lend you all assistance, and you are, of course, his senior. His name is Groener.'

'Yes sir. I feel I should point out that Herr Feutlanger was not very happy at having to take orders from me. Will Herr Groener be more amenable?'

'Whether he is or not, he is an agent of the Reich, and will obey his orders. As will you, Anna. Now, it may be necessary from time to time to give you additional information or instructions. These will come through Groener. However, he is not to be informed of your overall objective at any time. I expect great things of you. Now, off you go and get me some results.'

'I am sorry, Fraulein,' Bartoli said. 'I have received nothing further from London. When do you leave for Moscow?'

'Next week.'

'Then we must assume that your orders stand. I will wish you good fortune. Will I be seeing you again?'

'When I return to Berlin. But that may not be for a few months. I will wish *you* good fortune.'

She went to her apartment. She had gone straight to the boutique from Gestapo Headquarters knowing that as it was Saturday it would be open late. It had been one of the longest days of her life, and there had been quite a few of those.

She thought she could still taste Gabriella's lips, and she was sure she could taste the capsule, although she knew that had to be impossible, or she would also be dead. But it would have to be replaced. Not that she supposed there was the least risk of her being arrested by the NKVD; she would be a fully accredited German Embassy official, and even if they found cause to be suspicious of any of her activities, they could only deport her back to Germany.

She paid off the taxi and entered the lobby. 'Countess?' The concierge was agitated. 'I did not expect you until Monday.'

'Prague was rather boring,' Anna said.

'Ah. Yes. Shall I inform Fraulein Gessner?'

'I gave her the weekend off; you mean she is there?'

'Oh, yes, Countess.'

'Well I am going straight up, so there is nothing for you to do.' She frowned as she saw his eyes dilate. She rode up in the elevator, as was her custom whenever her suspicions were aroused, running over in her mind all the various possibilities. But there was only one. Was Birgit entertaining someone? The young woman had always appeared totally sexless. She thought it might be rather amusing.

She unlocked the apartment door, crossed the lobby and entered the drawing room. She gazed at the coffee table on which there were two empty schnapps glasses. She could hear voices coming from the kitchen, and again frowned, because both of them were female. Birgit and...?

She walked along the corridor. The kitchen door was open. She stood in the doorway, gazing at Birgit, who was in the midst of cooking, and Marlene, both of whom were naked. *When the cat's away*, she thought.

They seemed to notice her at the same time.

'Countess?' Birgit gasped.

'Anna!' Marlene cried.

'We...' Birgit began.

'Did not expect me back until Monday? When did you move in, Marlene?'

'Well ... I was so lonely...' Marlene was blushing.

Anna's heart was pounding. Coming on top of the Gabriella Hosek incident, seeing the two attractively naked young women in front of her, knowing what they must have been doing, had her emotions seething again. At the same time she was furious. The fury was mainly directed at herself for being turned on, but it still made her want to hurt, to

140

destroy. And did this creature not deserve to be destroyed? It could be done now. All she had to do was pick up the telephone and tell Heydrich that the girl was again not measuring up, and she would be gone forever. In fact, she could execute her here and now, and explain to Heydrich afterwards.

Emotions apart, she had so many problems to be attended to that the removal of even a potential one would be a great relief. And what was she concerned about? Just twenty-four hours ago she had killed two men and destroyed a third. And nine hours ago she had executed Gabriella Hosek. Executing Marlene would certainly be protecting herself, and possibly other MI6 agents such as Bartoli.

And the girl was an SD operative, however much she might be on probation. But she knew she was not going to do it. The fact was that she was desperate to prove, if only to herself, that she was not an indiscriminate murderess.

Birgit and Marlene had insensibly moved towards each other and were now holding hands; if one was going to be punished, so would the other. Anna surveyed them, and realized that they both smelt faintly of her very expensive perfume. 'Do I understand that you have been having sex in my bedroom?'

'I ... we ... it is such a lovely bedroom,' Marlene stammered.

Again Anna had a powerful desire to punish

her, at least physically, to stretch her across the bed and whip her insensible. But she knew herself too well. If she once allowed that destructive urge to control her, she would do the girl a serious injury. And in fact her violent emotions were beginning to calm. But at the same time, she would need to keep a very close eye on her.

'You were sent to me on probation. I wish you to remember that your very existence hangs by a thread. Now return to the barracks, collect your things and come back here. I will allow you an hour. You will remain here until we leave Berlin. I think the dinner is burning, Birgit. Turn off the stove, and then strip my bed and remake it with clean sheets. When Marlene returns she will clean the bathroom. When you have finished making the bed you will prepare a fresh meal. Remember that, as of now, you are also on probation.'

She went into the drawing room to pour herself a glass of schnapps. Then she sat on the settee. She had sat here for her first embrace with Clive Bartley. She had also sat here with her arm round Gottfreid Friedemann's shoulders, her pistol resting on the nape of his neck, before executing him.

That had been just under two years ago. She wondered if she had advanced or declined since that day. She also wondered if she had just made a mistake. Only time would tell.

★　★　★

'I just dropped in to say cheerio,' Clive said. 'They have at last got their act together, and I am off tomorrow. Gibraltar then Cairo.'

'How is Belinda?' Baxter asked.

'Browned off.'

'While you are like a dog with two tails. Before you push off, something has come in which I thought might interest you.'

Clive sat down and waited.

'We heard this morning that Operation Tomorrow has collapsed.'

'Just like that?'

'There seems to have been some kind of battle at Prague central railway station. Janos and Petar were shot dead, Reiffel was taken prisoner and somehow the Gestapo got on to Hosek.'

'Shit! Did they take her?'

'Apparently not, thank God, but she's also dead. She committed suicide when she was arrested.'

'What a waste. Was it worth it? For Meissenbach?'

'The Czechs thought it was. But that is not really what concerns me. The matter has been rather blanked out by the German news media, which means of course the Czech news media as well. But Razzak was at the station. He was not involved in Tomorrow, he was there as an observer. And naturally he made himself as scarce as possible. But he saw what happened. The shoot-out was a trifle one-sided. Janos and Petar did get off a shot each and one of Meissenbach's bodyguards was hit, but before they could fire again they were both cut down by four shots, each of which hit. Those shots were fired by a young woman who had just got off the train from Dresden.'

Clive frowned.

'She left the train,' Baxter went on, 'in the company of Reiffel. And then suddenly demolished him with a couple of highly sophisticated blows, took his pistol, and opened fire with, as I said, consummate speed and accuracy. Razzak says that Reiffel is not dead, but was paralysed by a blow to the neck, which has left him unable to articulate. Obviously the Gestapo are going to do their damnedest to fix him up, but at least that gives us time to pull the others out. I wonder if anything in this pattern of events is familiar to you?'

'Shit!' Clive muttered.

'Just in case it isn't,' Baxter went on, 'Razzak was able to give a description of the young lady who committed the mayhem: tall, slender, long golden hair, and strikingly handsome features.' He stared at Clive.

'What the devil was she doing in Prague?'

'Killing our agents. You won't believe how it happened. According to Razzak, Hosek learned that Meissenbach was planning to entertain a young woman he had met in Berlin, and told Hosek to arrange her train passage for the weekend. Razzak and his people immediately realized that this was their chance to get right up to the target. So Reiffel picked her up on the train. Can you

144

believe it? I mean, if you were going duck-shooting in a swamp, would you take a croco-dile as company?'

'Hold on. You are not suggesting she was sent by the SD? There is no possible way they, or she, could have known of Tomorrow. She was protecting Meissenbach.'

'Well there must be some kind of link. And I suggest you find out. All I can say is thank God she is going to Russia. That should at least keep her from bumping off any more of our people in Central Europe, however in-advertently. You know how the boffins are always chattering about how one day they will be able to create the ultimate weapon of mass destruction. They don't realize that we already possess it, and that it is quite out of control. Anna is your baby, Clive. You virtu-ally created her. Now it is up to you to sort her out. You had better get to Moscow before she does, just in case she takes a dislike to any of our people there. I am thinking especially of poor Sprague. Have a good flight.'

Five

Moscow

'Mr Bartley!' The Flying Officer ticked Clive's name off a list on his desk. 'Welcome to Gibraltar. You're for Cairo.'

'That is correct. ASAP.'

'Everyone wants everything ASAP. The problem letter is the P. However, you're in luck. Your flight leaves at 1800.'

Clive looked at his watch: it was just after eleven, or as this bloke would have it, 2300. 'That is nineteen hours away,' he pointed out. 'I really am in a hurry.'

'Everyone is in a hurry. You really don't want to go flying the length of the Mediterranean in daylight, old man. Musso may not be up to much, but he does have an air force, and you won't have any fighter protection. Have a good night's sleep and a restful day. I am sure Cairo can exist for another twenty-four hours without you.'

It's not Cairo that bothers me, Clive thought. 'And where do you recommend I have this good night's sleep?'

'Accommodation ... Ah, Parkyn!' he called.

'Sir?' A young woman, trim in her WAAF

146

uniform, appeared in the doorway. She had pleasant features, a solid figure, and short yellow hair. Everyone's concept of the girl next door, Clive supposed.

'Would you attend to this gentleman, Mr...' He checked his list again. 'Mr Bartley. He needs accommodation until 1700. Perhaps you could also arrange to have him picked up at that time and brought back to the station.'

'Of course, sir.' Miss Parkyn smiled at Clive and then at her superior. 'Will that be all for tonight, sir?'

'Oh, indeed. You may go off then.'

'If you'd come with me, sir.'

Clive picked up his suitcase and followed her into another office presently unoccupied. 'Do sit down.' She sat herself behind the desk.

Clive took a chair, glancing out of the open window. It was a brilliantly starry night, and so delightfully warm. He had a sudden feeling of relaxation. The flight over Biscay had been tense because of the possibility of German planes coming out from the French coast. They had seen none, but he had still been very pleased to land. The airstrip lay across the neck of land between the fortress and the Spanish mainland, and to their left the lights of Algeciras had glowed with all the brightness of a typical Spanish evening.

'Are you a VIP?' Miss Parkyn asked.

'Not really.'

'You're not in uniform. And yet you have the use of RAF transport. Or am I being too

147

inquisitive?'

'I'm afraid the answer has to be yes.'

'Ah. Hush hush. But I need to have some idea of where to put you. *If* I can put you anywhere.'

'Somewhere inconspicuous. Not the Rock.'

She began telephoning while he studied her, although he really wanted to think about Anna. Anna was a huge question mark. He knew that she had turned to him entirely by chance. He had happened to reappear in her life at the very moment when she had been 'disciplined' by her German employers, and had been a bundle of angry and humiliated nerves. Contrary to Baxter's supposition he had not created Anna: Anna had created him for her own purposes. She had loved him, physically, with all the intensity that made her at once the most desirable, and equally the most deadly woman in the world. How much, and how honestly, she had accepted his tutelage and then his leadership, he did not know. Perhaps he would never know. Baxter certainly was not yet convinced that she was genuinely committed to the Allied cause. *He* believed in her, but was that because he so desperately *wanted* to believe in her?

Yet the questions continued to cluster about her. What had she been doing in Prague? He did not really believe she had been a bodyguard for Heinz Meissenbach. There was nothing in his knowledge of her to indicate that she had ever been employed in that capacity by the SD, or that she had ever

148

met Meissenbach – yet she had apparently been intending to spend the weekend with him. He simply could not afford to be jealous of a woman like Anna, but it was difficult. And why was she going to Russia? He knew it could not be for so simplistic a reason as to obtain current Russian opinion. No doubt that mystery at least would be resolved when he finally saw her.

Which could be within the next couple of days. Cairo, Athens, probably some town in southern Russia, and then Moscow – not more than a week, depending upon how many officious flight controllers he encountered. And how soon after that would he hold her in his arms? It was one of those thoughts that could leave a man breathless, but which had to be resisted. He could not argue with Baxter's opinion that he was an utter scoundrel. But his excellence at his job was based upon an often ruthless single-mindedness which he liked to think was almost, if not quite, in the class of Anna herself. Spending the next week dreaming of Anna would be extremely distracting, and could even be dangerous. But here was this rather appealing, if alarmingly normal, young woman, who wore no rings, and was now smiling at him.

'I'm afraid the situation looks a bit grim, Mr Bartley. You see, since Italy entered the war, the garrison here has been more than doubled, and in addition, it is the staging post for everyone trying to get to Malta or the Middle East. So...'

'I sleep on a park bench, is that it? Is there a park in Gibraltar?'

'There's the beach front. But it would be a little uncomfortable.' She gazed at him, as if considering the situation, but he had an idea that she had already reached a decision. She was a serving soldier, and had to be circumspect in her relations with all other servicemen – or women – and that apparently now comprised ninety per cent of the Rock's population. But he was not in the services, at least as far as she knew. 'I could find you a bed...'

He waited.

'I share a room with another girl, but she has a furlough and has gone up into Spain. She apparently wants to see a bullfight.'

'One room?'

'I'm afraid so. If sharing isn't really your sort of thing, well...' She gave a pretty little blush.

'My dear Miss Parkyn, I don't seem to have much alternative. But I don't think I'd want to take the alternative, even if it was offered. Are you quite sure you want to put up with me for the next twelve hours or so?'

'I'm sure that you are a gentleman, Mr Bartley,' she said enigmatically.

'Well then, at least tell me your Christian name.'

'Thistleton-Brown,' announced the handlebar moustache, who wore the insignia of a Wing-Commander.

150

'Bartley.'

Thistleton-Brown looked him up and down as best he could in the gathering gloom. 'Diplomatic wallah?'

'That's one way of putting it,' Clive agreed.

'And you're for Cairo?'

'If that's where this plane is going.'

'Been here long?'

'Overnight.'

'Did you have any sleep? Not a bed in the place.'

'I managed to find one,' Clive said modestly. He had in fact slept very well, and as Alice Parkyn had told him to make himself at home when she had left for the station that morning, he had had a very comfortable and relaxing day. Then she had returned for him as arranged, and had just dropped him off in the small car she had the use of. 'I really am grateful,' he had said, 'for your generosity.'

'I am grateful too.'

'For having me hanging around?'

'For your being a gentleman,' she had said a trifle wistfully.

Perhaps he had missed something there. But it had not been the time, and he already had at least one woman too many on his mind.

'Gentlemen,' said the Flying Officer. 'All set? Malta in two hours, for fuel. Cairo by dawn.'

It was a very small aircraft and Clive and the Wing-Commander were the only passengers, sitting one in front of the other. 'Not

151

nervous, I hope?' Thistleton-Brown asked over his shoulder.

'Should I be?' Clive asked innocently.

The noise of the engine precluded further conversation, and they climbed into another disturbingly bright night, with the lights of Spain blazing away behind them. Clive tried not to think about anything, and especially not Anna. She was there, and he was going to her.

'Gentlemen,' said the pilot over the Tannoy, 'I'm sorry to say that we have company. I am going down. We stand our best chance of avoiding interference close to the sea.'

The plane dropped sharply. Clive looked out of his window but could see nothing. They descended for several seconds, then straightened out again. 'I think we've lost the buggers,' the pilot said.

But just then there was a tearing sound. Clive twisted his head and saw a large rent in the fuselage behind him. The plane swerved violently and began to climb again. Another tearing sound and he felt a sudden jolt. *My God!* he thought. *I've been hit!* The night suddenly became very dark.

Anna gazed out of the window at the seemingly endless Polish plain. The soil was black; the harvest had recently been gathered, before the onset of the autumnal rains.

She was glad to have put Warsaw behind her. The pinewoods the train had passed through on its way to the capital had brought

152

back her visit to her mother and sister too vividly. She turned her thoughts to what lay ahead: the Soviet Union – and Chalyapov. If it had been amusing to hear Heydrich say that the Russian wanted a totally uninhibited woman, and that she was clearly such a woman, she wondered for how long she could maintain that façade. She had been required to do it on a day by day basis for nearly a year with Ballantine Bordman, but he, being a totally inhibited Englishman, had been easy to satisfy. Heydrich had indicated that Chalyapov might just fall into the satyr variety.

And then there was Meissenbach. And his wife. She had met the lady when boarding the train, and had been formally introduced. Frau Meissenbach was a rather plump woman of slightly above average height, though several inches shorter than Anna herself. She wore her hair bobbed, perhaps to make her rather severe features more severe yet. As Heydrich had indicated, Meissenbach could only have married her in the first place for her money, so it was simple to understand why he could not keep his hands off any available woman. She had regarded Anna with the deepest suspicion. 'This lady is your assistant?' she had enquired coldly. 'Have we met, Countess?'

'I do not think so.'

'Your voice is familiar.'

Anna had glanced at Meissenbach, who was standing behind his wife, waggling his eyebrows in desperation. 'I am afraid you are mistaken, Frau,' she had said.

'I am never mistaken, you have a very distinctive accent,' Frau Meissenbach announced, and boarded the train.

'Here's to a jolly journey,' Anna remarked.

'It will be all right,' Meissenbach assured her. 'She really does not like travelling.'

Anna raised her eyebrows.

'I will try to see you on the train.'

'I'm sure you will, Heinz; there is only one dining car. I think that if you do not join your wife now, she may come back to look for you.'

He had hurried off, and she had made sure that Marlene and Birgit were settled in their second-class compartment. They seemed to have become inseparable in a couple of days. There was also the extreme intimacy of lovers between them, the occasional secret glance or touch of hands. Should that be cause for concern? She had actually considered calling on Heydrich, or at least Glauber, to supply her with an additional agent to keep an eye on them, but had decided against it. It would inevitably have led to questions, and the agent would necessarily have had to be a woman if she was to share a railway couchette compartment for three days. In any event, both had been totally subservient and anxious to please during the week before their departure from Berlin. Now they were both highly excited.

'This is a Russian train, Countess,' Birgit said in a stage whisper.

'Well of course it is. It is going to Moscow.'

154

'Will we be all right?' Marlene had asked.

'If there is any trouble, report to me. I shall expect you both in my compartment at six o'clock this evening.'

If she had to deal with a crisis, she was prepared to do so, ruthlessly. She had given them their second chance, to obey her in all things without question, which was more than they would have received from any other SD agent.

She nodded off, found herself dreaming of Clive. She wondered if he would be in Moscow before her. But as she did not see how he could get there except via the Mediterranean and the Black Sea, that was unlikely.

She was startled by a knock on the door. She had lowered the corridor blind to ensure complete privacy, but had not locked the door. It now slid back without invitation and a shaggy head looked in.

'Tea, Fraulein?' the guard asked in German. Like all Russian trains, at least in the first-class carriages, there was a huge samovar always bubbling away at the end of the corridor.

'That would be very nice, thank you.'

He returned in five minutes carrying a large pewter container with a handle, inside of which was a pint glass of steaming tea. He did not offer either sugar or milk.

'Thank you,' Anna said faintly. 'Will you tell me who makes up my bed?' She gestured at the bunk opposite; the pillow and blankets were on the net tray above it. Presumably the sheets were already in place.

'I do, Fraulein. I will do it while you are having dinner.'

'Ah. Thank you.'

She assumed he would now leave, but he hesitated. 'You are the Countess,' he proclaimed.

'That is correct.' She wondered if she was to be handed over to the nearest NKVD agent.

'I have a message for the Countess,' he announced.

But perhaps he was only seeking some form of identification, or a tip, before delivering his missive. 'How nice,' she said. 'Will you not tell me what it is?'

'It is from Herr Meissenbach. He invites you to dine with him. At eight o'clock. We will be in Brest-Litovsk by then.'

'Is that important?'

He regarded her with some contempt. 'It is where the change takes place.'

'You mean we change to another train?'

'No, no, Countess. You stay on this train all the way to Moscow.' His tone indicated that in Soviet Russia such wonders of modern science were commonplace. 'But it is necessary to change the gauge, you see.'

Anna did not see at all, but she said, 'You may tell Herr Meissenbach that I shall be pleased to join him for dinner.'

Again he hesitated, now definitely expecting something.

'Is it not illegal either to offer or receive tips

156

in Russia?' she asked innocently.

'Everything in Russia is illegal, Countess.'

'Or immoral, or it makes you fat,' Anna suggested. The guard looked bewildered, so she tipped him anyway, and he left.

The main part of Anna's luggage was in the guard's van, but in the two suitcases she had had delivered to her compartment she had packed three evening gowns. Punctually at six Birgit and Marlene arrived to help her dress. There was no possibility of a bath, and even topping and tailing from the tiny washbasin was a lengthy process. But the two girls worked enthusiastically and were just drying her when the train clanked to a halt.

They had of course drawn the blinds over both the windows and the door, but from the virtually incomprehensible shouts on the platform, she gathered that they were in Brest-Litovsk. It was disconcerting that she recognized so little of what was being said, but she reminded herself that a country as vast as Russia would obviously have a vast number of local dialects.

They heard stamping feet in the corridor and a succession of thunderous raps that now arrived at her door. Anna had only got as far as putting on her cami-knickers. Birgit hastily wrapped the towel around her mistress's torso, just before the door opened to reveal the conductor backed by a man in a green uniform and side cap, armed with a rifle.

Marlene gave a shriek of alarm. Birgit gog-

157

gled at him, still trying to hold the towel in place. Anna assumed her most imperious expression. 'What is the meaning of this?'

'Passports,' the conductor said. 'You must show your passports.'

'In that bag, Marlene,' Anna said. Marlene delved into the handbag and handed the passport to the conductor who passed it to the soldier. He gave it no more than a perfunctory glance, preferring to gaze at Anna, whose legs were totally exposed. As he seemed speechless, the conductor spoke for him. 'And the other ladies?'

'Their passports will be in their compartments, as you well know,' Anna said severely.

'Then they will have to come with us.'

Anna nodded and took control of the towel herself. 'Go along then. May I have my passport back?'

The conductor returned the passport. The soldier had not taken his gaze from Anna.

'I assume your friend has seen a woman before?' Anna enquired, speaking Russian for the first time.

The soldier's head jerked. He flushed and saluted, then moved along the corridor followed by the conductor.

'My God!' Marlene remarked. 'Will this sort of thing happen often?'

'Very probably,' Anna said. 'Now off you go before they place you under arrest. Just remember to come back as quickly as you can.'

★ ★ ★

In what Anna had to suppose was a remarkable feat of engineering, the entire train was now shunted on to a huge turntable and in some incomprehensible manner moved from the narrow gauge of the European railway system to the broad gauge of the Russian. The shunting process took an hour, with a succession of jerks and thuds and sudden stops. With some difficulty she finished dressing, and with even more difficulty completed her make-up. Birgit and Marlene, still outraged, returned to help her do her hair. Then at eight o'clock she made her way to the dining car.

The car was little more than half full, and only a few of the people present, all men with the exception of Greta Meissenbach, were wearing dinner suits. Anna estimated that this minority was the German passengers, the men in lounge suits being Russian. But all their heads turned to watch Anna make her way up the centre aisle, having to pause every few steps to place a gloved hand on the back of a seat; the train was now moving again.

Meissenbach was on his feet to greet her. 'My dear Anna, how charming you look.'

'Thank you, sir.' Anna took the indicated banquette seat beside his wife. 'What a lovely dress,' she lied convincingly. Actually, Greta was wearing a most attractive dress, but it did very little for her rather heavy figure.

'Thank you, Fraulein.' Anna raised her eyebrows and Greta smiled at her. 'Heinz has no secrets from me.'

'Really,' Anna said. 'What a remarkable man.'

Meissenbach sat opposite them, looking apprehensive. 'I felt I should put my wife into the picture. As far as possible,' he hastily added, and signalled the waiter for menus.

'Which is not actually very far,' Greta remarked. 'What exactly is it you do, Fraulein?'

Meissenbach coughed.

'What exactly does your husband do?' Anna asked. 'I mean, what is he going to Moscow to do?'

'Why, he is going to Moscow to take charge of the personnel and organization of the Embassy.'

'Then that is what I am also going to do. Under his supervision, of course.' As Meissenbach did not appear to be ordering aperitifs, she filled her water glass from the carafe on the table, drank and all but choked. 'My God!'

The waiter was now standing beside them, pad and pencil poised. 'Fraulein?'

'What in the name of God is that?'

'It is vodka, Fraulein.' He spoke excellent German.

Greta snorted.

'The Russians drink vodka with everything,' Meissenbach explained.

And you never warned me, Anna thought. 'Well, I would like a jug of water.'

The waiter looked sceptical and then at Meissenbach, who nodded. 'They are an uncouth lot,' he remarked, as the waiter

160

departed. 'But we will have to put up with their little ways.'

'Apparently. Were you visited by the border guards?'

'Indeed. Outrageous. I intend to raise the matter with Count von Schulenburg. But I don't suppose it'll change their detestable habits.'

It was one of the least enjoyable meals of Anna's recent life. But at last Greta needed to powder her nose. Having made this announcement, she waited for Anna to accompany her, but as Anna made no move to do so, she set off by herself, steam emanating from the back of her head.

'I think we are in for a difficult time,' Anna said, stirring her coffee. She had had several glasses of vodka, and now had to contemplate some extremely poor brandy. With her training it took a good deal of alcohol to make her tight, but it could easily make her irritable.

'Please do not let her upset you.' Meissenbach's hand slid across the table to hold hers. 'Anna, I adore you. I must see you again.'

'Aren't you seeing me now?'

'You know what I mean. Listen, I will come to you tonight.'

'Are you out of your mind?'

'There is nothing to be afraid of.' He flushed. 'I don't suppose you would be afraid, no matter what happened. But Greta takes a sleeping pill every night when travelling; any motion, either from a train or a boat, keeps

161

her awake. Midnight.'

Anna looked past him at Greta, just entering the car, and withdrew her hand. But Greta had enjoyed her discomfort over the vodka, not to mention her obvious distaste for caviar. She had it coming. 'I shall look forward to that,' she said softly.

Thanks to the alcohol she fell into a deep sleep, and awoke with a start at the knock on her door. This time she had locked it and had to get out of her couchette. It was a double compartment, and Birgit had thoughtfully laid a dressing gown on the other seat. She put this on, opened the door, and was immediately in his arms. He was certainly anxious; Anna had to reach past him to close and lock the door, and switch on the light.

While she was doing this, he got inside the dressing gown to caress her naked flesh. 'How I have dreamed of this,' he said into her ear. 'You and I on a train together, making love.'

Having sex, she thought. 'Why, Heinz, I thought you had gone off me.'

He sat beside her on the bed, continuing to caress her, moving the dressing gown from her shoulders so that it slipped down her back. 'I was overcome. I admit it. And then Gabriella ... The way you kissed her.' He gazed at her with wide eyes.

'It is my way,' Anna smiled. She had anticipated this question at some stage. 'She was a pretty woman. I like pretty things.'

'But you also like destroying them?'

162

'Sometimes.'

'You are a woman to fear. But then, to be loved by you ... Anna, will you hold him, as you did in Prague?'

That seemed a quick solution to his problem. She slipped her hand inside his pyjamas, and only a few seconds later was washing it in the basin, while he lay back with a sigh. 'Anna, you are a goddess! Anna, if I were to divorce Greta...'

Anna dried her hands and sat beside him. 'Dear Heinz, we are going to Moscow to work. I am, anyhow.'

His eyes, which had been closed, now opened. 'No one has ever told me what that work is. When I think of what you can do ... You do realize that if you were to shoot someone in Russia, it could lead to an international incident?'

'I told you, I am not being sent to Russia to shoot anybody. I am assuming that there is no one in Russia who is going to try to shoot *you*.'

'I should hope not. But you are not going to pretend you are really coming as my aide. Can you type? Can you file? Can you handle public relations? Make appointments, refuse appointments without giving offence, which is often the more important?'

Anna squeezed in beside him on the narrow bunk. 'I have not been trained to do any of those things, but you must pretend that I am indispensable. I am going to Russia to observe and report. General Heydrich, which means the Secret Services, which means the highest level of the Reich Government, wishes to know how the Russians are thinking. He also wishes,' she added thoughtfully, 'to learn whatever he can of the relations between the Russians and the British and the French. So you see, I need to mingle with the diplomats of all of these countries.'

'How do you propose to do that?'

She kissed him. 'You are going to arrange that, Heinz. I wish to be included in all receptions thrown at the Embassy. I wish to be found invitations to all receptions thrown by other embassies, or by Russian diplomats and politicians, to which any Germans are invited.'

'That is a tall order.'

'If it proves at all difficult, I wish you – and your wife, of course – to throw a succession of parties. Dinner parties would be best, to which you will invite anyone of the least importance. I am sure you agree that I will be an attractive guest.'

'I don't know that Schulenburg will be pleased with that. As for Greta...'

Anna again slid her hand inside his pyjamas. 'You will be doing it for the Reich. And for me, of course.'

Belinda Hoskin opened her door to the knock, and gazed at her visitor in astonishment. She had met Billy Baxter before, and she knew that he was Clive's boss, but he had never attempted to contact her before. Now she immediately knew he was the bearer of bad news. 'Mr Baxter?'

'May I come in?'

'Of course, do forgive me.' She stepped back, and closed the door behind him. 'It's about Clive.'

Baxter advanced into the room, looked at the sideboard. 'Shall we have a drink?'

Belinda poured two scotches. 'Tell me.' Baxter sat down and took a long sip. Belinda also sat, the glass held in both hands. 'He's dead.'

'He's in hospital. His plane was shot down, and he is suffering from extreme exposure, as well as various other injuries. I am informed that his condition is not life-threatening, but it may be a little while before he is fit again.'

Belinda had an instinctive feeling that he was lying. 'Shot down? Where was he shot down?'

'Now, Miss Hoskin – Belinda – you know I cannot tell you that. I can tell you that he was on a mission for the Department.'

'And shot down. Am I allowed to see him?'

'Ah ... I'm afraid that is not practical.'

'Why not? You mean ... My God, he's burned!'

Baxter took his pipe from his pocket, regarded it for a few seconds as a drowning man might regard a lifebelt that had suddenly been thrown to him, and then replaced it in his pocket. 'Clive has not been burned, to my knowledge.'

'You mean you have not seen him either?

He's in intensive care?'

'I understand that he was in intensive care, yes. But as I have said, he is now off the danger list.'

'But he was on it. And I'm not allowed to see him.'

'It is simply not practical.'

'So when will he be coming home?'

'As I told you, not for some time.' Baxter finished his drink and stood up. 'I just felt that you should understand the situation.'

'I do *not* understand the situation. Who was with him on this plane?'

Baxter could tell where her thoughts were heading. 'I am not in a position to give you that information. But I can tell you that there was no one on the plane that you know, or have ever known. I will be in touch when I have some more information.' He closed the front door behind himself.

Belinda stared at it for several seconds then hurled the still full glass of whisky at it.

'This place is a dump,' Marlene complained.

Anna had to agree with her. The Kremlin was starkly dramatic, but lacked any suggestion of architectural beauty. At the top end of Red Square were the magnificent, multi-coloured onion domes of St Basil's Cathedral, but they seemed an ornament stuck on the front of a very plain face: the church was no longer used for any religious purpose, and in any event, she had been educated at the Vienna convent to regard Russian Orthodoxy

166

as even more obnoxious than Protestantism.

Surrounding the square were some sub-stantial buildings, such as the GUM depart-ment store, open only to non-Russians as long as they spent their own currency, and the Historical Museum, but neither of these was the least attractive to look at. On the west bank of the Moscow River were several other large buildings that could almost be called palaces; these were, in the main, the foreign embassies. For the rest, there were endless streets of very ordinary houses, and worse, on the outskirts of the city were a mass of drab high-rise apartment blocks.

'It is utterly soulless,' Marlene continued.

'Sssh!' Anna recommended, for their In-tourist guide was approaching them; it had been decided that their first duty was to be shown the sights of the city.

He was a nervous young man named Dmitri who spoke German with a pro-nounced accent. 'Now here, Frauleins, is Red Square, the centre of the city.'

'Why is it called Red Square?' Birgit asked. 'There is nothing red in it.'

'Red does not refer to the colour,' Dmitri said severely. 'In Russian red means brave, courageous, bold. Now, I am going to take you on a tour of the Kremlin. You will see all the art treasures, as well as the great bell and the huge cannon with which our ancestors repelled the Mongols.'

Anna reflected that they were going to get a very one-sided view of history: to her knowledge the Russians had never succeeded in repelling the Mongols.

'But first,' Dmitri went on, 'we will visit the tomb of our great leader.'

'Herr Stalin is dead?' Marlene asked.

Dmitri raised his eyes to heaven. 'I am referring to Vladimir Lenin, the founder of the Communist State. Over here.'

He led them across the cobbles to the Kremlin wall towering some forty feet above them. Let into the wall were a series of niches, each fronted by a portrait. 'In those,' he explained, 'are the ashes of all our great leaders, who have sadly departed from this world.'

Anna could not resist the temptation. 'You mean men like Marshal Tukhachevski and Nicolai Bukharin?' They were two of the Bolshevik leaders executed by Stalin three years before.

'I was speaking of our great leaders, not criminal deviationists,' Dmitri said stiffly.

'Oh, I am sorry. I always thought that Marshal Tukhachevski was the greatest of all Soviet soldiers.'

'A criminal deviationist,' Dmitri insisted firmly. 'Come along, Frauleins.'

'This is going to take all day,' Marlene muttered as they approached the wall and the end of a long line of people.

Anna had to suppose she was right. But Dmitri merely led them up the line to the front, repeating in a loud voice, 'Intourist! Intourist!' and everyone immediately stepped

168

aside.

'Pays to have friends in high places,' she murmured.

There were two armed soldiers slowly goose-stepping up and down outside the entrance to the tomb. Inside the darkened chamber there were more armed guards. The three young women were escorted to the railing to look down past the glass casket at the dead hero reclining on his back with his hands on his chest. He wore a three-piece grey suit and black shoes, and his goatee beard reminded Anna of Reiffel.

'Gosh!' Birgit said. 'When did he die?'

'Sixteen years ago,' Dmitri told her.

'But...'

'He's embalmed, silly,' Marlene said.

As they left the tomb it began to rain. 'This is going to be a long winter,' Anna commented.

Weather-wise she was absolutely correct. At the beginning of September it started to rain seriously; at the beginning of October it started to snow and by the beginning of November the temperatures were well below zero.

'How long does this last?' Marlene enquired of one of the Embassy staff.

'It may start to thaw in April,' he told her.

'Jesus!' she muttered.

Yet they were not uncomfortable, certainly within the Embassy. Anna was given a spacious apartment, to which she was shown by Countess von Schulenburg herself, who explained that this was a wing of the building which had been recently modernised. It contained three bedrooms, the master bedroom being en suite, while the other two had a bathroom between them, a sitting room with a dining table at the far end, and its own small kitchen, so that they did not have to attend meals in the mess hall unless they wished. The original heavy furniture and tasselled brocade curtains remained.

Nor were they bored, at least for a while. In keeping with the role Anna was required to play, Meissenbach allotted her an office of her own where she and Marlene could be surrounded by typewriters and filing cabinets, and even found them work to do, handling various internal affairs of the Embassy. In the evenings they were often escorted to the Puppet Theatre, or the Bolshoi ballet, or concerts at the Moscow Conservatoire, which sometimes included performances by Shostakovich.

To Anna, brought up in Vienna, the work of even the Russian genius was heavy and unexciting, probably due to the fact that everything he wrote had to be approved by a Party official. This applied even more to the film industry, which produced an endless succession of bowdlerised and turgid romances about young women falling in love with young men who were heroes of the Soviet Union for having dug five tons of coal more than their comrades.

The overall word for the society in which

she found herself was grey. Even the cocktail parties to which Meissenbach saw that she was regularly invited were grey affairs in her opinion. The liquor consisted mainly of vodka and Russian 'champagne', which was hardly more than fizzy water. The conversation was so carefully non-committal as to be puerile. Nor did the various commissars appear terribly responsive to her charms. In fact she got the strong impression that the average Russian did not like the average German. Or even the exceptional German.

The atmosphere was slightly better, overall, at the small parties Meissenbach threw in his own quarters, but from Anna's point of view they were rendered less than attractive by the presence of the hostess, whose dislike for her became more evident every day.

But the most important, and disappointing, aspect of her situation was that she was not getting any real work done, on either front. She thought her big moment had come at a party in early October when almost as soon as she entered the room she recognized Chalyapov, standing some distance away, smoking a cigarette and talking to several men. As the young Embassy official who was escorting her obviously did not know who Chalyapov was, and therefore could not be asked to provide an introduction – and as Heydrich had warned her not to be forward, but to let events take their course – she could do nothing more than slowly work her way closer to her target and wait to be noticed. But suddenly, when she was still some ten feet away from him, with quite a few people between them, Chalyapov left the room, apparently without seeing her at all. She scanned the guest lists for every Embassy party, but his name was never on it, while on the one occasion she managed to get hold of a list of staff at the British Embassy, Clive Bartley was also not to be seen. Nor was any attempt made to contact her.

Which was not to say that she lacked male attention. Count von Schulenburg himself clearly enjoyed the view, although equally clearly he was far too much of an old-fashioned gentleman ever to consider taking off after an employee, however attractive. The Count was also disturbed by her very presence. 'This is most unusual and irregular, Countess,' he had remarked when he received her in his office. 'We have never had an SD agent here before, and these instructions that you are to have carte blanche, as it were...' He peered at her. 'I mean, you are really very young to be given such responsibility, and, well...'

'I am also a woman, sir,' Anna said softly.

'Isn't the SD a counter-espionage department? I had no idea they employed women at all.'

'That is one of their secrets, Your Excellency, and we are, after all, a secret department. As regards both my gender and my age, I am merely carrying out my orders. As we are all required to do.'

He frowned at the implied rebuke. 'And I

172

am not to know what those orders are. That is most unsatisfactory.'

'I am sorry, sir. You are of course quite entitled to take the matter up with Herr von Ribbentrop, or indeed with General Himmler, if you so wish.'

'I may take that under consideration, Countess. But I will say this: I will allow you carte blanche to pursue your allotted task, but I will not have the workings of this Embassy – and even more the good relations I have established with Monsieur Molotov and the Soviet Government – in any way disrupted. Please remember that. Good morning.'

If that was ominous, what was even more disturbing was the fact that she definitely did attract Hans Groener. Even if he had no idea what her mission was, there could be no doubt that he had a predatory eye for beauty. Sadly, with his tall, lanky frame, his moon face, and his bristly Prussian hair cut, he was not the least attractive as a man.

He made his move early on, summoning her to his office only a week after her arrival. 'You understand, Fraulein, that I am in charge of Embassy security. And in this regard I require absolute compliance from every member of the staff.'

'That must be very interesting,' Anna said agreeably, sitting before his desk with her knees crossed.

Groener opened the file in front of him. 'There are a few things I need to verify.'

'One of them should be that I am the Countess von Widerstand,' Anna said.

He regarded her for several seconds. 'You are Anna Fehrbach. You are a secretary in the Gestapo. It says so here. Thus you are my junior. But I am informed that you are here in a special capacity, which places you outside my jurisdiction. I wish to know what this is.'

'I am here as Personal Assistant to Herr Meissenbach in whatever capacity he requires of me.'

Another long stare. 'What possible assistance could he expect from a Gestapo secretary?'

Anna smiled at him. 'You will have to ask him that, Herr Groener.' She decided to drop Heinz into it, as that was the easiest solution for her. 'He arranged for the posting.'

Groener's nostrils twitched. 'You have known Herr Meissenbach a long time?'

'It seems that I have known him a very long time,' Anna replied, being absolutely truthful.

'I see. Well, I shall keep an eye on you, and Herr Meissenbach. We do not wish any scandal. I assume Frau Meissenbach is also an old friend?'

Anna smiled again. 'Wives are never close friends with their husband's female aides, Herr Groener.'

It was disconcerting to feel that she was regarded with such suspicion by her own people, but she could do nothing more than ignore them, especially as she had not yet found herself in a position to commence her mission. But it was Groener who came to her at the beginning of December and placed an envelope on her desk. It was addressed to the Countess von Widerstand and marked Top Secret. 'From Berlin,' he announced.

Anna turned the envelope over to look at the seal, which appeared unbroken.

'I have not opened it, Countess. But I am entitled to ask you to inform me of the contents.'

Anna broke the seal and took out the single sheet of paper; it bore Heydrich's personal crest.

I am disappointed not to have heard from you. The situation changes every day, and while I recommended patience, that is now no longer possible. You must make contact with your quarry by Christmas. Inform me the moment this is done. Heydrich.

'Well?' Groener inquired.

Anna struck a match and carefully burned the letter.

'What the hell...?'

'This is a personal message from General Heydrich to me. If you feel entitled to know what was in it, I suggest you contact the General and ask for a transcript.'

He glared at her for several seconds, then turned and left the room.

★ ★ ★

Clearly Heydrich was growing impatient. So was she, but her impatience was more to discover why Clive had not turned up – and, if his visit had been cancelled, why no one from the British Embassy had attempted to make contact. However, satisfying Heydrich had to take priority, only she did not see what she could do about it.

It was Meissenbach who inadvertently provided the answer. He had not been making life any easier for her. As Greta was now firmly on dry land, as it were, she no longer took sleeping pills, and thus he found it impossible to get away at night. It was obviously even more difficult for them to get together during the day. He came to her office regularly, which was reasonable, but here again he always found Marlene in situ. It was only a few days after Heydrich's letter that he paid one of his calls.

'Apparently Count von Schulenburg is very proud of the Embassy's Christmas parties. I would like you to handle the invitations for this year's. It's very simple. It seems we invite exactly who we invited last year.'

Alarm bells immediately started jangling in Anna's brain.

Meissenbach was now bending over her shoulder, as if continuing his instructions. 'Can't you get rid of her?' he whispered. 'I don't understand what she is doing here in the first place. Do you need an assistant?'

'My superiors feel that it is necessary.'

'For what purpose? Don't tell me she is also

a professional assassin?'

'I would not call her a professional any-thing. Neither would I call myself an assassin. You should think of me as a bodyguard.'

'I only wish to think of you as the most desirable woman in the world. Anna, I've got to have you. I am going mad.'

For the time being he had to be humoured. She squeezed his hand. 'Let us see what can be done.' The idea was crystallising; every-thing she sought, on both fronts, could be dropping into her lap. All that was required was to keep this lovesick oaf happy. 'Marlene, would you go down to the Records Office and find me the guest list for last year's Christmas party?'

'Of course, Countess.' Marlene hurried from the room.

'I cannot offer you more than fifteen min-utes,' she said.

'I can prolong it,' Meissenbach said, and picked up her telephone to dial the Records Office. 'Ah, Bluther? Will you come up to my office, please? There is something I wish to discuss with you. Thank you.' He replaced the phone. 'It will take Bluther ten minutes to get up to the office, where Frau Estner will tell him that I am not there. She does not know where I have gone. He will probably wait for at least five minutes to see if I return, and then he will go back to Records. By that time Fraulein Gehrig will be waiting to access the document she requires. Then they will have to find it before she can return here. I would

177

say we have half an hour.'

'You are an organisational genius. But...' Anna looked around her. In addition to the filing cabinets, and two tables with typewriters on them, the office contained two desks, each with a reasonably comfortable but not very large chair, as well as two straight chairs. 'I do not have much to offer you.'

'You have everything I wish,' he declared, sweeping blotting paper and pens from her desk. Then she was stretched across it, her dress around her waist, her cami-knickers pulled aside, and he was inside her. *The things I do for Germany*, she reflected. Or was it for England? But it enhanced her image as a woman who could not resist the offer of sex, and she felt that might come in very handy later on.

They were again fully dressed, and her desk restored, before Marlene returned, even if Heinz was still breathing somewhat heavily.

Anna glanced down the invitation list. 'These are all Russians and Americans.'

'Well, we are in Russia. And the Americans are neutral.'

'They are such boring people. So are the Yanks. Don't you think it might be rather amusing to invite a few people from the British Embassy?'

Meissenbach raised his eyebrows. 'You wish to invite British Embassy officials to come here?'

178

'Why not? They are not likely to arrive with guns in hand, shooting at us.'

'But we are still at war.'

'Isn't the war just about over? What military activity has there been, except at sea or in the air, since July?'

'They are certainly shooting at the Italians in Libya.'

'The Italians.' Anna got all the Aryan contempt she could into her voice.

'I know. As allies they are not worth a damn. And they are making a complete mess of their so-called invasion of Greece. But I imagine the British lump them together with us.'

'I still think it may be amusing, and it could well be informative to entertain them.'

'And you will be present?'

'Well, I would hope so.'

'Anna, to the British you are a traitor.'

'And do you suppose they will endeavour to arrest me? They have no jurisdiction anywhere in Russia, outside of their own embassy. In any event, I should not think any member of the British Embassy has any idea who the Countess von Widerstand is. The famous spy who escaped from England in May was the Honourable Mrs Ballantine Bordman.'

He stroked his chin.

Anna pressed home her advantage. 'Do you know, I could even try vamping one of them...'

'Anna, you are incorrigible. But I adore

179

you. Invite who you like. Just let me have the list before you send the invitations. You do understand that I will have to submit both the idea and the guest list to the Ambassador?'

Anna kissed him. 'Tell him it is my idea.'

'This place is impossible,' Marlene complained when Meissenbach left. 'Herr Bluther was not there, and no one knew where he was. So I had to wait. Then when he returned he told me that he had been summoned to Herr Meissenbach's office. But when he got there, Herr Meissenbach was not there, and no one knew where *he* was. Well, I could have told him that. But he hung around Herr Meissenbach's office for ten minutes before coming back down to Records! How we won the war defeats me.'

Anna sat behind her desk. 'Well, I have another job for you. I wish a complete list of everyone who is employed by, or at, the British embassy.'

Marlene's eyes became as large as saucers. 'You mean we are...'

Anna rested her finger on her lips. 'We are going to invite them to the party. Some of them, at any rate.'

Marlene bustled off. Anna glanced at the previous year's list and frowned. There was no Chalyapov! But Meissenbach had told her to invite whichever of the Russians she chose. On the other hand, if Clive *was* in Moscow, she did not really want them both meeting her at the same time.

Marlene returned fifteen minutes later with another list. 'Do you think any of them will come?'

'I am sure of it.' Anna hoped the girl could not hear the pounding of her heart as she scanned the names. None of them meant anything to her. Damnation! Of course he might not be risking his own name. But as far as she knew he had never previously operated in Russia, nor was he even widely known in the Gestapo. Certainly she did not think that Groener, who had been in Moscow for some years, would ever have heard of him.

But on the fairly safe assumption that, for whatever reason, Clive had not yet arrived, or might not be coming at all – she had only the code word Belinda to work on – she owed it to both her employers to get on with her mission.

'Well then,' she said. 'Let's see. We'll start with the ambassador and his wife, with this chap...' She ticked each name. 'And this chap and his wife. And this chap: a Commander Sprague; he sounds interesting.'

Marlene took the list, looking increasingly sceptical.

'Now for the Russian guests.' Anna spread the previous year's list in front of her and again began ticking names. 'I think we'll just add one: Ewfim Chalyapov.'

'You haven't ticked Marshal Stalin,' Marlene pointed out.

Stalin's name was certainly on the previous

list. 'Well, of course we shall invite Marshal Stalin,' Anna agreed, although she saw from the cross beside his name that he had declined last year's invitation. Molotov had come, though.

As Anna had anticipated, a summons to the Ambassador's office soon arrived.

'You are a very enterprising young woman, Countess,' Count von Schulenburg remarked. A copy of the guest list lay on his desk. 'Herr Meissenbach tells me you are hoping to obtain some information from these people. I know, of course, that you are carrying out an instruction given to you by General Himmler. I just wish to repeat that I will permit nothing that may jeopardize the standing or the reputation of the Reich here in Moscow. I am sure, having spent three months here, you appreciate that the Soviet Regime is confoundedly suspicious of everything that does not seem to them to be above board. The point I am making is that there is almost as much hostility and mistrust between Moscow and London as there is between London and Berlin. Were the Soviets to become suspicious that the Wilhelmstrasse was attempting any kind of negotiation with Whitehall, the repercussions could be serious.'

He was entirely missing the point, for which she was grateful. 'I do understand that, Your Excellency. But throughout all history has it not been the accepted custom for warring states to maintain diplomatic contact in neutral capitals?'

'It is hard to regard the Soviets as neutral in any form. I will ask you this: were you sent here to open any such negotiations?'

Not in any sense that you might appreciate, Anna thought. 'No sir. I was sent here to obtain the general feel of the Soviet Government not only as regards us, but as regards Great Britain. I consider that to bring British and Russian diplomats together under our roof and in our presence, in a strictly social environment, may be interesting.'

'You are a singularly precocious young woman. Is it true that you are not yet twenty-one?'

'Yes sir.'

'And you have this much confidence placed in you by General Himmler?'

'I was trained by General Himmler,' Anna said reverently, reflecting that it was no lie, as Heydrich, Glauber – and even Hannah Gehrig – were all Himmler's creations.

'Well then, I must be content to leave the business in your hands. But I will also hold you responsible should anything unfortunate result from this scheme of yours.'

Anna was content, although again she saw some very large storm clouds on the horizon when she misbehaved herself, as it would certainly be interpreted by the scandal-conscious old gentleman.

But first the party. The invitations went out and she awaited the replies with some anxiety. The British Ambassador declined but the other invited members of his staff accepted, no doubt on his instructions. The Americans all accepted, as did the Russians, with the exception of Stalin. This was clearly a disappointment to Meissenbach, but Anna reckoned he would only get in the way.

'Am I coming too?' Marlene asked.

'You are not invited,' Anna pointed out.

'I am just a dogsbody,' she grumbled.

'This party is for diplomats and senior officials. Your time will come,' Anna assured her.

Commander John Sprague looked up from his desk at the figure standing before him. 'My God!' he remarked. 'I had given you up for lost. I was advised by London that you had been put out of action for the foreseeable future.'

Clive Bartley sat before the desk. 'I thought I had been put out of action as well. You wouldn't believe it, but the plane I was travelling on was shot down by Italian fighters off Malta. Spent two days in a rubber dinghy drifting about the place with a bullet in my back and a chap dying on either side of me.'

'Sounds rough,' Sprague agreed. 'But you were all right?'

'Unfortunately not. I spent six weeks in a hospital, being bombed almost daily. It was worse than the Blitz.'

'May I assume that you are now again fit?'

'Entirely.'

'Well, I will wish you better fortune going back.'

'My dear fellow, I am not going back until I have done what I was sent here to do.'

Sprague gave him an old-fashioned look. 'Whatever you were sent here to do, it was four months ago. It cannot possibly still have any relevance.'

'It is just as relevant now as it was then. Perhaps more so. I am to make contact with one of our people serving in the German Embassy.'

Now Sprague was frowning. 'We have an agent in the German Embassy? Why was I not informed of this?'

'Because it is the most closely guarded secret MI6 currently possesses. This ... ah ... agent is one of our very best people and is carrying out a mission of the utmost importance.'

'And how do you propose to contact him?'

'Is there no liaison between the embassies at all?'

'Not so you'd notice. Although, oddly enough, half a dozen of us have been invited to their Christmas party. His nibs isn't happy, but he's agreed that we can go, providing we keep our noses clean.'

'Brilliant,' Clive said. 'I'll come with you.'

'My dear fellow, you haven't been invited.'

'Do you think they will turn me away?'

'It could happen. They have a new Chief Secretary, a chap named Meissenbach. He used to be in Prague. Earned himself a

185

reputation as a hard man. The Czechs even tried to bump him off. You must know about that.'

'We set it up,' Clive said, his brain spinning. 'And you say Meissenbach is now in Moscow?'

'Running the embassy. He sent the invitations, or at least his sidekick did. Some Countess or other. Supposed to be quite a dish. I haven't seen her myself. I suppose she is one of these big-titted Valkyrie types. I say, old man, are you all right?'

'John,' Clive said, having got his breathing back under control. 'I am going to attend this party and take my chances.'

Six

The Party

Anna found herself becoming increasingly agitated as the date of the party approached. She had no real expectation of making any progress with the British, unless they used the opportunity to arrange contact. But Chalyapov ... She told herself that he was only a man, surely more interesting than Bordman had ever been. But possibly far more intelligent, and therefore more difficult to hoodwink on a continual basis.

And suppose he did not, after all, find her sufficiently attractive to seduce her? Heydrich had refused to contemplate that possibility. She wore her favourite pale blue sheath, with its deep décolletage, her gold earrings and crucifix, which sat so entrancingly in the valley between her breasts. The ruby ring was unnecessary as she was wearing elbow-length white gloves. 'I think you would look even better with your hair up,' Marlene suggested.

Anna stood before her full-length mirror and scooped her hair away from her neck. 'Do you know, you could be right.'

'Nothing should be allowed to detract from

187

your face,' Birgit said enthusiastically.

They consider me some kind of gigantic doll, Anna thought, merely to be played with. But she had to agree that it was a good idea; she could always let her hair down when the opportunity arose.

Her coiffure completed, she hurried to the ballroom to make sure everything was going according to plan: the white-gloved waiters, the champagne already opened and waiting on ice, the silver trays of canapés arranged in mouth-watering expectation in the pantry.

'Anna! You look superb.' Meissenbach kissed her gloved hand. 'I have never seen you with your hair up.'

'Then perhaps you have never seen me at my best. Frau Meissenbach.' She bestowed a gracious smile upon Greta, who was looking more out of sorts than ever, in high-necked brown velvet, dripping with what Anna considered vulgar jewellery. 'Excuse me.' She hurried across the room to greet Count von Schulenburg and his wife, who had just entered. 'Your Excellency! Countess! I hope everything is in order.'

Schulenburg kissed her glove. 'I have no doubt of it.'

'And you look absolutely charming, my dear,' Countess von Schulenburg said. She was a tall, gracious woman who must have been a beauty twenty years before, Anna estimated. She did not know if the Count had confided any of his disquiet at her presence in Moscow to his wife, but the Countess had always been unfailingly pleasant to her.

Then she found herself facing Groener. 'Did I invite you?' she asked. 'I don't remember doing so.'

'I do not require an invitation. I am on duty.'

'I do not think a Christmas party is a suitable place for a policeman to be on duty.'

'But my dear Countess, you are a policewoman. Are you not also on duty?'

Anna glared at him, but the room was starting to fill with senior embassy staff members and their wives; it was time to form the reception line. Anna had not supposed she should be involved in this, but Schulenburg insisted. 'This is your party, Countess. You organized it.'

So she found herself number five, next to Greta Meissenbach, who produced a monumental sniff.

The Americans arrived first, and came slowly down the line. Anna was not very interested in them, until one man, who was not accompanied by a wife, bent over her glove. 'I have waited a long time for this privilege, Countess.'

Anna stared at him. He was tall, quite handsome in a somewhat cynical manner, and very well dressed, but she could not remember having seen him before. 'Have we met, sir?' she asked.

He was still holding her hand. 'Sadly, no. But I saw you at the Cheltenham race meeting, two years ago.' He smiled. 'Your name, as

I recall, was the Honourable Mrs Ballantine Bordman.'

Anna felt vaguely sick. 'Are you sure you are not mistaken, Mr...?' His name had been announced, but she had not been listening.

'Andrews, Countess. Joseph Andrews. And I do assure you that no man could possibly mistake your face once he has seen you.'

Anna withdrew her hand. 'I look forward to having a talk with you, Mr Andrews. Later on.'

'I am looking forward to that, too.'

He went on to join the other guests, and Anna let her breath go in a vast sigh. She supposed something like this had always been bound to happen. But what repercussions might there be? If he had known about Anna Bordman, he would know that she was a German spy. That would only matter here in Moscow if he felt obliged to pass the information on to a local contact. But why should he do that? As far as she knew there was no great love lost between Russia and the United States at this moment.

Her reverie was interrupted by the arrival of the Russians, and a few minutes later she was gazing at Ewfim Chalyapov, who was in turn gazing at her.

'Countess von Widerstand.' His voice was quiet, his German faultless. 'They told me the most beautiful woman in Europe was working at the German Embassy, and I did not believe them.'

'Because you possess sufficient beautiful

women of your own, Herr Chalyapov?'

He looked into her eyes. Perhaps, she thought, he does not like women who can riposte. But then he squeezed her fingers. 'No man could ever possess a beauty to equal yours, Countess. Will I see you later?'

'I shall be circulating, Herr Chalyapov.'

'And I shall be waiting, Countess.'

He moved off. Once again she was breathless. But it had seemed almost too easy.

The English guests were arriving. She glanced along the line before they reached her, and this time felt quite paralysed.

'Commander John Sprague, Countess,' the Commander explained. 'And this is an associate who has just arrived in Moscow, Mr Clive Bartley. I know he was not invited, but the Ambassador seems to feel he is acceptable.'

'Of course.' Anna kept her voice at its normal pitch with some effort. She could hardly believe this was happening, and her usual quickness of thought and decision had for the moment deserted her. 'Welcome to Moscow, Mr Bartley.'

'I had intended to visit the city some time ago,' Clive said. 'But I was delayed. Now I feel it was almost worthwhile.'

Sprague had moved on. Clive opened his mouth again, and she said softly, 'Wait.'

He followed Sprague into the throng. There were still more guests to be greeted and it was fifteen minutes before the reception line broke up and she was able to move away. She took a glass of champagne from a passing tray and went into the crowd of people, having to stop and chat with most of them, while she took her bearings, acutely aware that Groener was watching her. Chalyapov was standing, as she remembered from the previous occasion she had seen him, against the far wall, smoking, as usual surrounded by several people. They were talking animatedly, and he appeared to be listening, but like Groener he was watching the room and she knew he was looking for her. Their eyes met, and he gave a little inclination of his head. She responded and began to move towards him only to find herself joined by both Clive and Andrews, who seemed to know each other.

'Small world, Countess,' Andrews remarked.

'And growing smaller by the moment, Mr Andrews,' she agreed. 'Do I gather you are acquainted with this gentleman?'

'You could say we're in the same line of business,' Andrews acknowledged. 'But of course you and Mr Bartley know each other.'

Anna raised her eyebrows.

'There, you see, Clive old boy, she's forgotten you.'

'We met in Berlin in 1938,' Clive said. 'When I was there with your husband. He is still your husband, is he not?'

'Perhaps, just about,' Anna said. 'I know he sued for divorce, after I left England. But as that was only seven months ago, I do not know if the matter has been concluded as yet.'

'Bit tiresome if nobody troubles to inform you,' Andrews suggested.

Anna shrugged. 'It is of no matter. In Germany, and here in Russia, I have reverted to my maiden name, the Countess von Widerstand.'

'But surely, even in Germany, you cannot marry again until your divorce is finalized?'

'I have not considered the matter, Mr Andrews, as at this moment I have no desire to marry again.'

'Point taken. Did you ever get close to catching the Countess, Clive?'

'That is a state secret. And definitely not cocktail party conversation,' Clive said with a smile. 'Countess, I hate to be gauche, but I am not used to this cold weather. Would I be arrested if I went looking for a bathroom?'

Anna smiled back. 'Very probably. We could not have an English Secret Service agent wandering about the corridors of the German Embassy, now could we? If you will excuse us, Mr Andrews, I will just indicate to Mr Bartley where he should go, and find him an escort. Mr Bartley?'

Clive followed her to one of the exit doors. 'God, it's been too long. When?'

'I will walk in Gorky Park tomorrow at eleven.'

'It's twenty below.'

'I'm sure you can borrow a fur coat. We meet by accident. Ah, Gustav...' She summoned a footman. 'This gentleman needs to use the bathroom. Will you accompany him please? And bring him back to the ballroom.'

Gustav gave a brief bow.

'You have been very kind,' Clive said. 'I would hope to see you again, Countess.'

'I'm sure you shall, Mr Bartley.'

Anna waited for a few seconds before re-entering the ballroom. She was not used to having her emotions in such a jangled state, at least when she had not recently engaged in any extreme action. She had almost given up hope of seeing him again. Apart from the emotional loss she had been growing increasingly anxious about the way she had apparently been dropped by MI6. But he was here, and she would see him tomorrow, even if in the middle of a snowstorm. What might happen after that she was prepared to leave up to him. She had no doubt that he wanted to get together with her as much as she wanted to get together with him. Love? Or lust? Or just a desperate need to know that somewhere in the world there was someone who actually cared about her? That was her need, certainly; the problem was she did not know if it was his.

But meanwhile, back to work. She arranged her features and entered the room, paused, looked around her, and had a sudden spasm of sheer panic. Chalyapov was nowhere to be seen. If he had made one of his sudden departures, she was in deep trouble: there was no saying when she could arrange for them to meet again.

Then she saw him. He had moved to the far side of the room and had his back to her. She hurried towards him, smiling at people and resisting as politely as possible their desire to have her stop and talk with them. Groener was in turn moving towards her, but she neatly side-stepped him. 'Herr Chalyapov.'

He turned, frowned, and then raised his eyebrows; as always, he had a cigarette in his fingers.

'I just wanted to make sure you were being looked after.'

Now his face relaxed. 'And I thought you had forgotten all about me, Countess. When I saw you leave the room with that fellow ... He was with the English party, was he not?'

'I think so. Believe it or not, he wished to relieve himself.' She chose her words with care: according to Heydrich, this man wanted earthy women. 'And I could not merely direct him. He is an enemy of the Reich.'

'So did you accompany him, and hold his ... hand?'

'I handed him over to one of our people. You have not told me whether you are enjoying yourself.'

'Frankly, no – up to this moment. Do you think things will change for the better?'

'I would like to think so, Herr Chalyapov. It is my business to see that our guests have all they require.'

He put the cigarette to his lips and inhaled

195

deeply. 'What I require may not be acceptable to you.'

Anna lowered her eyes. 'Tell me, and I will do my best to find it for you.'

'Your company, Countess. Shall we say supper?'

'Tonight, sir?'

'Why not? You have surely done everything that you possibly can to ensure the success of the party. Now you must enjoy yourself.'

'But not here?'

'A man and a woman can only truly appreciate each other's company when they are *tête à tête*.'

'I take your point. But you will have to be patient. I cannot possibly leave the party until it is over.'

He smiled and stubbed out his cigarette on an adjacent ashtray. 'But you will be leaving with me. I do assure you that no one will attempt to stop us.'

Anna hesitated briefly. But she had already deduced that he was not a man to take no for an answer, without at the same time taking offence, and she was under orders. If a crisis with either Schulenburg or Meissenbach would therefore happen sooner rather than later, it would just have to happen.

'It is snowing outside,' he said. 'You will need a coat and heavier shoes.'

'Give me ten minutes.' She hurried from the room, praying that she would not encounter Clive. She ran upstairs to her apartment where Birgit and Marlene were playing chess.

'Oh, Countess!' Marlene cried. 'Is it going well?'

'I think so.' Anna took her mink and matching hat from the wardrobe, slung the coat over her arm and tucked the hat under it, added a silk scarf, and smiled at them, 'Don't wait up.'

As the party was still bubbling, few people actually observed Chalyapov and Anna leave the ballroom for the lobby. Clive was back in the room, and endeavoured to catch her eye, but she merely smiled at him and went on. Chalyapov helped her into her coat, watched while she wrapped her scarf round her neck, adjusted her hat in the mirror and then stooped to slide her feet into the boots she kept in the porter's office. The two guards on duty pretended not to notice them. She slipped her dainty shoes into the mink pockets.

'Is the rest of you as elegant as your clothes, Countess?'

'Perhaps one day you may be able to form a judgement on that.'

'In Russia,' he said, 'we learn to live for today.'

Anna was still digesting this as they approached the waiting limousine. She slipped on the icy ground as she reached the car and would have fallen had Chalyapov not grabbed her round the waist with one hand, opened the door with the other, and then placed the same hand on her buttocks to thrust her in. She gave a little shriek as she landed on her knees, half on the seat. The door slammed and the car moved away, but Chalyapov's hand remained grasping her bottom to push her up on to the seat, still on her knees. While she gasped for breath, face pressed into the back cushions, he slid his hand under the coat and the gown to feel her calves. 'You are frozen,' he said solicitously.

'All over,' she panted.

This was a mistake, as he now turned her round, released the belt of the coat, opened it and was inside her décolletage before she could do anything to stop him. Although he was not at that moment smoking, she was enveloped in an aroma of stale tobacco. As she had never smoked herself, she found this extremely off-putting.

His hands were also cold, but not as cold as her frozen nipples. 'You are enchanting,' he murmured, and kissed her, not brutally, but with extreme passion.

She pushed him away, drawing great breaths. She could see his frown even in the darkness. 'You do not like me,' he protested.

'Of course I like you, Herr Chalyapov. But you must give me time to breathe.' *And to understand what is going to happen to me.* But whatever it was, it had to be accepted, endured, and if possible enjoyed. Certainly it was an experience outside anything she had previously known. Quite apart from never having had sex in the back of a car before, she had never been quite so manhandled. Again, there was no brutality in what he did, but his hands seemed to be everywhere at the same time, moving with irresistible purpose. He did not bother to remove her coat, but had her long skirt up to her thighs in a moment. She was wearing nothing under her gown, and she got a brief glimpse of the driver adjusting his rear-view mirror before Chalyapov had released his pants, and had her sitting astride him, surging to and fro while he nuzzled her breasts, fondled her buttocks, and kissed her mouth.

It was all rather quick. As she felt him spend, she kissed him and removed herself.

'The moment I saw you,' he said, 'I knew I must have you.'

'And you do everything immediately,' she suggested.

'If I can. Now, we shall go to my home, and make love all night.'

Oh Lord, she thought. It was only eight o'clock. 'You said something about supper.'

'Oh, there will be food. But I would rather make love.'

'I will be better after I have eaten.'

'You could not be better. But I want you naked. Do you know what I am going to do to you?'

She wasn't sure she wanted to find out. 'You will have to tell me.'

'I wish to lick you, from head to toe.'

It was three in the morning before Anna got home. The embassy was in darkness, save for the lobby, where two different night guards were on duty.

'Countess?' They peered at her. She knew she must look a sight. Chalyapov had released her hair and had proceeded to play with it, leaving it a tangled mess. She had no make-up left, her cheeks were still flushed, and although her mink hid the ruination of her dress, they could have no doubt that she had spent a thoroughly tousling evening.

She smiled at them and went up to her apartment. The debris of the party had already been cleared away, and she encountered no one. She had taken off her boots in the lobby and entered the suite on tiptoe, so as not to disturb the girls, and locked her bedroom door. Then she threw her clothes on the floor and stood beneath the hot shower for several minutes. This was necessary because she had again become very chilled on the drive home, but it was also important if she was ever going to feel clean again. As he had soon resumed smoking, her hair stank of it.

The disturbing fact was that she had enjoyed most of what had been done to her. When Chalyapov had said he wanted to lick her all over, he had meant it. He had revealed a remarkable knowledge of the female anatomy, and of its requirements, and had brought her to orgasm with his tongue, before resuming what she might consider normal sex. She supposed he must have entered her about six times, and in between had never stopped playing with her. And he wanted to see her again, and again and again. As she must want to see him. But if indeed he liked to maintain a mistress for a year, she supposed this might be considered some sort of punishment for her sins.

And in the meantime, crisis. On several fronts.

She could only take each one as it came. The girls were in a state of high excitement, which increased as they sorted out her discarded clothing and examined the torn dress. 'Burn that,' Anna told them. 'And I shall need a dressmaker. Have you anything to report?'

'Oh, Countess...' They both started speaking together. Apparently Meissenbach had visited the suite when the party ended, looking for her, and they had felt obliged to tell him that she had gone out. 'He seemed awfully put out,' Marlene said.

'He is always put out about something or other,' Anna remarked. She breakfasted, dressed and went down to her office. The Embassy was just waking up, and those people she passed on the stairs or in the corridors gave her nervous smiles. She sat at her desk, took out a sheet of her personal notepaper, and wrote two words: *Contact! Wow!* As she addressed and sealed the envelope, marking it Private and Confidential, she wondered if Heydrich had any sense of humour.

She took the envelope along to the Gestapo offices, received another anxious smile from the woman secretary at the outer desk, and entered Groener's office after a brief knock.

'Countess? I am told you left the Embassy without permission or notifying anyone last night, and that you did not return until three o'clock this morning. I wish an explanation.'

'I left the Embassy on official business for the Reich,' Anna said coldly. 'Business which, as you are aware, is known only to the SD. I have a message here for General Heydrich which I wish to go off in today's pouch.' She laid the envelope on his desk.

He gazed at it. 'I do not think I can permit this.'

'Herr Groener, I am giving you an order as an officer in the SD. If you wish to disobey that order, I will have to report the matter to General Heydrich.'

'I intend to report the matter to the Ambassador,' Groener snapped.

'That, Herr Groener, is your prerogative. But if General Heydrich does not receive that letter tomorrow, I will not answer for your future.'

She returned to her office and found Meissenbach waiting, a terrified Marlene cowering behind her desk. 'Where were you last night?' he demanded.

'Out.'

'You walked out in the middle of the party with one of those Russian louts. I saw you go. I could not believe my eyes. And you had not returned three hours later.'

'You know this because you checked. I will not be spied on, Heinz. Spying is my business, not yours. Nor will I be treated like some schoolgirl Cinderella. What I do, and whom I do it with, is my business. If it will reassure you, it is also the business of the Reich.'

Meissenbach stared at her with his mouth open, his cheeks turning red. 'And you expect me to continue the charade of having you work for me?'

'Of course. That also is for the Reich.'

The telephone jangled. Marlene hurried across the room to pick it up. 'Countess von Widerstand's office ... Oh. Ah ... Yes of course. Immediately.' She replaced the receiver and looked at Anna. 'That was Count von Schulenburg's secretary. The Ambassador wishes to see you immediately, Countess.'

'I would say your days are numbered,' Meissenbach said smugly. 'Or are you going to attempt to tell the Ambassador to mind his own business?'

'If I have to,' Anna said.

'Sit down, Countess,' Schulenburg invited.

Anna did so and crossed her knees.

'I have received a most serious complaint from Herr Groener. Would you like to explain it to me?'

'I had to go out last night, for a prolonged period, sir.'

'With a senior Russian official?'

'Yes sir.'

Schulenburg looked down at the paper on his desk. 'Groener states here that his security people reported that you did not return until three o'clock this morning, and that you were...' he hesitated '...in a dishevelled state.'

'I'm afraid I was. Yes sir.'

'And you do not feel able to give me an explanation?'

'I cannot, sir.'

Schulenburg leaned back in his chair. 'That you absented yourself for some seven hours, at night, in the company of a commissar, is apparently known throughout the Embassy. Which means, I have no doubt, that it is rapidly becoming well known throughout Moscow. I warned you that I would not tolerate any scandal that could bring this Embassy into disrepute. I regard your behaviour as being unacceptable.'

'Are you placing me under arrest, Your Excellency?' Anna asked in her most dulcet tone.

'I am today going to make a full report of this incident to Herr von Ribbentrop, and request that he instruct General Himmler immediately to recall you from Moscow.' He stared at her.

'You will do as you think fit, Your Excellency.' Anna looked at her watch. It was ten o'clock. 'Now, sir, if you will excuse me, I must leave the Embassy again.'

'And if I refuse you permission to do so?'

Anna stood up. 'I would reflect very seriously as to whether that would be a wise step to take, Your Excellency, in the absence of any instructions from Berlin.' She stood to attention. 'Heil Hitler!'

It was a great relief to get out of the Embassy, even if it was well below freezing outside. Anna was thoroughly wrapped up; apart from her furs, she wound a thick woollen scarf round her face from the nose down, and she wore dark glasses and ear-muffs. But the pleasure was more than physical. She actually disliked verbal confrontations, and to have three in rapid succession was disturbing. Nor did she truly know what the outcome would be. But she was carrying out her orders as faithfully as she could.

The park was deserted, save for the odd keeper, and she saw the unmistakable figure of Clive at a distance. 'Isn't this a terribly public place?' he asked.

'Not today. And we are meeting by accident, are we not? Did you enjoy last night?'

'No. Did you?'

She fell into step beside him. 'I was working.'

'I sincerely hope so. I understand that Russian chap you left with is quite important.'

'He is very important.'

'And you seduced him.'

'As I said, I was working. I hope you are not going to carp?'

'I wouldn't dream of it. Even if ... Shit, Anna, the thought of you in another man's arms makes me, well...'

She squeezed his hand. 'Listen. Matters are

a little fraught right now, but I hope they will be resolved within three days at the most. By the end of that time I shall either have been recalled to Berlin, or my position here will be unchallengeable. I am, of course, anticipating the latter. Now, that being so, I must continue and build on my relationship with Chalyapov. If it will relieve your mind, this is not a very entertaining prospect.'

'But you will carry it out to the best of your ability.'

'I do what has to be done, Clive, to the best of my ability at all times. That is my motto, and it is the key to my survival.'

'Even if it involves shooting two of our people in Prague.'

'I did not know they were your people. And in any event I was in my capacity as an SD agent. I hope you did not come here to quarrel.'

'I came here officially to find out just what you are at. And to see you. And...'

'You will, and I will give you a complete account of what I have been, and am, doing. But there is no need for me to see Chalyapov every night. What you must do is take a hotel room somewhere in Moscow, and I will come to you whenever I can.'

'You will be able to do this?'

'I've told you. In three days' time I shall either be back in Berlin, or my own mistress.' She squeezed his fingers. 'I would rather be your mistress. If you will walk here again in four days' time, I will be here, if I am still in

Moscow. If I am not here, you will know that I have been recalled. If I am here, you will give me the address to go to, and I will come to you whenever I can.'

'Four days' time is Christmas Day.'

'Well then, we shall be a Christmas present to each other.'

He stopped walking and gazed at her. 'If the Russians...'

'All they can do is expel me.' Another smile. 'And you, perhaps.'

'You know, I am supposed to be controlling you.'

'Try it from the other side, just for once. You may enjoy it.'

'Anna, I adore you.'

'And I look forward to adoring you.' She released him and walked away.

'Dicey,' Sprague commented. 'She could be setting you up.'

'She isn't.'

Sprague regarded Clive for several seconds. 'It is highly irregular for one of our people to live in a hotel instead of the Embassy. You do understand that the Reds have almost every hotel room bugged, and also make irregular checks.'

Clive grinned. 'The mysterious midnight phone call. I know a bit about bugs.'

'Well, I will have to inform the Ambassador. He may not like it.'

'I am travelling as an ordinary business-man,' Clive pointed out. 'If anything happens to me, you simply deny all knowledge of me.'

'Even if we know you are on your way to a gulag via the Lubianka. These chaps play pretty rough.'

'So do I,' Clive said. 'When I have to.'

Groener entered Anna's office, and without a word placed the envelope on her desk. Then he stared at her for several seconds, turned and left the room again.

'Ooh!' Marlene said. 'I thought he was going to arrest you.'

'In which case he would have arrested you as well,' Anna told her, and broke the seal on the envelope.

Congratulations! I have cleared the air for you. These instructions are not to be confided to anyone, even your assistant. Circumstances continue to change every day, and your position must change with them. The political attitude of the Soviets towards Germany is no longer of great importance. We wish you to obtain information about the dispositions, morale, and commanding officers of the Soviet Army, particularly those on the Western frontier. You will of course be discreet. It is also important that you gain access to Marshal Stalin, which will require a working knowledge of the interior of the Kremlin. Inform me the moment this has been achieved. Burn this immediately. Heydrich.

Anna remained gazing at the note for some time. She was aware of a peculiarly chilled sensation across her shoulders. Heydrich could have no doubt that she was an intellectual genius. Therefore he must know that she would be able to interpret what he had just told her. Therefore the matter had to be urgent.

She struck a match and carefully burned the paper. As she did so the telephone jangled. Marlene picked it up. 'The Countess von Widerstand's office. Yes, sir,' she put her hand over the mouthpiece. 'Herr Meissenbach,' she hissed.

She took the receiver. 'Good morning, Heinz.'

'I wish to see you.'

'In your office?'

'Yes. Now.'

'Now.' She handed the phone back to Marlene.

'Is there going to be trouble?' the girl asked.

'No,' Anna said, and went to the door.

'This is an intolerable situation,' Meissenbach announced.

Anna sat before his desk and crossed her knees. 'In what way, Heinz?'

'Berlin has virtually placed you in charge of the Embassy.'

'Of course they have not. They merely wish me to be allowed to carry out my duties without interference.'

'The Ambassador is furious. He is seeking further clarification from the Foreign Minister. It is quite unacceptable that he should not have ultimate jurisdiction over every member of his staff.'

'I am sure any clarification he requires will be provided. As you know, I can only carry out my orders, and this I intend to do.'

'By seducing every commissar you can lay hands on, is that it? Do you intend to turn the German Embassy into a brothel?'

'You have my word, Heinz, that I intend to seduce no one within these walls. But I would appreciate it if your interference in my affairs ceases now. And you should also require Herr Groener to do the same.' She smiled at him. 'I am sure this new arrangement will make Greta very happy.'

Seven

The Betrayal

Clive, with his irrepressible sense of humour, had chosen the Hotel Berlin as his Moscow residence, but there was method in his madness. It was a large, bustling place, its foyer dominated by a huge stuffed brown bear. There was always a crowd of people coming and going, even after dinner. No one paid the least attention to Anna when she entered; wrapped up against the cold as she was, even her beauty could not be noticed, while her obviously expensive clothes – she was wearing her mink – precluded any suggestion that she might be a prostitute looking for business.

Clive had given her his room number when they had met on Christmas Day. She crossed the foyer to the lifts. 'Five,' she told the attendant.

'Yes, comrade.' He pressed the appropriate button and they rode up. He gazed at her, but she did not remove any of her protective clothing, not even the scarf over her nose and mouth, although it was perfectly warm inside the hotel.

She left the lift and walked along the empty corridor. She knocked on the door, and was soon in his arms. He lifted her from the floor and carried her into the room, kicked the door shut while he kissed her mouth as she pulled the scarf away. 'I think I have waited all my life for this moment.'

He released her and she unwrapped herself, took off her hat, and shook out her hair. 'What actually kept you?'

'Would you believe that I was shot down?'

She had been laying her mink across a chair, but now she turned sharply. 'Where?'

'Over the Med.'

'But you're all right?'

'Well, obviously; I'm here. But I was a bit bashed up at the time. I stopped a bullet in the back of my thigh, and as it was a couple of days before I was rescued, I needed God knows how many blood transfusions. I spent a couple of months in a Maltese hospital, which put things back a bit.'

'God, I have been so worried, not knowing if you were coming at all.'

He stood against her, to slide his hands over her dress and down her back to caress her buttocks. 'Were you worried for me or for you?'

She kissed him. 'I have never lied to you. Are we alone?'

'I've taken out two rather obvious bugs.'

'Which you were meant to find. I think we need to be up close and personal.'

'I won't say no to that.'

212

They undressed facing each other, and then she was again in his arms. 'The thought of you in—'

She kissed him. 'No names. Let's get into bed.' He slid in beside her, and she put her hands down to hold him. 'We should have sex first. Or this chap will get in the way. How long is it since you had a woman?'

'I told you, I've been in hospital or recuperating for the last few months.'

'Umm. That means you're going to be away in seconds.'

'But we have all night. Haven't we?'

'Most of it. So, how would you like to start?'

'Well ... Do you know, I have no idea what you do. What turns you on?'

'Everything turns me on, when I wish to be turned on. And I do everything. And I love you. You must not be shy with me. You want something we have not done before, and perhaps you do not do with Belinda. So do it with me.'

Clive took a deep breath. 'Would you suck me?'

She raised her head. 'You do not do that with Belinda?'

'Belinda is a rather old-fashioned woman. Don't get the wrong idea. She enjoys sex, but she likes to, well, close her eyes and let events take their course.'

'I think you were sex-starved even before your swim in the Med. Of course I will fellate you. But I think you wish to watch.'

She threw back the covers, and he caught

213

her hand. 'What I would like most is ... ah ... well...'

Anna gazed at him for several seconds, and then gave a gurgle of laughter. 'You shall have what you wish, sir, and we will see who can get the other off first.' She rose to her knees, turned her back on him, swung her leg across his chest to straddle him, and tossed hair from her eyes before lowering her head.

He lay with his arm round her, her head on his shoulder; for the moment their passion was spent. 'Tell me about Chalyapov.'

'He is a job of work.'

'Which is also my work.'

'Of course. What do you wish to know?'

'What precisely are your instructions?'

'They have changed, but I do not know how important you will think them. I came here to gain what information I could about Soviet feelings towards the Reich.'

'You did not find this odd?'

'Why should I?'

'Well, my darling, with the greatest possible respect, you are twenty years old, you have been trained to seduce men and you have been trained to kill. I don't think any of those accomplishments can have properly prepared you for evaluating political currents.'

'Perhaps you are right. In any event my instructions have now been changed, as I told you. I am now to use my intimacy with Chalyapov to discover as much as I can about Soviet troop concentrations.'

'And?'

'Well, I have not actually started yet. I am going to work on him the next time I meet him, which is the day after tomorrow.'

'He can provide this information?'

'According to Heydrich, he is one of Stalin's closest associates, and has access to the most sensitive information.'

'And have you drawn any conclusions from this?'

'Yes. I think Hitler is preparing for a war with Russia.'

'It certainly seems like it.'

'Will that help Great Britain?'

'Well, obviously, if Germany and Russia went to war it would take the heat off us, at least for a while.' He stroked her hair.

'Would it not provide you with an ally? A very powerful ally?'

'That's difficult to say. As to whether the Soviets would prove a worthwhile ally, I have no idea. They lost all their top generals in 1937, and they made very little impression on the Finns last year.'

'There are an awful lot of them.'

'A lot of men do not automatically make a successful army. And then there is the question of whether the Government, our Government, will ever consider an alliance with Communist Russia. I think Winston hates them even more than he hates Nazi Germany. Still, that is a pretty important piece of news, and I shall certainly relay it. What happens if your friend suspects what you are after? I mean, how does he regard you?'

She laughed. 'Ewfim Chalyapov believes that he is God's gift to the female sex. He selects every beautiful woman who drifts into his orbit, and expects them to fall madly in love with him. I am just following fashion. He knows absolutely nothing about me except that I am an employee of the Embassy.'

Clive hugged her protectively. 'And is he God's gift to womankind?'

'He is very virile. But he is also very rough and ready, and totally uncouth in his personal habits. And he smokes like a chimney and stinks of tobacco. Every time I have been with him, I stink too.'

She sat bolt upright as there was a knock on the door. Clive squeezed her hand as he got out of bed and put on a dressing gown. 'It's only the night porter.'

'What? Checking up?'

Clive grinned. 'No. I told him to bring up a bottle of champagne at midnight.'

'Suppose I hadn't come?'

'Then I'd have drunk myself insensible. But you did come. Now we are going to toast the future. Our future. You just snuggle down beneath the covers and keep out of sight.'

He went to the door.

It was three in the morning when she sat up again. 'I think I should be getting back.'

He put his arms round her waist to nuzzle her. 'I am going to see you again?'

216

'Next Tuesday.'

He sighed. 'That seems a hell of a long time away.'

'Six days.'

'During which—'

'It is a *job*! Are you not pleased with what I have told you? Who knows what I may have for you next week?'

He released her and lay back. 'I am being very schoolboyish. Seriously, it's what Heydrich wants you to do that seems more important than what you get out of Chalyapov. How often do you hear from him?'

Anna got up and started to dress, but continued to speak in a whisper. 'Whenever he wants something specific. Unless the situation changes again, I do not expect to hear from him for a while. He may have something he wants from Stalin.'

Clive sat up. 'Stalin? What has he told you about Stalin?' he hissed.

Anna peered into the mirror to freshen her make-up. 'Only that he wants me to persuade Chalyapov to introduce me, and that I should obtain a working knowledge of the Kremlin.'

Clive swung his legs out of bed. 'Holy Jesus Christ!'

Anna turned. 'Sssh! What is wrong with that?'

He came over to stand against her. 'My darling, how can a working knowledge of the Kremlin and access to Marshal Stalin be of any value to the Reich, unless we put that alongside the fact that the person obtaining this knowledge and this access is a trained assassin?'

Anna slowly sat down on the dressing stool.

'Just as Heydrich commanded you to assassinate Churchill last May, which is why we had to get you out of England, remember? This is a death sentence. We can't manipulate things here in Russia.'

Anna got up again, put on her hat and her mink.

'What are you going to do?' he asked.

'I cannot disobey Heydrich.'

He took her in his arms. 'And I cannot let you die.'

She kissed him. 'It may not come to that. Chalyapov apparently tires of women as enthusiastically as he takes them up. I must make him tire of me as rapidly as possible, after I have discovered those military dispositions. Once he does that I will no longer have access to the Kremlin, and then there will be no reason for me to remain in Russia.' They gazed at each other, and kissed again. 'That is what we must believe. I will see you on Tuesday.'

For the first time since that terrible March day in 1938, she was frightened. She lay in bed, unable to sleep, staring into the darkness. It was snowing outside, and for all her warm clothing she had become chilled on the walk home. Now she found herself shivering. She could not doubt that Clive's analysis was correct; she should have worked it out for herself. But up till now her Russian adventure had been no more than an enjoyable caper, in which she had been able to use her authority to its utmost. But no one was ever given such authority without being expected to earn it.

The situation was very similar to that in England the previous year. When she had received the dreadful command from Berlin, she had felt in an impossible position. To kill Churchill would have meant her execution, and once she had been executed there would be no more reason for the SD to keep her family alive. The same applied now. But not to carry out her instructions, and save her own life, would equally have condemned her family to death. So, as the outcome was inevitable in either case, why should she not save her own life? And live with those deaths on her conscience for the rest of that life?

She remembered thinking back then that at least the English were gentlemen. She would not have been tortured, and even the act of placing the noose over her head would be carried out with the utmost courtesy. She could expect no courtesy in Russia.

She finally fell asleep just before dawn, and awoke with a start to find Marlene sitting on her bed and peering at her.

'Countess! Anna! Is something the matter?'

Anna blinked. For the past hour she had been sleeping so heavily that she was unsure where she was. The curtains had been drawn back and the room was filled with bright

219

winter sunshine.

'Anna!' To Anna's consternation, Marlene threw both arms round her to hug her and began nuzzling and kissing her neck. Then one of the hands closed on her breast. 'Oh, Anna, I adore you so. I admire you so. I *love* you so. Anna—'

Anna threw her off violently. Marlene gave a little shriek and collapsed on the floor. Anna sat up. 'Do not do that again. What time is it?'

'Nine o'clock,' Marlene gasped, her cheeks crimson.

'Oh my God!' Anna threw back the covers and leapt out of bed. Marlene stared at her; she slept in the nude. 'Has anyone asked for me?'

'There is a message from that man Chalyapov.'

Anna went into the bathroom to shower. 'I will be down in five minutes.'

Marlene stood in the doorway to watch her. 'Anna! Please! Do not be angry with me. Mother told me...'

Anna stepped out of the stall and towelled herself. 'Whatever your mother told you about me was a lie. And my name is the Countess von Widerstand. Only my friends may call me Anna. And if you ever touch me again I will break your neck.'

She was more upset than she had supposed she would be. But the girl was definitely proving a nuisance. At the same time she had no wish further to upset the internal working of the Embassy by asking Heydrich to recall her.

Anyway, she had more than enough on her plate to get on with. The situation was actually easier than she had dared hope. Chalyapov was certainly overboard. He wanted to see her as often as possible, which was a bore, but his adoration was also productive.

'Our army?' he asked, holding her on top of him as he liked best, so that he could wrap his legs around hers. 'What does a pretty girl want with an army?'

'I adore armies,' Anna said, shaking her head gently to and fro so that her hair trailed across his face. 'My grandfather was a famous soldier. And I have heard so much about the great Red Army. I should love to see some of it.'

He kissed her. 'And so you shall. But the Red Army is everywhere, and getting about in this weather is very difficult.'

'Don't you have some units on the border?'

'Well, of course. We have three fronts situated on the border.'

'What is a front?' Anna asked innocently.

'It is what you would call an Army Corps.'

'And you have them on the border? Who are you going to fight?'

He grinned. 'As you said, every country needs to have units on its borders. We have no desire to fight anyone in Europe.'

'And outside of Europe?'

'Ah, well, the Japanese are a threat. Do you not know that we have been fighting an undeclared war with Japan along the border with Manchuria for the past three years?'

'I did not know that,' Anna said more innocently yet.

'Well, we don't publicize it. But we generally win the battles. On the other hand it is something we have to sort out eventually. Those little yellow men seem to wish to take over all of Asia. We could never allow that.'

'I wish I were a Russian,' Anna said dreamily, wriggling her hips as she felt him hardening beneath her.

'I have never heard a German say that before.'

'But you are so immense, so strong, so unbeatable.'

He chuckled. 'Are you speaking of me or the country?'

'You are the country,' Anna assured him and spread her legs.

'Now that is very interesting,' Clive said. 'If Russia and Japan were to start a real war, that would change quite a few things.'

'Is England not friendly with Japan?'

'God, no! We were once, but since 1922, when we went along with the USA in reducing the strength of all navies at the expense of Japan, they have been increasingly hostile. And since this war started they have been flexing their muscles more and more contemptuously. They feel that we cannot fight Germany and Japan at the same time. And the damned thing is they are right. They are even giving us orders, like telling us to close the Burma Road through which Chiang Kai-Shek's army obtains most of its supplies. And we have felt obliged to do that to avoid any risk of a clash. That really is a bitter pill.'

Anna kissed him. 'You will work it out. Does not Great Britain always win the last battle?'

He ruffled her hair. 'So they say. I assume you are reporting all of this to Heydrich?'

'I have done so, certainly. But I have not heard anything further from him.'

'And what about the Kremlin, and Stalin?'

'I am about to start working on that.'

'I wish to God you wouldn't.'

Anna got out of bed and began to dress. 'You know I must,' she whispered. 'I will see you next week.'

'Well?' Groener demanded. 'What do you want?'

Marlene stood in front of the door. 'To speak with you, Herr Groener.'

'You? What do you have to say to me? You work for the Countess von Widerstand.'

'I am required to do so, yes, Herr Groener. But my loyalty must be to the Reich.'

Groener stared at her for several seconds. 'You have something to tell me about the Countess?'

'There is something I think you should know.'

'Is she not your friend?'

'She is not my friend, Herr Groener. She is nobody's friend. She is an utterly selfish

223

person, as cold as ice.'

Groener stroked his chin. 'I see. So what would you like to say about her? I know that she has been away these past few weeks. I understood that she had gone to the country with Herr Chalyapov.'

'Yes sir. But now that she has returned, she has begun leaving the Embassy just about every night and staying out till three in the morning.'

Groener snorted. 'Do you think I don't know that, you silly girl?'

'Do you also know where she goes?'

'She meets Herr Chalyapov, of course. He appears to be totally infatuated with her. Count von Schulenburg seems prepared to accept this relationship. He and I have received instructions from Berlin that she is not to be interfered with, so I assume they think she is obtaining information from this lout. Perhaps she is. But surely you know all this as you are her assistant? Even if,' he added, 'you seem to have fallen out with her.'

Marlene ignored the implied criticism. 'Suppose I was to tell you that she does not always go to Chalyapov?'

Groener raised his eyebrows. 'Where else does she go?'

'I do not know.'

'Then what are you saying?'

Marlene advanced right up to the desk. 'Herr Chalyapov is a heavy smoker. When the Countess returns from him, her clothes stink of cigarette smoke, but at least once a week when she comes in, there is no smell.'

'And that is proof that she has been with someone else? Perhaps Chalyapov does not smoke every night.'

'He is a chain-smoker, Herr Groener.'

Groener considered. 'Then she is no doubt servicing some other Russian as well. One who does not smoke.'

'Perhaps. But don't you think it is something you should know about?'

'I have told you that I have been given specific instructions, from General Heydrich himself, that under no circumstances am I to interfere with Fraulein Fehrbach's activities. That includes interrogating her as to those activities.'

Marlene looked as if she was about to stamp her foot. But she kept her temper. 'Not even if she is betraying the Reich?'

'You have given me no proof of that. Provide me with proof that she is engaged in some subversive activity, and I will act.'

Marlene regarded him for several seconds, then she said, 'You are asking me to risk my life.'

'Now you are being melodramatic.'

'I do not think you know this woman, Anna Fehrbach.'

'I know all I need to know: that she is a glamorous little bitch who enjoys the patronage of the head of the Gestapo. That is not difficult to understand, in view of her looks. That he chooses to employ her as a whore is his business, just as the fact that she appears

225

to enjoy it is hers.'

'Then you are unaware that she is a trained killer.'

Groener leaned back in his chair. 'You are starting to irritate me, Fraulein. How can a twenty-year-old girl be a trained killer?'

'Are you aware that my mother was Commandant Hannah Gehrig of the SD?'

'Which is no doubt why you have been given a position in the service. Yes, I know of your mother, Fraulein. I also know that she is presumed dead.'

Marlene nodded. 'I believe that she is dead, too. But perhaps you do not know that when she disappeared she was Fraulein Fehrbach's controller, and that before then she had personally supervised Fraulein Fehrbach's training, both as an agent and as an assassin. She told me that Fraulein Fehrbach had killed several times, before she was even twenty.'

'And she was never arrested for these crimes?'

'They were carried out on the instructions of the SD, of General Heydrich himself. All except one, which she claimed was in self-defence.'

'I will say again: if you feel that Fraulein Fehrbach is doing something, anything, that could harm the Reich, prove it. Unless you can do that, do not trouble me again.'

Marlene stared at him. 'I would like a weapon.'

'What?'

'I have told you, if I am to secure the proof

226

you wish, I will have to endanger my life. I need to be able to protect myself.'

'You mean to shoot Fraulein Fehrbach.'

'If I have to.'

'And you understand that should you kill her without providing proof of what you claim, you will hang.'

'If I have to shoot her, it will be because I have secured that proof.'

Groener considered for a last few moments, then opened a drawer in his desk, took out a Walther PPK, and held it out. Marlene gazed at it. 'That is only a five millimetre shot.'

Groener shrugged. 'It will kill, if accurately aimed and fired at not more than twenty-five metres.'

Marlene remembered shooting at the man in the training camp, with a pistol exactly like this, and being unable to hit a vital part. But she did not think she would be unable to kill the bitch who had so arrogantly rejected her. She took the pistol, and tucked it out of sight beneath her blouse. 'I shall also need permission to leave the Embassy as I choose at any hour of the day or night. Written permission.'

Once again Groener considered for several seconds. Then he pulled a block of headed notepaper towards him and began to write.

'So where have you been the past month?' Clive asked. 'Last Tuesday was the loneliest night of my life.'

'Except, surely, when drifting around the Mediterranean with a bullet in your backside,' Anna suggested. She kissed him. 'I have been working.'

'I am sure. On exactly which part of Chalyapov's anatomy?'

'You are in a grouch. I have been with Ewfim to inspect the troops.'

'Say again?'

'He took me to Brest-Litovsk, and then up and down the border. They have an awful lot of troops concentrated there. He even introduced me to the various generals and showed me over some of their units.'

'And you have relayed this information to Heydrich?'

'That is my job, just as I am now relaying it to you.'

'I don't imagine even a vast Russian army perched along the Polish border is about to invade Great Britain. Do you think they are planning a war with Germany?'

'Ewfim says definitely not.'

'Then why are they there?'

'He says because they have to be somewhere, and because Stalin is paranoid about his borders.'

'You believe him?'

'Well, the troops I saw did not look as if they were preparing to go to war. Mind you, it is still ten below.'

'And in another month or so it may be up to zero. What do you think Heydrich will make of this information?'

'I have no idea. It may even put his, or Hitler's, plans back a bit. Which can't be a

228

bad thing. But I am sure I will receive follow-up instructions in due course.'

'And what progress have you made in that other direction?'

'Two days ago I took tea with Marshal Stalin.'

'You what?'

'Fact. I have virtually the run of the Kremlin. Everyone adores me. I told Ewfim that I would like to become a Russian citizen and he is working on it. He told Stalin about me and I was invited to tea. Have you ever met him? Stalin, I mean.'

'You are operating out of my class.'

'He is a charmer. He speaks through that huge moustache and makes me think of my grandfather. My real grandfather, not the invented one.'

'And because of this "charm", you are going to commit suicide?'

'I would rather not. I am working on it. Now, let us make love. We have talked business long enough.'

'Oh, my darling girl.' Clive held her close, kissed her forehead, her chin, her cheek, her eyes, her nose, and then her mouth. 'To have you here, and know—'

'You know nothing,' Anna said fiercely. 'I have received no instructions as yet, except that I should become acceptable in the Kremlin. This I have done. When I receive further instructions, I will tell you, and we will discuss it.' She looked at her watch. 'Now

I must go. I will see you next Tuesday.'

She got out of bed, and he caught her hand. 'I won't be here next Tuesday.'

Anna paused in the act of pulling on her cami-knickers. 'Where will you be?'

'I have been recalled to England.'

'Why?'

'Presumably they are happy with the way things are going here.'

'So who will be my contact?'

'Commander Sprague.'

Anna smoothed her dress. 'He's not really my type.'

Clive got out of bed to take her in his arms. 'You don't have to go to bed with him. In fact, I would prefer it if you didn't. But he'll be here on Tuesday nights. All you have to do is bring him up to date, have a drink, and then push off.'

'Does he know about you and me?'

'I haven't given him chapter and verse, but he's not a fool. On the other hand, he is a gentleman. He won't bring it up unless you do.'

'Um.' She put on her mink and held him close. 'When do you leave?'

'Tomorrow morning.'

'And you're telling me now?'

'My instructions only arrived on Friday, and there was no way of getting in touch.'

'I wish you weren't going. Your being here gives me a sense of security, a feeling that I'm not entirely alone.'

'Is that all I give you?'

230

'You know it isn't.'

'Well, your being here gives me the heebie-jeebies. I want you to start work on irritating Chalyapov just as soon as you can, as we agreed. If he drops you, you'll be no more use to the Nazis here, so they'll have to recall you, and you'll be off the hook.'

She nodded, released him, and put on her hat.

'Promise?' he asked.

'Promise.'

She kissed him and left the room. It was just after two, and the hotel was quiet. She was in a hurry to get back to the Embassy and into the privacy of her room. She felt quite shattered. It was absurd, of course. She had existed in Moscow for four months without Clive, without even knowing whether he was going to appear or not. It was illogical now to feel that she was being abandoned, just as it was illogical ever to feel that his presence in any way protected her. She had to be her own salvation, as she had always been in the past. But how often in the past had she felt no less lonely?

She stepped from the elevator, wrapped her scarf round her face, and crossed the now empty foyer towards the swing doors.

'A word, comrade.'

Anna turned her head. The night porter had left the reception counter to approach her.

'You have been in Room 507.'

'Is that important?'

'To me, no. But to others, who knows?'

'You mean the NKVD?'

'I do not think so, as yet.'

'Would you explain that?'

'Well, I am required to report to the police anything that I consider may be of importance.'

'And you have reported me. But you do not know who I am.'

'I know that you are not a resident in the hotel, and I know that you regularly visit the Englishman in 507.'

'I see. And you have reported this to the NKVD.'

'No, comrade. I have reported it to the Moscow police, as I am required to do. Whether they have considered it necessary to inform the State Police I do not know. But I doubt it. I told them that a foreign lady comes to the hotel every Tuesday night, and spends several hours with an English resident, and then leaves again. The NKVD are usually only interested when a foreigner has an assignation with a Russian.'

'I see,' Anna said again, sizing him up. He was a pleasant-looking man, in early middle age, chunkily built as were so many Russians, and had somewhat sleepy – but also sly – eyes. Presumably he also had a wife, and perhaps children. But he had suddenly become a threat. 'I still do not understand why you are telling me this, but I am grateful. Would it be possible to reward you?'

'That would be very nice, comrade. But I have something else to tell you. Something more important, perhaps.' He gazed at her.

'Then I shall certainly reward you.' Anna opened her handbag.

'I do not wish money, comrade.'

'Ah. Well then, tell me what this more important matter is, and I will decide just how great a reward you will have.'

The man hesitated, as if wondering whether he should claim the reward first. Then he said, 'There was someone asking after you tonight.'

Anna frowned. 'The police?'

'No. A foreign lady like yourself. In fact, she had an accent exactly like yours.'

Anna felt a slow tensing of both her mind and her stomach muscles. 'What exactly did she ask you?'

'She said she was looking for a tall, very beautiful, yellow-haired woman who came regularly to the hotel. She wished to know if I remembered such a lady, and if I could tell her why she came here.'

'What time was this?'

'Before midnight.'

'I see. And what did you tell her?'

'Well, she had obviously been watching your movements for some time. So I said you were a visitor to one of our guests.'

'You did not tell her who?'

'No, comrade.'

'Thank you. And you do not feel that this lady was a member of the NKVD or the police.'

'No, no. The lady was definitely a foreigner.

233

As I told you, she spoke very like you. But you are more fluent in Russian,' he added ingratiatingly.

That narrowed it down to a field of one: Marlene. The Berlin was a hotel for foreign visitors to Moscow, not Russians. That eliminated the possibility that she had been visiting another Russian commissar. Much would depend on who Marlene told of her investigation, and how soon. But in any event, that she should be spied upon by her own assistant was unacceptable. And in the circumstances there could be no question of merely writing Heydrich and requesting him to recall the girl for being no good; Heydrich might just be prepared to listen to what Hannah Gehrig's daughter had to say.

As for this poor fellow... 'You say that you have known of my visits to the gentleman in 507 for some time.' She was using her most innocent, but anxious, voice. 'Who else knows of these visits, apart from the police?'

'Well, comrade, I may have mentioned it to my assistant, who comes in on my nights off.'

'Was he interested?'

'Not very, as I remember.'

'And no one else? When I arrive the foyer is always crowded.'

'That is exactly it, comrade. No one else has noted your entry, because there are so many people coming in and out. But I am always here when you leave.'

'And how do you know which room I have been to?'

The porter winked. 'You come every Tuesday night. And every Tuesday night the gentleman in 507 orders a bottle of champagne. A gentleman never orders a bottle of champagne to drink all by himself. He is entertaining a visitor. And every Tuesday night you are a visitor to the hotel. Am I not a detective?'

'You are brilliant,' Anna smiled. 'Well then, what would you like your reward to be?'

'I would like to know if you are as beautiful as that woman said.'

'I think we should go into your office if I am to take anything off.'

'Oh, yes.' He was positively panting. He raised the flap and she went behind the reception counter. As she did so his hands closed on her buttocks, massaging them through the mink. Her feelings of sorrow for what she was about to do evaporated.

She went into the little office, turned and unwound the scarf from round her face. 'Oh, yes,' he said. 'The woman's right. You are superb.'

'You say the sweetest things,' Anna said, and hit him on the side of the neck. He saw the blow coming, but it was delivered at such a speed and with such force that he could do no more than get his hands half up before he lost consciousness. He hit the floor with a thump. Anna knelt on his chest to hold his body in place, grasped his head in both hands and gave it a violent twist with all her strength. She heard the snap. She stood up

235

and made the sign of the cross. Then she closed the office door behind her and left the hotel.

She regained the Embassy at three. The guards by now regarded her with a mixture of embarrassment and apprehension. She smiled at them and went upstairs to her apartment. There was no sound but the light was on in Marlene's bedroom. She went to her bedroom and undressed. Then she opened the bag in which she kept various essential supplies, and took out a bottle of strong sleeping pills. Carrying this she returned to Marlene's room and opened the door, immediately closing it again behind her.

Marlene had been sitting at her table writing on several sheets of paper. She looked up and gave a little gasp; it was not Anna's normal practice to wander around the apartment in the nude. 'Countess?'

Anna stood next to her. 'Are you writing your autobiography? Or a confession? Or merely an observation?'

Marlene opened her mouth and closed it again.

'No matter,' Anna said. 'You are not looking well. You have spent too much time out in the cold night air. I think you need a very good night's sleep. What is left of it. Here. I have brought you these. They are very good.' She held out the bottle invitingly.

Marlene stared at it as a rabbit might have stared at a snake. 'I do not like to take pills.'

'But I insist. I know what is best for you.'

Marlene licked her lips, and glanced at her bureau.

'Ah.' Anna stepped to the chest and opened the top drawer. Marlene stood up, and then sat down again; she knew better than to take on Anna at unarmed combat.

Anna took out the Beretta. 'How nice,' she remarked. 'Where did you find this? Under a bush?'

Marlene was trembling.

'Or was it given to you by a friend? So tell me, if you had had it handy, would you have shot me?'

'I...'

'Of course. You would have claimed that it was self-defence. But why should I attack you physically when I can destroy you with a few words? Who gave you the gun?' Her voice was suddenly crisp and harsh.

'Herr Groener.'

'I see. You have been a busy little bee. But it is very obvious that you are distraught. Now, take these pills and go to bed. I will have the doctor examine you in the morning.'

'I ... I...'

'If you do not obey me,' Anna said, 'I will be forced to write to General Heydrich and have him recall you to Berlin, where you will be sent to an SS brothel. I do assure you it will be better for you to do as I ask. Go into the bathroom and pour a mug of water.'

Slowly Marlene got up and went to the bathroom. Anna went with her to watch.

Marlene poured the water, and Anna again held out the bottle. This time Marlene took it. 'I think four should do it,' Anna told her.

Marlene unscrewed the cap, dropped four of the tablets into the palm of her hand, cupped them into her mouth and drank the water. She made a face and put down the mug beside the bottle.

'There,' Anna said. 'Now undress and go to bed.'

'I am undressed,' Marlene protested.

'You will feel better for sleeping in the nude like I do,' Anna assured her.

Another hesitation, and then Marlene took off the nightdress and got into bed. Anna pulled the sheet to her throat. 'Now close your eyes and have a good long sleep.'

She stood above the girl and watched her eyes droop shut. Then she sat at the table and read what Marlene had written. It was, as she had supposed, a long, somewhat rambling denunciation of her, listing all the suspicions Marlene claimed to have felt since their first association, relating how she had tracked her to the hotel on several occasions, and how this very night she had discovered that her quarry always visited the same room and that there could be no question of her meeting another Russian commissar. There was no indication as to whether the wretched girl had confided her suspicions to anyone else, but obviously she must have done so to Groener. But as she was only now compiling her report, which would now never be read,

Anna did not feel that was relevant.

She collected the sheets together neatly and turned to look at the bed. Marlene was breathing slowly and evenly. She was certainly in a deep sleep. Anna went into the bathroom and listened at the other door; there was no sound from Birgit's room, and she remembered that the maid was a heavy sleeper. She turned on the bath water, then she returned to the bedroom, took the sheets of paper into her own room and carefully burned them, collected the ashes and flushed them down the toilet.

Next she returned to Marlene's room, stood above the sleeping girl for some moments, then threw back the covers, and with an effort lifted the inert body. Her brain was as always ice-cold and entirely concentrated on what she was doing, on what she had to do. But she felt that self-horror was lurking. Killing an armed man, or woman, or in self-defence she could accept. Cold-blooded execution left her very nearly a nervous wreck, and this was the second this night.

But it *was* again self-defence, and the defence of her family. That single essential dominated her life. She carried Marlene along the corridor into the bathroom, carefully lowered her into the water and very gently pressed on her shoulders. Marlene went under. For more than a minute there was no reaction, then her eyes suddenly opened, as did her mouth. Anna retained her grip, still gently, but sufficient to keep the head from rising, now up to her elbows in very cold water. Marlene tried to lift her hands to strike but her arms were held in place by Anna's grip. Then she kicked several times, and water splashed about the room and over Anna's body. But very quickly the kicks subsided. It was over inside three minutes.

Anna held her there for another few minutes then stood up and dried herself. She left the lights on and the open bottle of pills, which now had Marlene's fingerprints on it over hers. Then she carefully wiped the pistol free of prints and restored it to the drawer, returned to her bedroom and got beneath the covers. She was shivering and tears rolled down her cheeks.

Eight

The Plot

Surprisingly, Anna slept heavily, but she knew she was emotionally exhausted by the events of the evening. She wished she could have warned Clive of what had happened, but it would have been too risky to linger in the hotel, and she believed the porter's claim that he had told no one of his deductions; he had been too anxious to see what profit he could achieve for himself. There would of course be a great fuss when the body was found, but there would be no immediate reason for any of the guests to be implicated, and Clive would surely be back in England before the investigation could get very far.

She awoke to a piercing scream, sat up and pushed hair from her eyes just as Birgit burst into her room, still wearing her nightgown, her face white and her hair dishevelled.

'Countess! Countess! Oh, Countess!'

'What in the name of God...?'

Birgit panted, 'Marlene! In the bath...'

Anna threw back the covers and got out of bed, reaching for her robe. 'There has been an accident?'

'Yes. No. I don't know.'

Anna grasped her shoulders and shook her. 'Pull yourself together. You are saying that Marlene has fallen in the bathroom?'

'No, Countess! I do not think so. She's dead.'

'What?' Anna ran from the room, Birgit behind her. She stood above the bath and looked at Marlene. The body was almost blue from its prolonged immersion in the near-freezing water. The eyes and mouth were still open, and there were also deeper blue marks on her upper arms. These had to be accounted for immediately. 'What are those marks? They look as if someone held her there.'

'I tried to lift her up,' Birgit wailed. 'When I saw her ... I could not believe she was dead. I tied to lift her up. I thought I held her wrists, but I must have held her arms as well. I don't remember. I was so horrified...'

'Of course you were,' Anna said sympathetically. 'And you did entirely the right thing in trying to help her. Just tell Herr Groener, when he asks you, exactly what happened. I will support you. Now, I think you should go back to bed; you do not look very well.'

'But...'

'I will deal with this.'

'Your breakfast...'

'I will get my own breakfast. Off you go.'

Birgit stumbled from the bathroom. Anna closed the door and returned to her bed-room, picked up the telephone. 'Herr Meis-

242

senbach's apartment, please,' she told the switchboard operator.

Anna decided against dressing; when confronting a room full of men she knew she was at her best wearing only a dressing gown. And the room very rapidly became filled with men, and even some women. Anna sat in a corner and sipped coffee.

'When did it happen?' Meissenbach asked.

'I have no idea. Can't the doctor tell us that?'

'No, he cannot. How long a body has been dead can usually be ascertained by taking the rectal temperature, because all bodies cool at a fixed rate after death. But this system is useless when the body has been immersed in cold water since death.'

'My people say that you came in at three o'clock,' Groener said.

'That would be about right.'

'What did you do after coming in?'

'I was both tired and cold. I came straight upstairs and went to bed.'

'And you noticed nothing out of the ordinary?'

'I noticed that Marlene's light was on. But that was not out of the ordinary. She often sat up late, reading.'

'But the bathroom light was also on.'

'Apparently. I cannot see that bathroom door from my room.'

'Did you know,' Meissenbach asked, 'that Fraulein Gehrig possessed a pistol?'

Anna frowned. 'I did not know that. Anyway, it is not possible. We were not issued with firearms for this assignment.'

'Nevertheless...'

Groener cleared his throat. 'I do not think her possession of a weapon is relevant: she did not shoot herself. The doctor thinks that she took a dose of strong pills from the bottle on the table beside her bed.'

'Oh, my God!' Anna cried, and leapt to her feet, scattering her dressing gown and revealing a great deal of flawless leg.

'Countess?'

Anna crossed the room and opened her medical bag. 'Those are my pills. She must have taken them while I was out.'

'And having taken the pills she got into a cold bath to drown herself?' Meissenbach asked.

'The bath must have been hot when she got in.'

'The important point,' Groener said, 'is why should Fraulein Gehrig commit suicide in the first place?' He looked at Anna, who sat on her bed.

'Well?'

'It is very embarrassing,' Anna said in a low voice, hunching her shoulders.

'You mean you know why she did this thing?' Meissenbach demanded.

'Well ... Marlene had a lover. Or at least, she was in love. But the person she loved did not respond. Could not respond.'

'You mean he was a married man? Someone here in the Embassy?'

'It was not a man.'

The two men stared at her.

'Marlene was in love with me,' Anna said.

'What?'

'I feel so bad about it,' Anna said. 'But...' She gazed at Meissenbach. 'I am not ... well ... when she made advances, I rejected her. Perhaps I was too brutal about it. I told her that if she ever attempted to come to my bed again I would inform General Heydrich and have her recalled to Berlin. She was in any event on probation. She failed her training course, and was due to be degraded. But because her mother and I had been friends I interceded for her, and begged for her to be given a second chance. But she knew that if she was returned from here in disgrace she would be dismissed from the service and sent to an SS brothel. In view of her ... well, sexual interests, this would have been a virtual death sentence. I did not mean it, of course; I was just very angry at the time. But she must have taken me seriously. I feel so very unhappy about it. I mean, I may as well have shot her myself.'

The two men exchanged glances. 'Well,' Meissenbach said, 'I must compliment you on your frankness, Countess. No doubt you will inform your superiors of what has happened.'

'Would you stop by my office, Herr Meissenbach?' Groener requested.

'Certainly.' Meissenbach accompanied the policeman to the Gestapo office. 'Are you not satisfied?'

'Have a seat.' Groener sat behind his desk. 'May I ask how long you have known this so-called Countess?'

'Not very long. I met her for the first time last July.'

'But you know something of her background?'

'I'm afraid I know nothing of her background. I was merely told that she was to accompany me to Moscow as my aide.'

'You did not find her absurd name suspicious? Countess of Resistance?'

'Well, yes I did. And I was told that it was not my business to ask questions. That the Countess was being sent to Moscow to carry out a mission for the Reich, and her position as my aide was to provide her with a cover.'

'Hmm. You were not informed that she was a Government assassin?'

'What?' Meissenbach cried, as convincingly as he could. 'A twenty-year-old girl? How do you know this?'

'I was informed ... by Fraulein Gehrig.'

This time Meissenbach's consternation was genuine. 'And you believed her? Who is she supposed to assassinate? Or, indeed, who *has* she assassinated?' Groener stared at him, and he gulped. 'You cannot be serious. I mean...'

'Oh, it was a totally professional job, and we will never be able to prove that it was not a suicide. But that is what I would expect from a professional killer.'

'But, if Gehrig made advances ... I can tell you that the Countess is not a lesbian.'

Groener raised his eyebrows, and Meissenbach flushed. 'Well, I have been fairly close to her for several months.' Then he frowned as he recalled the loving way Anna had kissed Gabriella Hosek just before beginning to torture her – and just before Hosek had bitten the cyanide capsule. But he felt it might be unwise to confide any of the events in Prague to this man. Groener was regarding him with interest, and he hurried on. 'What I mean is, even if they were lovers who had quarrelled, that was surely no reason for her to murder the girl.'

'It is my opinion,' Groener said, 'that Fehrbach – you know her real name is Anna Fehrbach?'

Meissenbach nodded.

'Well, Gehrig became suspicious of her activities, and confided her suspicions to me. She was convinced that Fehrbach was seeing somebody else in addition to Chalyapov when on her midnight jaunts. I'm afraid I was sceptical about the importance of this, but I gave her permission to see what she could find out. I also gave her that pistol to use in case she needed it; if she had been able to shoot Fehrbach it would have solved all of our problems. However, as I was saying, I believe Fehrbach found out about her suspicions and killed her. Sadly, she does not appear to have been able to use the weapon.'

'My God! What are we to do?'

'As I have said, Herr Meissenbach, there is nothing we can do. This woman is a creature of the SD, and they will not permit anything to happen to her, certainly not until she has completed her mission. I just wished you to understand the situation, so that, if the opportunity arises, we can work together.'

'Of course. But we must inform the Ambassador.'

'That is what we must *not* do. He has been sufficiently shocked at the news that Gehrig killed herself. He is an old-fashioned Junker, whose gods are honour and duty. If he knew we suspected Fehrbach of murder he would feel compelled to take the matter to the highest level, which could well bring the SD into our midst in force, and God knows what would happen then.'

Meissenbach considered, then nodded. 'I understand. But to think that we have a cold-blooded murderess right here in the Embassy...'

'Patience, Herr Meissenbach. Patience is a policeman's most effective weapon. All criminals make a mistake, eventually. Fehrbach may be a cold-blooded killer, but she is still only a girl of twenty. She will make a mistake, sooner rather than later. And then we will have her. I ' – he added with thoughtful anticipation – 'will have her. But you may watch, Herr Meissenbach.'

'I hope you are glad to be home,' Baxter commented.

'No, I am not,' Clive said. 'I hate leaving unfinished business.'

'Well, I'm sure Belinda is pleased to have you back in one piece.'

'I'm not too sure about that either. She seems to feel that I was away unnecessarily long.'

'An opinion with which I entirely concur. However, I'm sure you'll be interested to hear the latest despatch from Sprague.'

'I'm not sure that I will be.'

'You mean you don't want to know about his cavortings with your beautiful protégée? Well, I can put your mind at rest in that direction. Sprague has seen neither hair nor hide of the young lady since your departure.'

'Good Lord! She did say that he wasn't her type...'

'Clive, we are running a secret service department, not a knocking shop. I find her reluctance to communicate with Sprague both annoying and disturbing. However, there may just be a logical if not excusable reason. I presume you are aware that there was a murder in the Hotel Berlin the night before you left?'

'Oh, yes. There was the devil of a flap. Someone mugged the night porter.'

'As you say, someone mugged the night porter. Sprague has been able to get some detail on the crime. Time of death 0230.'

Clive frowned.

'Quite. I assume, as it was your last night in

Moscow, you had company between the sheets?'

'Well...'

'And what time did the lady leave you?'

'Jesus,' Clive muttered. 'But that can't be right. Why on earth should Anna kill the night porter? The time has to be a coincidence.'

'If it's a coincidence, she must certainly have seen the killer. But it wasn't a coincidence.'

'You mean she's been arrested? Oh, Christ!'

'Relax. The Moscow police have no idea who the assassin was, although they apparently feel fairly sure that it was a man. Apparently the porter had a reputation as a lady killer, and they are working on the theory that the crime was committed by an outraged husband or boyfriend. There was absolutely no one around at the time. Only we know differently.'

'Oh, come now, Billy. Simply because Anna *may* have passed through the lobby at about the time the murder was committed? Isn't it most likely that she saw two men together, perhaps quarrelling, perhaps even fighting, and decided to get out of there before the noise attracted attention?'

'That would be a valid point, except for one thing: the reason the police are certain it was a man. The porter died as a result of two acts of supreme power and violence.'

'Eh?'

'He was laid out by a karate blow to the neck, and then was killed by having his head twisted until his vertebrae snapped. According to the police, only a man would – or indeed could – have done something like that. But again, we know better, don't we?'

Clive stared at him. 'Hannah Gehrig died like that!'

'Go to the head of the class.'

'But why?'

'I would say that he found out about Anna's midnight trysts with you and decided to capitalize on it, by requesting either money or favours as the price of keeping his mouth shut. The world is full of sex-hungry men who believe that innocent-looking, pretty young girls are there for the taking. Sadly, in most cases, they are absolutely right. This unfortunate character, exactly like poor Reiffel, had no idea he was snuggling up to a hungry lioness who was also engaged in secret and highly dangerous business.'

Clive sighed. 'That poor girl.'

Baxter raised his eyebrows.

'All right,' Clive conceded. 'So she reacts violently when she considers herself in danger. You know that. What you don't know is how vulnerable she is.'

Baxter snorted.

'How desperately lonely,' Clive went on. 'And she was upset at my leaving.'

'You'll have me crying my eyes out in a minute. What you are saying is we should be grateful that Moscow is still standing.'

'Anyway,' Clive said. 'Let's look on the bright side. The only person in the world who can possibly relate Anna to that murder, apart from you and me, is Anna herself.'

'I haven't finished reading Sprague's despatch.'

'Oh my God! What now?'

'There has been a suicide at the German Embassy.'

Clive stared at him. 'No,' he muttered. 'No!' he shouted. 'It cannot be!'

'Simmer down. It's not Anna.'

'Then...'

'It was a young woman. However, she is listed as being secretary to the Countess von Widerstand. And this suicide apparently took place on the same night the porter was murdered. You'll never guess what the girl's name was. Marlene Gehrig.'

Once again Clive stared at him.

'As I recall,' Baxter said, 'Hannah Gehrig was in her forties when Anna broke *her* neck. This girl is reported as being in her late teens. I would suppose she must have been a daughter. I mean, it would be too much of a coincidence to suppose that Anna would employ as a secretary someone with the same name as her old enemy who was not actually a relative.'

'But would she employ a relative of the woman she killed?'

'She never mentioned this girl to you?'

'No, she did not.'

'Hmm. She certainly does like to keep her secrets. The point is that she seems to be discovering too many people who appear to

252

be finding out, or are on the verge of finding out, too much about her. Which leads us to the question: is she becoming too vulnerable for us to continue employing her?'

'You think that again, and my resignation will be on your desk in one hour,' Clive told him. 'And when I retire I am going to write my memoirs – fuck the Official Secrets Act. We have just touched the tip of the iceberg as to what this girl can deliver. Don't we now know that Germany intends to invade Russia? Probably as soon as the thaw sets in. I presume you have passed this information on?'

'It went to the Boss, and thence to the War Cabinet, and thence to the PM himself.'

'Who no doubt chose to disbelieve it.'

'He did believe it, Clive. He took it very seriously, and conveyed it to Marshal Stalin in a personal letter. Unfortunately, Stalin did *not* believe it. Or at least, he chose not to do so. We shall just have to wait and see what evolves.'

'But it was Anna who gave us that information, and who will give us a great deal more. Obviously right now she's lying low because of what happened at the Berlin Hotel and what happened to that girl. Are you supposing that she killed her as well?'

'It would seem logical. The girl was apparently found drowned in her bath, the bath having been taken in the middle of the night. Do young girls normally take baths in the middle of the night? In mid-winter? I know that my daughter doesn't.'

'I should get back there.'

'Forget that. The last thing we want is for one of our people to get involved in whatever shenanigans are taking place in the German Embassy. I'll go along – at least for the time being – with the idea that she'll surface when she feels it's safe to do so.'

'If only,' Clive mused, 'we could have some idea of just what she's doing now.'

'Tea,' Josef Stalin remarked, beaming through his moustache. 'It is the greatest of drinks, the ultimate solace of mankind. And womankind, of course. Do you not agree, Countess?'

'Absolutely,' Anna purred.

'But it should never be adulterated with such things as milk, or lemon, or sugar, as they do in the West.'

'I couldn't agree with you more, Your Excellency.'

'You are a woman of taste. So you know, here, in the privacy of this office, I would like to call you Anna. May I call you Anna?'

'Of course, Your Excellency.'

'And you must call me Josef, when we are in this office. Anna is a good old Russian name. We had an empress once named Anna. She was very successful.'

'Were not the tsars, and the tsarinas, terrible people?' Anna asked, at her most innocent.

'Of course. But rulers need to be terrible. One of our tsars rejoiced in being *known* as the Terrible.'

As you are terrible, Anna thought. She

254

knew that this charming old man had ruthlessly executed everyone he distrusted during the past ten years. But then, had she not done the same in a much shorter time?

'The tsars,' Stalin went on, 'were a necessary part of Russian history. They created the nation. They declined, of course, as time went by, and became corrupt and had to be eliminated, but without them none of us would be here. But you know, I did not invite you here to talk politics. You have now experienced a Russian winter. And you are about to experience a Russian spring. Already the ice is breaking. In a week or two there will be green shoots everywhere, and soon after that the entire country will erupt in colour and song. A Russian spring is the greatest natural event in the world. It truly fulfills the criteria of the old gods, that in winter the earth dies, but in spring it is reborn again.'

And it may be the last you will ever see, Anna thought. And it may be my last too. She had received no further communication from Heydrich. Not even a comment on the death of Marlene. She had been cast entirely adrift, by both her employers.

Her position in the Embassy was more equivocal than ever. All pretence of finding her something to do had been dropped; Marlene had not been replaced as an assistant, and the senior staff did their best to pretend that she wasn't there. Whether they suspected that she might have been involved in Marlene's death she had no idea, but even

Meissenbach never came near her, and she was no longer invited to any dinners or cocktails parties. This was no longer important, as she remained Chalyapov's mistress, but the only company she enjoyed inside the Embassy was Birgit, and enjoyed was hardly an appropriate word in this context. Birgit seemed more terrified of her than ever, and she also clearly mourned Marlene, and also clearly kept worrying if she had, inadvertently, by word or deed, contributed to her lover's decision to take her own life.

That left Chalyapov, who remained as enthusiastic as ever. But now she was embarking upon the plan she had agreed with Clive – that of becoming an increasingly demanding, querulous and generally irritating little woman, in the hopes that he would decide to drop her so that she could be returned to Germany...

There was a knock on the door, which then opened.

Stalin did not turn his head, but he said quietly, 'I gave instructions that I was not to be interrupted when I was entertaining the Countess von Widerstand.'

'Comrade Molotov said that you would wish to be informed immediately, Comrade Stalin. He has received an urgent despatch from our minister in Belgrade.'

'What can be happening in Belgrade that is so urgent?'

'It is under attack, Comrade.'

'What?' Now Stalin did turn, while Anna

put down her tea cup with a clatter. 'Attack by whom?'

The secretary gave Anna an anxious glance 'It is being bombed by the Luftwaffe, and it is reported that an army corps of the Wehrmacht has crossed the frontier and is advancing on the city.'

'What steps is Comrade Molotov taking?'

'He has summoned Count von Schulenberg to a meeting and will ask for an explanation.'

'Very good. Thank Comrade Molotov for informing me so promptly, and tell him that I would like to see him at the conclusion of his meeting with the ambassador.'

The secretary withdrew, and Stalin looked at Anna. 'You did not know of this?'

'Me? I do not think anyone at the Embassy can have known of it. It does not make sense. Prince Paul, the regent for the boy king, is a supporter of the Reich.'

'So I have always understood. Well, clearly he has either changed his point of view, or more likely, he has been replaced as regent.'

'But why? And why should the Fuehrer wish to invade Yugoslavia? They have never been our enemies.'

He regarded her for some seconds, but he could have no doubt that she was as bemused by what had happened as anyone. 'And the country has little of value,' he remarked at last. 'Except...' He got up and went to the huge map of Europe pinned to the wall, studied it. 'It provides the only practical route for a large armed force to take through the

Balkan mountains to the Aegean Sea. To Greece, in fact. I think we will find that your Fuehrer will say that he wishes to send an army to help his friend Mussolini beat the Greeks, which they are not doing, especially now that there is a British army fighting on the Greek side.'

'But you do not believe that is the true reason?'

'The true reason, my dear Anna, is that Herr Hitler intends to complete the conquest of all Europe, apart from Spain and Sweden, by occupying the entire Balkan Peninsula. Only then will he feel able to bring his full might to bear upon Great Britain. Yes. That is excellent.'

Anna felt like scratching her head. 'This does not concern you, Comrade Stalin?'

'Josef,' he reminded her. 'Concern me? It pleases me very much.'

'But ... if Germany controls all of mainland Europe, her borders will be contiguous with yours.'

'We already have a contiguous border with the Reich. In Poland. There is no difficulty on that. Soviet Russia and Nazi Germany have a twenty-five-year non-aggression pact, with which we are both totally content. You require our oil and coal and iron ore; we require your expertise. We share the future. Now I will tell you why I am pleased. A state secret, eh? I actually received a communication from the British Prime Minister, Mr Churchill, to the effect that he had positive proof that Germany is planning an attack on Russia.'

Anna drank the last of her tea, which was by now cold.

'I did not believe what he said, of course. The British have been trying to embroil us with Germany for years. Since before the war even started. But at the same time, our agents reported to us considerable German troop movements to the East. You do not mind my admitting to you that we have agents inside your country?'

'I am sure that we have our agents inside Russia,' Anna said faintly.

'Of course. It is all part of the game, eh? But now it is all explained. Your troop movements to the east were to facilitate your takeover of the Balkans. As I have said, it is always good to have a conundrum resolved, especially when it is resolved in such a satisfactory manner. Do you know, I feel like a holiday. I should be able to get out of Moscow for a week or so, next month.' Stalin poured more tea. 'Then I generally go down to my dacha in the south, where I can relax. I would be delighted if you were to accompany me.'

Anna turned her head sharply. Although she had known from their first meeting that he had been very taken with her, he had remained entirely avuncular in their relations. She found it difficult to imagine having sex with any man over fifty. And this man ... She wondered what Chalyapov would make of that. Or Clive? Or Heydrich?

'I am sure that you would enjoy it there,'

Stalin continued. 'You would be able to meet my children. My son Jacob is in the army, but my daughter Svetlana is still a girl. I am a widower, you see,' he added ingenuously.

My God! she thought. He can't be serious! But he very evidently was, at least at this moment. She drank tea, and spoke absently. 'I have a birthday next month.'

'What is the date?'

'The twenty-first.'

'And how old will you be?'

'Twenty-one.'

'Twenty-one. Ah, to be twenty-one again. But, twenty-one on the twenty-first. That is capital. You will spend your twenty-first birthday with me.'

Time for a decision. 'I'm sure that would be most enjoyable, Your Excellency.'

'Josef,' he reminded her.

Was he living in never-never land, or could he possibly be right? Anna wondered. But he was the master of a great country, and had been that master for more than a dozen years. He had to be used to evaluating, correctly, the acts and indeed the words of other governments. But if Germany had only ever been intent on occupying the entire Balkans, what of Heydrich's orders to her, to find out all she could about Russian attitudes towards Germany, and her troop dispositions along the border? But, she realized, they too could be explained, if one was determined to do so: clearly Hitler had been concerned about

Russian reaction to his projected move to the south-east.

In which case the information she had given Clive, and the inference the British had drawn from it, had been entirely erroneous. And Churchill had gone for it! He would now be hopping mad. So, where did that leave her as regards MI6?

For that matter, where did she stand in any direction? Her sole desire was to get out of Moscow. Before her week with Stalin? She just could not imagine what that might be like. But she could not refuse him now, although there could be no doubt that Heydrich had to be informed. She could not imagine *his* reaction either, save that if Stalin's judgement was accurate, there was simply no reason for her to remain in Moscow.

'I think your mind is elsewhere.' Chalyapov threw her off him with some violence, so that she rolled across the bed and lay on her back.

'I am sorry, Ewfim. Would you like me to leave?'

'You are becoming bored with me. You are seeing another man.'

'Of course I am not.'

He got out of bed. 'I do not like women who cheat on me. Or who lie to me. Give me his name.'

'There is no other man.'

'Very good. Roll over.'

Anna sighed, but obeyed. When he entered her from behind it was always painful. She spread her legs, closed her eyes, and waited for him to raise her thighs from the mattress. Instead she heard a swishing sound. She opened her eyes again and turned her head. Chalyapov had drawn the heavy leather belt from his pants. 'What are you doing?' she asked.

'I am going to beat you. I am going to make that delightful little ass of yours bleed.'

Anna rolled over and sat up. 'Please do not do that, Ewfim. I do not like to be beaten.' The last person who had flogged her was Hannah Gehrig, and she had had the assistance of three men.

'If you liked being beaten,' Chalyapov pointed out, very reasonably, 'there would be no point in doing it. Lie down!'

'Ewfim,' she said, also speaking very reasonably, 'if you attempt to hit me, I shall break your arm.'

'You?' He gave a bark of laughter. 'Very well. If you wish me to mark your tits...' He swung the belt.

Anna caught the flailing leather in both hands. The shock of pain only increased her anger, but her brain remained ice cold. As she caught the belt she rose to her knees and threw herself sideways. The combined jerk on the belt and her roll pulled Chalyapov off balance; his knees struck the bed and he fell across it. Anna leapt off the bed and got behind him. The temptation to hit him was enormous, but she felt that to kill him might be a mistake. While he was trying to push

262

himself up she knelt on his back, grasped his right arm, which still held the belt, and pulled it behind him and across while shifting her knee to his shoulder. Chalyapov uttered a scream of pain as the arm was dislocated, then Anna released him and stepped away.

He rolled to and fro, groaning and holding his arm. 'Bitch!' he moaned.

'I did warn you,' Anna pointed out, dressing herself.

'I am going to have you—'

'Before you get carried away,' Anna said, 'I should tell you that you are quite right in supposing that I am seeing another man. His name is Josef Stalin.'

She closed the door behind herself.

It was only when she regained the Embassy that she realized she had wanted to hurt Chalyapov, as much as possible, ever since that first evening in his car, when he had, to all intents and purposes, raped her. Why had she not done it before? Because she had needed an excuse. Now that it was done, she could surely ask to be relieved. She sat at her desk and wrote to Heydrich.

I deeply regret that this should have happened, but the fact is that his treatment of me has grown increasingly brutal, and indeed, sadistic, over the past weeks. I have accepted this in order to carry out my mission, but when he threatened to beat me until I bled, I am afraid something snapped. I do not think I have done him any permanent injury, but I would say that he is unlikely to wish to see me again. I may also say, and it is an opinion in which I hope you will concur, that he has exhausted his potential as a source of information.

She considered for some moments before continuing. It was very necessary to remind her boss of her continuing value.

However, Herr Chalyapov has now become entirely irrelevant. I have become very close to Marshal Stalin himself, and have tea with him every Friday afternoon, in complete privacy; I come and go in the Kremlin as if I belonged there. I have also been invited to visit with him at his dacha in the Crimea. I will admit that he has not yet divulged any information of much value, other than that he is confident of maintaining good and friendly relations with Germany, but as we grow more intimate I am sure I will obtain results. I can in any event assure you that he is perfectly content with our moves in the Balkans and sees no reason why these should drive a rift between our two nations. I would be very happy if you would confirm your approval of my present activities, although I am sure you understand that should you feel I have served my purpose here I am ready to return to Berlin. Anna.

She realized her heart was pounding. If Clive were right, and her German employers had designs upon Stalin's life, she was virtually inviting them to use her. But if Stalin were right ... and Stalin had to be right.

She sealed the envelope and took it to Groener for inclusion in the Diplomatic Pouch. He regarded it for several moments. 'It is some time since you heard from General Heydrich, is it not?'

Sharks, she thought, waiting for me to fall into their pool. 'My orders from the SD, Herr Groener, are ongoing. However, I am sure you will be pleased to know that my mission here is all but completed, and that I shall shortly be recalled to Berlin.'

She prayed that it might be so.

Over the next few weeks Anna continued to be invited to tea; she had become such a regular visitor that she was no longer even searched before being admitted to the inner sanctum. Not that it would have mattered as she never carried a weapon. On the other hand, the invitation to accompany the dictator to the Crimea was not repeated. Either Stalin had been upset by what she had done to Chalyapov – although he remained unfailingly pleasant to her – or his invitation had not been serious in the first place, or events in the Balkans were not turning out quite as favourably for Russia as he had anticipated. On the whole she was relieved, although there was just a hint of disappointment: it would have been quite an experience, she had no doubt. More disturbing was the absence of any reply from Heydrich. So she celebrated her twenty-first birthday alone in her apartment with Birgit.

But Stalin was certainly right about the weather. June was a delight, the more so because of the tremendous contrast provided by warmth and sunshine to the grey skies and biting winds of only a few weeks previously. Anna took up going for a daily walk in the park; it was such a pleasure to be able to wear a summer frock and a big hat and feel the gentle breeze caressing her legs, even if she now found herself awakening each day with increasing apprehension. She had no doubt that something was going to happen this summer; her sole ambition was to get back to Germany before it happened.

'Countess! What a pleasant surprise.'

The man was speaking English! But the American accent was unmistakable. Anna turned her head. 'Mr Andrews? I did not know you were still in Moscow.'

'Like you, I guess, I go – and stay – where I'm put. But I sure thought you had gone, seeing as how you haven't been at any parties recently. And here you are, prettier than any picture I have ever seen. As always. May I walk with you?'

'Certainly, after such a nice remark.'

He fell in at her side. 'You know that fellow Bartley has returned to England? A couple of months ago.'

'I had heard. I thought Mr Bartley was a friend of yours?'

'Like I said, we're in the same line of business.'

'Military intelligence.'

'Well, intelligence. Spy-spotting.'

Anna was happy to take the bait. 'And catching?'

'Sure. When it's possible. And convenient. May I ask you a question?'

'I don't have to answer it.'

'Are you really a Nazi spy?'

'As I said, Mr Andrews, I don't have to answer your question. When I lived in England, I was married to Ballantine Bordman. Sadly, it didn't work out.'

'And when it didn't work out, you returned to Germany.'

'What else would you have me do? Germany is my home. Or at least, Austria is. My family now lives in Germany.'

'But you had become a British citizen.'

'Bally wished me to. But I retained German nationality.'

'Which I guess has put you in rather a spot regarding the British.'

'That may well be so. But as I am not in England, their feelings towards me are hardly relevant.'

'I heard someplace that your mother is actually English. Is she happy with this?'

'My mother is Irish.'

'You never did answer my question. Were

you a spy? The Brits sure thought you were.'

'I never said I would answer that question, Mr Andrews.'

'But you're here, at the Embassy...'

'I have a living to earn. Thus I work for the German Government. I suppose in your eyes that makes me a Nazi. I can only say that in Germany today, it is the best thing to be. I would also hope that that does not make me your enemy.'

'Not mine. At least not right now. But you're not afraid of what may happen? One day?'

How little you know, she thought. 'What do I have to be scared of, Mr Andrews?'

'You don't think it's odd, that fellow turning up in Moscow and coming to your party?'

'What fellow? Oh, you mean Mr Bartley. I am sure he had some other reason for coming here. Apart from me, I mean. He surely knows that here in Russia I am outside of his jurisdiction.'

'I guess you're right,' Andrews said thoughtfully. 'Say, Countess, would I be completely out of court if I asked you to have dinner with me? I mean, June in Moscow, with the trees blossoming and the birds singing...' He paused, anxiously.

'Why, Mr Andrews,' she said. 'I think that is a perfectly charming idea.'

'This has been one of the pleasantest evenings I can remember,' Anna said, with considerable truth. Her moments with Clive had always been the highs of her emotional life, but they had always been stolen. They had never shared a quiet evening at a restaurant together, never been to a dance together, never strolled in a park together, except as conspirators. Now she sat on a terrace over-looking the river, dining on carp, drinking white wine and discussing sweet nothings.

She had no doubt that he was dying to ask more questions, but so far he had restrained himself, preferring to talk about the United States, about his home in Virginia, the more so as she had confessed that she had never been to America, and knew very little about it. 'You'd love it,' he promised. 'And America would love you.'

'Even if I work for the Nazis?' she asked in an unguarded moment.

'You have convinced me that it is just a job of work, a means of earning a living. Not that you truly believe the ideology. Heck, I work for a Democratic administration, even if I've always voted Republican.'

She made a moue. 'I still cannot believe that I would be very welcome in your country.'

'You would be. One thing about us, we adore beautiful things. And you would be just about the most beautiful thing any of them would ever have seen. I do apologize. I did not mean that you are a thing.'

'But I am a spy, am I not? The British say so.'

'Well, you know, the Brits aren't always right in their judgements. I find it very difficult to accept that you are anything other than what you seem: a very beautiful and very charming young lady.'

Anna stared at him with her mouth open, and he flushed.

'Again I apologize. Heck, no. I don't. I ... well, I'd sure like to get to know you better.'

'If you did that, you might not like me at all.'

'I'll take my chances on that. May I be extremely rude, and ask a personal question?'

'That depends on how personal the question is.'

'Someone at our Embassy has the idea that you are still in your early twenties. Can that possibly be true?'

Anna sipped cognac. 'My twenty-first birthday was a fortnight ago.'

'You're putting me on.'

'Do I look that much older?'

'Heck, no. I mean...' He was flushing. 'Didn't you marry that fellow Bordman three years ago?'

'I was eighteen when I married Bally, yes.'

'Wow! Well, I guess that puts the kybosh on the crazy idea that you could have been a spy.'

'You say the sweetest things,' Anna commented.

'Listen! I would like you to know that if things ever turn out bad, you can count on me. I mean...' One of his flushes. 'If you ever feel you have to get out of Germany, you can call on my help, and I'll see you find a home

270

in the States.'

Anna smiled. 'In Virginia?'

'I'd like that.'

Anna squeezed his hand.

'Do you have something to tell me?' Heinz Meissenbach asked. However much they had briefly been thrown together by the death of Marlene Gehrig, he had, like most Germans, an instinctive dislike and distrust of the Gestapo.

Groener closed the office door, pulled a chair in front of the desk, and sat down. 'I would like an update on your current relationship with Anna Fehrbach.'

Meissenbach raised his eyebrows. 'We greet each other when we meet.'

'But she works for you. You must see her every day.'

'I see her as little as possible, Herr Groener. She no longer works for me. What she does with her days I do not know; I assume she is following some agenda dictated by the SD. What she does with her nights ...Well, I think we all know that.'

'And there is still nothing you can do about her.'

'You know that as well as I. If you have a solution, tell me of it.'

'I think she is a menace. I think we need to do something about her before she gets us – gets the Reich – into serious trouble. If she has not already done so.'

'And I have just reminded you that there is

nothing we can do. Or have you found some proof to link her to the death of the girl Gehrig?'

'I do not suppose we shall ever know the truth of that. Unless...' He gave a sigh of hopeless anticipation. 'Unless I were to be given the right to interrogate her. However, as I have told you, I am always prepared to watch, and wait, and listen, and gather straws...'

'I am a busy man, Herr Groener.'

'I have a contact in the Kremlin.'

Meissenbach frowned.

'He is a menial, of no importance whatsoever. But he is there. And yesterday he reported that Herr Chalyapov, who has not been seen for a month, has just returned from hospital. Where, Herr Meissenbach, he was being treated for a badly dislocated shoulder. There is a rumour that he suffered this injury in the course of one of his amours.'

'He probably deserved it. I never did like that fellow.'

Groener gave another sigh, this time of impatience. 'The point I am making, Herr Meissenbach, is that we know that Chalyapov, if certainly a womaniser, only ever has one mistress at a time, and for the past six months that woman has been Anna Fehrbach. We also know that Chalyapov is very high in the Soviet Government, and a protégé of Marshal Stalin himself. And thirdly, I also know, because Marlene Gehrig told me, that Anna Fehrbach is as deadly with her bare hands as with a gun. Lastly, we know that she is Heydrich's creature, who carries out his orders without question or hesitation.'

Meissenbach scratched his head. 'What are you trying to say? That Fehrbach was sent to Moscow to assassinate Chalyapov? She has taken a very long time about it. And he isn't dead. I can tell you that when Fehrbach decides someone should be dead, he or she dies, not left merely with a broken arm.' He flushed. 'I did actually know something of her background before we came to Moscow.'

'What? It is essential that I know everything about her.'

Meissenbach sighed. 'Did you hear about that incident in Prague, last year, when an attempt was made on my life?'

'Indeed. You were saved by the prompt action of your bodyguards. I congratulate you, and them.'

'My guards had nothing to do with it. I was saved by Anna Fehrbach, who shot and killed two of my assassins, after disabling their leader with a single blow, all in a matter of ten seconds.'

'You mean Gehrig was right? She is that good?'

'Why do you suppose she is so highly valued by the SD – by Heydrich himself?'

'I see. And you did not think it worth your while to tell me this before?'

'Well ... I was told the whole thing was top secret.'

'And of course you owe her your life. But

now you have turned against her. Why?'

'It would be more correct to say that she has turned against me, cast me aside like a worn-out glove.'

Groener stared at him. 'Hell hath no fury, eh? I always thought that applied only to women. However, perhaps you will now agree that we simply have to do something about the fair Fraulein.'

The man was starting to sound like a cracked record. 'I would entirely agree with you, Herr Groener, but for the simple fact that she is protected by General Heydrich.'

'I think it is worth the risk. I am saying this to you because I believe you are a man to be trusted, a man who has the good of the Reich at heart. Are you such a man?'

'Well … what exactly are you getting at?'

'I believe that General Heydrich may be following an agenda of his own, one which is not necessarily in the best interests of the Reich, and that he is employing his creature, Fraulein Fehrbach, to carry out that agenda. I believe that it is our bounden duty to the Fuehrer to find out just what that agenda is.'

'And how do you propose to do that?'

'Fehrbach uses the Diplomatic Pouch to communicate with her employer. Her letters are always carefully sealed, but I assume they contain whatever information she has obtained at the time. And he of course replies, his letters also being sealed. Now, it so happens that the last time she gave me a letter for inclusion in the pouch was a month ago, May sixteenth. That is the day after Chalyapov was taken to hospital. If we accept my hypothesis, that Fehrbach was responsible for his misfortune, then it is reasonable to assume that the letter she rushed off to Berlin the next day was to inform Heydrich of what had happened. Do you agree?'

'It would seem likely.'

'He did not reply immediately. But then, he never does. His reply arrived this morning.'

'Ah! Did Fehrbach seem concerned by its contents?'

Groener took the envelope from an inside pocket. 'She has not yet received it.'

Meissenbach gazed at him. 'You would be taking an enormous risk. Once that seal is broken...'

'I have been practicing for some time, and I believe I can reproduce this seal, at least sufficiently to stand up to a cursory inspection. I have never dared take the risk of doing this before. But I have observed that Fehrbach never does more than turn the envelope over to check the seal has not been broken, before herself breaking it. On this occasion, after a four-week wait and on a matter she will have to be apprehensive about, I believe she will be in such a hurry to see what her master has to say that she will hardly even check the seal.'

'If you are wrong, it will mean a concentration camp. At the very least.'

'And if I am right, and the letter proves that Heydrich is carrying on some clandestine negotiation with the Soviet Government...'

'Why have you told me all this?'

'Because, as I have said, I believe that you are a patriot, who wishes to protect the Reich, and the Fuehrer, from traitors.'

'You mean, because you are afraid to act on your own.'

'Because I wish you, the most senior member of the Embassy staff after the Ambassador, to know what I am doing, and why. And because I know that your feelings about Fehrbach are the same as mine.'

Meissenbach decided not to comment on the ambiguity of that statement. He knew that Groener dreamed of nothing more pleasurable in life than to have Anna strapped naked to a table in front of him, with the right to torment her as much as he chose.

Groener was studying him. He knew he had his man. 'It must be done very carefully,' he said. 'The seal must have only one break. Give me that paper knife.'

A last hesitation, then Meissenbach slid the knife across the table. Groener inserted the narrow blade beneath the seal, and exerted just enough pressure to break it. Then with equal care he slowly prized open the flap and took out the sheet of paper within. Meissenbach found he was holding his breath as he watched Groener's expression. 'Jesus,' the policeman muttered.

'What is it?'

Groener handed him the paper, and Meissenbach scanned the words. 'My God! This must go to the Ambassador immediately.'

'That would be suicide.'

'But...'

'To show the Ambassador would be to reveal that we had opened General Heydrich's secret correspondence. Anyway, would you not suppose that he already knows?'

'Count von Schulenberg? He would never be a party to something like this.'

'That is as may be. But to show him this letter would be to sign our own death warrants.'

'We have to do something.'

'I will tell you what we are going to do, Heinz. We are going to reseal this letter, and then we are going to deliver it to the young lady ... And then we will take certain steps.'

Nine

The Lubianka

'Good morning, Fraulein,' Groener said jovially, closing the office door behind himself before advancing to Anna's desk.

Anna raised her eyebrows; Groener looking pleased was neither a usual nor a pretty sight. 'Good morning, Herr Groener. May I help you?'

'No, no. It is I who am going to help you. I have a letter for you. From Berlin.'

'Ah!' Anna could not prevent her relief from showing, although the relief was also tinged with apprehension.

'Came in today.' Groener placed the envelope on the desk in front of her.

'Thank you.' She resisted the temptation immediately to pick it up.

'I think you have been waiting for this message, Fraulein.'

'I am always waiting for orders from Berlin, Herr Groener.'

She gazed at him, and he realized that she was not going to open the envelope in his presence. 'Well, then, I will leave you to it.'

He left the room, and Anna remained

278

gazing at the closed door for some seconds. Something was up. But whatever it was, it could not be half as important as discovering what Heydrich had to say.

She broke the seal, opened the envelope, took out the single sheet of paper and unfolded it, heart pounding.

My Dear Anna. Anna frowned. Heydrich had never begun a letter so affectionately in the past.

I most heartily congratulate you on what you have achieved, and I entirely agree that Chalyapov has become redundant in view of your progress. It now but remains for you to render the Reich the ultimate service. I wish to make it perfectly clear that while I most fervently hope to see you back in Berlin in the near future, should you find yourself unable to return, then once your mission is completed you will occupy an honoured, immortal place in Germany history, so long as there is a Germany.

Anna was suddenly aware of feeling cold.

I also wish you to know that once the news of the successful completion of the mission is received in Berlin, your parents, and your sister, will be immediately set free, to pursue their lives as and where they choose.

Now, your Friday meetings with

Premier Stalin are the key, together of course with the free access to his presence, plus the fact that you say you are alone during these meetings. Friday 20 June is the decisive day. On that afternoon it is necessary for Stalin to die. I do not anticipate that someone with your skills will find any difficulty in this. It should also be possible for you to complete the task and leave the Kremlin well before his body is found. You will proceed immediately to the address on the separate piece of paper that accompanies this letter. It is situated in the Kotay Gorod, which as you know is the busiest and most crowded part of Moscow. Memorize the address and then burn it together with this letter. You will be concealed there until it is possible to smuggle you out of the country. This has been arranged but may take a day or two to implement. It only remains for me, on behalf of General Himmler, and indeed the Fuehrer himself, to wish you Godspeed and every success. Heil Hitler. Your always admiring, Reinhard.

Anna remained gazing at the letter for some time. Just like that, she thought. Just like that. Next Friday, you will die. Just like that. So much for her dreams of escaping.

The problem with people like Heydrich was that they could never believe there were other people in the world with an intelligence equal to or greater than their own. The plan outlined was perfectly plausible. She did not doubt that she could kill Stalin and escape from the Kremlin before any alarm was raised; the Premier had made it very clear to his staff that he did not wish his sessions with the glamorous Countess von Widerstand to be interrupted. She knew she would even be able to gain the security of this apparent bookshop in the market centre. But that would be as far as she could go. It had apparently not occurred to Heydrich that she would realize there could be only one possible reason for wishing Stalin dead: as Clive had recognized so long ago, Hitler meant to go to war with Soviet Russia. There could be no doubt that Stalin's sudden death would throw the Soviet government into disorder for some time, if only because, due to his paranoia, there was no truly designated successor, and a power struggle would inevitably ensue, during which the Soviet military would also be paralysed.

And as the dictator's death had been fixed for a particular day, any German invasion, to gain most advantage from the ensuing chaos, would have to take place within at most forty-eight hours. Which would make it impossible for anyone to be smuggled out of the country. Or would it? It might just make it simpler.

She had to believe that. Because, as always, she had no choice but to carry out her orders, even if she was now realizing that this had to have been the true point of her mission from the beginning, from last June when she had first been appointed as Meissenbach's assistant. Stalin had always been her goal, and she had been planted, with infinite care and patience, to work towards that goal. And now she was there.

She felt cold and hot at the same time, while a million thoughts raced through her mind. She had known this moment had to arrive sometime, but the realization that it *had* arrived was still a shock to the system. She knew she had no right to indulge in any recriminations, even to herself. She had been taught to kill, and she had preserved herself by doing so, on too many occasions. To be called upon to die herself was perfectly fair. But there suddenly seemed so much to be done, and so little time in which to do it. But some things were more important than others.

Today was Tuesday. It was therefore her only chance to contact MI6. She did not wish to disappear entirely anonymously. She pulled her block of private notepaper towards her and wrote, quickly and concisely. The note she placed in a thick manila envelope, and then added to it her gold earrings, her crucifix, her ruby ring, and her watch; these were all of her that would remain, all that he would have to remember her by in the days to come.

She sealed the envelope, took it up to her apartment. She lunched with Birgit. They spoke little, but then they seldom spoke much nowadays; she did not imagine that

Birgit noticed anything different in her demeanour.

After lunch she went to bed for several hours; she did not feel like taking the risk of encountering anyone she might have to engage in conversation. Then she had a hot bath, dressed, and ate a light supper. Again, Birgit showed no great interest in this rather unusual behaviour. The meal over, she waited until nine thirty, then she placed the manila envelope in her handbag and left the Embassy, the guards as always carefully showing no concern at her movements.

She walked to the Berlin Hotel, enjoying the brilliant June evening, and arrived at ten. It was the first time she had entered the hotel since Clive had left. She could not resist the temptation to glance at the reception desk, but the man who was now standing there was unknown to her, and he did not seem the least interested in her; the foyer was as always crowded.

She took the lift to the fifth floor, and walked along the hall, so many memories crowding upon her. What a happy miracle it would be if Clive were to open the door.

She reached 507 and knocked. It was some seconds before the door opened, and she stared at the man in his shirt sleeves who stood there. He stared back, clearly as astonished as she was. 'Señorita?' he asked.

Anna recovered. 'I am sorry. I have the wrong room. Please excuse me.'

She turned, and he stepped into the hall.

'There is no need to be sorry, señorita. It is my pleasure to be disturbed by a beautiful woman. Will you not come in? I can offer you some wine.'

'Thank you, but no. I am looking for someone, and sadly you are not he. Good night, señor.'

She walked back to the lift, leaving the Spaniard staring after her in disappointment. She felt like screaming. But again, the fault was entirely hers. It was nearly three months since she had kept the rendezvous; she certainly could not blame Sprague for having given up waiting for her. But it seemed as if all the accumulated disasters and errors of her life were coming together in one climactic catastrophe. Now she would indeed disappear without trace, only the slightest twitch across the face of history.

She realized she was crying, and hastily patted her cheeks with a tissue from her bag. Her fingers brushed the envelope. Her last will and testament. It would now have to be thrown into the river.

'Countess! What a pleasure!'

Anna all but fainted as she turned. He wore black tie and had clearly been dining. 'Oh,' she said. 'Hello.'

'I have to be the luckiest man alive,' Andrews declared. 'I have just endured one of the most boring dinner parties of my life, and suddenly – *voilà*! The night has come alive.' Then he frowned. 'You're not with someone?'

'No. I was supposed to meet someone, but

he didn't turn up.'

'In that case he's a bounder, but am I glad he didn't show.' His forehead had cleared, but now the frown returned as he peered at her. 'This guy was important, huh?'

'Why, no. Not really.'

'Then why have you been crying?'

'Well, I ... should you ask a question like that?'

'I guess not. That was damned inquisitive of me. Would you let me make it up to you? A drink in the bar?'

Anna hesitated only a moment. This man's company was incredibly soothing. Presumably it came from being an American. 'A drink would be very acceptable.'

Andrews escorted her into the bar, which was uncrowded. 'The counter or a table?'

'I'd prefer a table.'

He seated her in a corner of the room. 'What do you drink after dinner? You have had dinner?'

'Yes. I think I'd like a glass of champagne.'

'Brilliant. Bring a bottle,' he told the waiter. 'And I want the real stuff. What do you have?'

'There is Taittinger, sir. But it is very expensive.'

'You worry about the liquor, and I'll worry about the cost.' He sat beside Anna. 'I have a strong suspicion that you have had some bad news.' He raised a finger. 'Don't remind me; I'm being darned inquisitive again. But you know what they say: a trouble shared is a trouble cured.'

'And you once said that if I was ever in trouble you would help me, no matter what,' Anna remembered, more thoughtfully than she had intended. Did she dare trust this man? Of course she could not, in real terms. But if he was prepared to do her a favour...

'And I meant it.' The ice bucket arrived and he inspected the label before pouring. 'Let's hope this isn't a fake.' He brushed his glass against hers. 'Here's to us. I have a positive notion that one of these days you and I may be able to get together. Don't take offence. If a guy doesn't dream from time to time he becomes a bore.'

'I don't think you could ever be a bore, Mr Andrews.'

'Don't press your luck. And how about calling me Joseph, if we're to share a secret? Although,' he went on, 'I prefer Joe.'

'Are we going to share a secret?'

'I sure hope so.'

'It would have to *be* a secret. My life could be involved.' There was a sick joke.

He gazed at her for several seconds. Then he said, now serious, 'That bad?'

'I want you to do something for me. But before I tell you what it is, I want you to promise that you will ask no questions, just tell me whether you'll do it or not. And that if you can't do it, you'll forget this conversation ever took place.'

'I promise.'

'How well do you know Clive Bartley?'

286

Now she had really surprised him. 'I don't really know him at all. No, that's not true. We worked together, once. We were both after the same thing, and as we were outnumbered by the bad guys, it seemed sensible to pool our resources.'

'And?'

Andrews drank some champagne. 'Hell, Anna, I thought he was one hell of a guy. You could say that without him I wouldn't be here now. On the other hand, I guess without me he wouldn't be here either. Don't tell me he's getting too close?'

Anna took the envelope from her bag. 'Can you have this sent to England in your Diplomatic Pouch, and delivered to Clive at MI6?'

Andrews did not move for several seconds. Then he said, 'You'll have to forgive me while I try to get my brain in gear. You want me to send this envelope to Clive Bartley? You?'

'You promised to ask no questions. Just tell me you can do it. Or not.'

'Of course I can do it. But Anna...'

'You promised.'

'So I did. I have got to be a nerd. But I'll keep my promise. I'd just like to get my facts straight. The British suspect that you are a German spy. In fact they have gone so far as to describe you as a reincarnation of Mata Hari. Right?'

'They flatter me.'

'I would dispute that. However, Clive Bartley is the MI6 officer who just failed to get

287

you before you left England. Right?'

'So I believe.'

'And you are sending him something, but you cannot do it through the British Embassy.'

'Of course I cannot. As you say, I am a German, and the British think I am a spy.'

'But you brought this envelope here tonight, to give to someone, who didn't show.'

'You're very close to breaking your promise, Joe.'

'Yeah. I'm sorry. I just need to be sure of one thing.' He fingered the envelope, could feel the solid objects inside. 'You wouldn't be sending him a bomb, would you?'

'There is nothing lethal in that envelope. I give you my word.' Except for the damage it just might do to his heart, she reflected.

'Okay. I'll believe you. This will go off tomorrow morning, and be in London tomorrow night. I'll have to write a covering note for our security people there, but I have a fair amount of clout. Clive should get it some time on Friday.'

And London is several hours behind Moscow, she thought. Whatever his reaction, it could not possibly take effect in time to alter the course of history. 'That would be very satisfactory. I can only say thank you.' She finished her drink. 'Now I should be getting back.'

He rested his hand on top of hers. 'Anna, I'm not looking for any reward, I promise. But would it be possible for us to have dinner together again, say next week?'

'Next week,' Anna said thoughtfully, and chose her words with care. 'I would like to think that could be possible.'

'Shall we say, right here, at seven on Monday?'

'I would like that very much,' Anna said, again telling the absolute truth.

Andrews placed the envelope on his dressing table, where he would see it first thing in the morning; the plane carrying the Diplomatic Pouch left at eleven.

He got into bed and switched off the light. But he knew he wasn't going to sleep; the envelope might as well have been giving off a brilliant white light. In view of the fact that it obviously contained some solid objects, he would have to enclose it in a larger envelope, marked Private, Confidential and Top Secret, and hope that he carried as much clout as he supposed.

So what exactly was he doing? Getting involved with a very beautiful spy was one thing. Getting mixed up in some clandestine exchange between said spy, working for Germany, and a senior member of the British Secret Service, was another. Which one was the traitor? And having been brought into the picture, as it were, could he now just close his eyes and pretend it wasn't really happening?

That was just not possible with a girl like Anna. Oh, Anna! To get together with Anna would be a dream come true. But could he ever truly get together with her unless he knew exactly what she was? It would mean betraying his promise to her. But he was a secret service operative. He lived in a world of secrets and betrayals, which could be matters of life and death, and for one's country as much as any individual. He had never allowed personal feelings to interfere with his duty.

He switched on the light, got out of bed, and took the envelope to his desk. It was sealed, but with ordinary wax; he could not make out any design, and he had sufficient wax to replace it. He broke the seal, unstuck the flap, and emptied the contents.

Her jewellery! He had known something was off about her tonight, but had been so fascinated by her very presence that it had not immediately registered: her ears, her neck, her hands and arms had been bare. And now she was sending these very expensive personal items to the man who was supposed to be her arch enemy?

He was suddenly reluctant to open the letter; he had the strangest feeling that he was about to look into Anna's soul. He drew a deep breath and unfolded the sheet of paper.

My dearest Clive,

I have received my final orders, and they are as you thought they might be, last January. And as I have not succeeded in extricating myself you know that I must carry them out. So much for hope. It is to happen when I take tea with you-know-who on Friday afternoon. H has of course devised a plan for my safe return to Germany, but I do not think even he believes that it will work. However, should it, I will be in touch as soon as possible. If it does not work ... I enclose these items which are very dear to me for you to remember me by. Do not weep for me, Clive. Does the Bible not say 'those that live by the sword shall die by the sword'? But I do wish you to know that throughout the horrendous events of the last three years of my life, the fact that you have been there to support me and encourage me and even, I hope, to love me, has alone kept me going. Give Billy and Belinda kisses for me, and ... see you in the hereafter. All my love, Anna.

Andrews remained staring at the sheet of paper for several minutes. He had uncovered one of the great secrets of modern espionage. And, even more important from a personal point of view, a woman who in addition to an almost unearthly beauty also possessed a quite unearthly courage and determination.

This was, to all intents and purposes, a suicide note. Only she did not intend to kill herself; she intended to die, because she knew she must, in carrying out some special duty.

Think, God damn you, he told himself. There could no longer be any doubt that she was a double agent, with the Brits. But if the Brits had given her a suicide mission, she would hardly be writing to Clive in these terms. Therefore it had to be her German masters. Thus the H she referred to would probably be Himmler, or more likely his demonic assistant, Heydrich. But what was the mission? Someone with whom she was going to have tea on Friday afternoon. Nothing could be more innocent than that. How could it turn into an event that might involve her life?

He pulled on his dressing gown and went downstairs to the Communications Room. The rather sleepy young woman on duty was painting her fingernails, and looked up in alarm as he entered. 'Mr Andrews?!'

'Hello, Carol. I need to send a telegram.'

'Yes sir. I'll get out the book.'

'No. I'll send it in clear.'

'Yes sir,' she agreed doubtfully.

Andrews sat at the table, regarded the form for a moment, then wrote rapidly.

mutual friend in deep trouble stop possibly terminal stop you know I don't stop Friday deadline stop letter in mail but do something now stop Joe

Carol regarded it. 'In clear,' she repeated. 'We don't have a wire address for anyone named Bartley.'

'We have one for MI6 in London, don't we?'

'Yes, we do. But ... well...' She peered at the form.

292

'Okay, Carol. Send that, and I'll square it with the ambassador in the morning. Okay?'

'Good morning, Mr Bartley.' Amy Barstow always greeted her boss brightly, even if he did not always respond.

'Morning, Amy. Anything from Moscow?'

He had asked this question, increasingly morosely, every morning since his return three months before, and she had been finding it rather tiresome. But today she was able to wave a sheet of paper at him. 'Came in overnight. In clear, believe it or not. Unless it's some code I don't recognise. It's certainly gobbledygook.'

Clive snatched the telegram, scanned it, and frowned. 'Oh, my God! Billy in?'

'Half an hour ago. Shall I call...?'

But Clive was already running up the stairs. Baxter was drinking coffee and reading the *Times*. 'What the hell...?'

Clive thrust the telegram at him. 'I have to get to Moscow. Today.'

'Just simmer down.' Baxter studied the form. 'Who the hell is Joe?'

'Joe Andrews. You remember him, Billy. His lot cooperated with us on that African business about five years ago. He's now running security at the American Embassy in Moscow.'

'And this is his idea of security, is it? I assume your "mutual friend" is Anna?'

'Yes. And...'

'Just tell me how he knows she is your

293

friend? And why she should be his?'

'Well … I know he met her at a reception at the German Embassy, and I could see he took a shine to her. Well, I mean, who wouldn't?'

'I can think of one at least. So are you telling me that she is now working for the Yanks, as well as the Germans, as well as us? As I have said before, this woman is a walking cataclysm waiting to happen.'

'Of course she's not working for the Americans, Billy. But somehow Joe has become involved. He'll explain it in the letter he says is on its way.'

'I hope he can. I would like to see it the moment it arrives.'

'Okay. You open it when it comes in. But I can't wait. *She* can't wait.'

'Can't wait to do what? Look, go and take a sedative and calm down, and bring me that letter when you get it. And hope that it does explain what's happening.'

Clive placed his hands on the desk and leaned forward. 'Billy, don't you remember my theory on why Heydrich should send Anna of all people to Russia just to find out what they're thinking? His most highly trained and successful assassin, just to hold a watching brief? Don't you remember my report back in January? For Christ's sake, you showed it to the PM, didn't you?'

'I did. And he was unwise enough to act on it. And got roundly snubbed by Stalin. And now we are well into the summer and there has still been no German invasion. I can tell you that the boss is not happy, because Winston is not happy.'

'I'm more interested in Stalin's reaction to the conclusion I drew from Anna's presence in Russia.'

'As to that, I have no idea. We decided not to use it.'

'For God's sake!'

'No, no, Clive. It is I who should be saying for God's sake. Did you seriously expect us to ask the PM to inform the head of another country – a country that has rejected any idea of an alliance with us, and with which, in fact, we have come close to being at war more than once in the past year – that we feel there is a chance he may be in line for assassination?'

'*May* be in line?'

'Well, I suppose someone like Stalin is in line for assassination every time he leaves the Kremlin, and is protected accordingly. But that is his business, not ours. And in any event, to attempt to explain that one of our people could be involved would be to open the biggest can of worms in history, certainly in view of Russia's paranoiac distrust of us and everything we do or say.'

'Billy, I am not talking about what may happen outside the Kremlin. Anna has gained virtually free access to Stalin.'

'And you seriously think she has been commanded to murder him? In her capacity as a Nazi agent? My dear fellow, that is madness. It would mean war between Russia and

Germany.'

'That is what I have been trying to convince you is going to happen for the past six months.'

Baxter picked up his pipe and his tobacco pouch. 'And you seriously think she would carry out such a command?'

'She would have no choice. You know that. There are lives she values more than her own: those of her family.'

'But it just isn't practical. She'd never be allowed to take a gun, or a knife, into the Kremlin.'

'Billy, you know as well as I that Anna does not need a gun or a knife. Think of Hannah Gehrig, or Elsa Mayers. Or the night porter at the Hotel Berlin.'

'And you think that this assassination attempt is fairly imminent.'

'According to Andrews, it is going to happen on Friday.'

'You said that Andrews doesn't know anything about Anna.'

'He doesn't, to my knowledge. But he has discovered that something involving Anna is going to happen on Friday. Something terminal, he says. That can only be the assassination. Billy, I have got to get to Moscow before then.'

Baxter struck a match, and puffed with great satisfaction. 'War,' he said, half to himself. 'Between Russia and Germany. Do you realize, Clive, what a help that could be to us? I mean, even if Germany wins, which I

296

suppose will be the most likely outcome, it'll still occupy her for a year or so. Maybe longer: Russia is a big country.'

'Billy, I hope, for the sake of our friendship, that you are not suggesting what I think you are suggesting.'

'Even if I let you go to Moscow, Clive, just what are you proposing to do? What *can* you do?'

'Just get me there, Billy. I'll think of something.' With Joe Andrews, he thought. Having been in a couple of tight spots with Joe in the past, he had the highest regard for the American's guts and determination, and more important than either, his ingenuity. But he decided against mentioning this to Baxter.

'Whatever you think of, the Embassy cannot be involved.'

'I have no intention of involving the Embassy.'

Baxter thought for a few minutes. 'You understand that the only way you can get to Moscow in a hurry is by the Med? Which is a hell of a lot hotter now than it was last year.'

'Lightning never strikes twice in the same place.'

'It's a philosophy,' Baxter conceded.

'But I do need the best you can get. Fast planes and no delays. This has to be top priority all the way.'

'Hmm. And Belinda?'

'You handle this right, Billy, and I'll be there and back before she knows I've gone.'

Baxter did indeed pull out all the stops. Clive just had the time to wire Joe the words *Expect me* and then he was at Hatfield where he was met by an anxious looking Flying-Officer.

'Glad to have you aboard, sir,' he said. 'Name's Revill.'

'Bartley.'

'Yes sir. Flown before?'

'As a matter of fact, yes.'

'Of course you have, sir. I meant have you flown a Mosquito before.'

'A what?'

Revill gave him an old-fashioned glance. 'This, sir. The machine you are here to try out. The de Havilland Mosquito.' His tone was reverent.

'Ah, yes. Of course.' A few pennies were starting to drop, although not all were landing right side up. 'Nifty little thing.' He had to hope it was, because its twin engines did not suggest a great deal of speed. 'The guns are concealed, are they?'

'There are no guns, sir.'

'Say again?'

'This is a PR machine, sir.'

'Ah, yes. I get it. Public Relations, eh? But I'm trying to get to Gibraltar ASAP. Will it do it?'

'PR means Photo Reconnaissance, sir,' Revill explained with great patience. 'Not a fighter. It is also a prototype; there are only a couple in existence. I believe there are plans to build a fighter version, and a bomber, if

298

these prove as successful as anticipated.'

'A prototype,' Clive said thoughtfully, wondering if Baxter was taking the easy route to get rid of him. 'And it'll take me to Gib? Without guns? What happens if we're attacked over the Bay?'

'We cannot be attacked, sir.'

'That is very solid reasoning, Mr Revill, but is it based on anything more solid than hope?'

'Speed, sir. Speed. The fastest Messerschmitt in the best possible condition cannot fly at much over three hundred and sixty miles an hour. This little gem will do four hundred and twenty. So if we are attacked, we simply fly away. When they get around to arming the new models, it will be the most formidable fighting aircraft in the world.'

Clive had to be impressed, but when he climbed into the cockpit – the two seats were placed side by side – he had a strange feeling. 'This is very odd material,' he remarked. 'I'll swear it's not steel. Or aluminium.'

'Well, no, sir. It's wood.'

'Hold on just one moment. You are proposing to fly a wooden machine at more than four hundred miles an hour? Won't it fall apart?'

'Good heavens no, sir. The wood is laminated and glued together under extreme pressure. There are one or two steel struts, of course. But it really is as safe as a house. And it has a range of fifteen hundred miles.'

Revill was proved right, and it was the most

exhilarating flight Clive had ever made, even if his heart was in his mouth most of the way. They flew so fast he wasn't sure whether or not they saw any other aircraft; certainly nothing got close enough to be a nuisance.

And there was Section Officer Parkyn waiting to greet him, as always as bright as a button. 'Well, hello,' she remarked. 'Am I glad to see you! There was a rumour that you had bought it, last year.'

'Nearly, but not quite.'

'And now you're using one of these new secret machines. You really must have clout. May I offer you a bed for the night?'

'I'd love to, Alice. But I'm off again in an hour. As soon as we're re-fuelled.'

'Ships that pass in the night,' she said sadly. 'But please don't get shot down again: the Ministry would never forgive you if you managed to lose a Mosquito.'

They were in Cairo by dusk having seen a number aircraft, both Italian and German, none of which could get near them.

'They'll all be scratching their heads,' Revill said as they walked across the burning tarmac. 'Well, Mr Bartley, it's been fun. I hope you enjoyed your flight, and I hope you'll give the machine a good report to your firm. Maybe I'll see you again some time.'

'Wait a moment. Aren't you taking me to Moscow?'

'Good lord, no. You don't think the bosses would let me fly a Mosquito over Russian air space? As for landing there ... we'd never get off again. No, it's back to Hatfield for me, tomorrow. Don't worry. They'll get you to Moscow in a couple of days.'

'A couple of days? I have to be there on Friday morning.'

'Well, in that case...' Revill pulled his nose. 'I reckon I should wish you luck.'

'Don't panic, Mr Bartley,' said the Wing-Commander. 'It's all arranged. You take off tomorrow morning, and fly to Teheran.'

'Why on earth am I going to Teheran?'

'Well, we can't over-fly Greece as it's in German hands. And the Turks won't allow us to use their air space. With a German army perched on the Aegean they are keeping to strict neutrality. Anyway, as I was saying, you'll leave Teheran on Friday morning, and should make Stalingrad that evening, with Moscow the next day. How about that?'

'Wing-Commander,' Clive said earnestly, 'I have got to be in Moscow on Friday morning.'

'I'm afraid that is simply not possible, Mr Bartley. Look, I've booked you into Shepheard's. Go and have a good meal and a good night's sleep. You'll feel better in the morning. After all, is twenty-four hours really going to make that much difference?'

'It's a gorgeous day,' Birgit commented as she served breakfast. 'It's hard to believe that only a couple of months ago it was freezing.'

301

'Um,' Anna commented. As it was only eight o'clock, presumably it was just dawn in London. Clive would not receive her letter for another few hours.

Did it matter? There was of course a tiny voice whispering away at the back of her brain, *maybe something will happen to save me*. But that thought had to be dismissed. Even if Clive tried to get to her immediately after reading the letter, he could not possibly reach Moscow before Tuesday, at the earliest. That was supposing there was anything he *could* do, or anything he wanted to do.

It was time to put all thoughts of Clive – of survival – from her mind. Simply go out in a blaze of glory.

'I feel lazy today, Birgit,' she said. 'I think I will stay in bed.'

'But are you not taking tea with Marshal Stalin, Countess?'

'Good heavens! I had forgotten. Yes, of course. But that is not until this afternoon. I shall have my bath after lunch.'

Lying there allowed her to relax. She could not stop herself thinking, of course. She could go through the program as outlined by Heydrich, envisage herself delivering the blows that would destroy the Soviet dictator – who had always been so nice to her – and then leaving his office, telling his staff that he did not wish to be disturbed for the next hour – would they suppose that he had had sex with her? – walking along those interminable corridors and out of the great doors, resisting

302

the temptation to break into a run, leaving the fortress and plunging into the crowded streets of the Kotoy Gorod, only a short distance away, reaching the bookshop, perhaps just as the alarm went in the Kremlin, being welcomed and concealed while all Moscow seethed about her, and then escaping ... It *could* happen.

She heard a familiar voice and sat up. 'No, no, Herr Meissenbach. The Countess is in bed.'

Meissenbach clearly ignored her, and a moment later the bedroom door opened. 'You *are* in bed.'

Anna held the sheet to her throat with unusual modesty. 'What do you want?'

'I went to your office, and you weren't there. It is ten o'clock!'

'I do not feel very well.'

'Oh! But is today not Friday? Do you not take tea with Marshal Stalin?'

'Is that any concern of yours?'

He glared at her, unable to stop himself looking at the body thinly protected by the sheet. 'So you are not going?'

'Of course I am going. It is not until this afternoon. I shall be better then.'

He gave little sigh. 'I am glad. I do not like to think of you unwell, Anna. I will wish you good fortune.'

He left the room, and Anna stared at Birgit. 'I am sorry, Countess. He just pushed me aside.'

'Don't worry about it, Birgit.' But what a

303

strange thing to do, she thought, after having hardly spoken to her for two months. And suddenly to be concerned about her health? It was almost as strange as Groener's quite unusual good humour on Tuesday, when he had brought her Heydrich's letter. Her instincts told her that it was something that needed thinking about. But she was not in the mood to think about anything save what lay ahead. In any event, whatever the pair of them were about, it was no longer relevant. By this evening she would be out of their range, one way or the other.

She lunched, had a bath, and dressed for the afternoon. She wore a summer frock, in pale green with matching high heels. In her handbag she stowed a pair of flat-heeled pumps, as she suspected she would have to travel as fast and as sure-footedly as possible when she left the Kremlin. She left her hair loose, but wore a broad-brimmed summer hat. She felt naked without her watch and jewellery, but at least she knew they were in good hands.

'Will you be in for dinner, Countess?' Birgit asked.

'Aren't I always?' She had a sudden urge to hug the girl, but resisted it; she had never shown her any great affection in the past.

She went downstairs, smiled at the various people she passed, and walked out into the bright June sunlight. It was only a short walk to the Kremlin, and she was there in fifteen minutes. The guards on the outer gate all knew her by sight, and saluted her with smiles.

She passed them, crossed the inner courtyard. There were quite a few people about, but none of them paid her much attention; if she had been admitted past the outer gate her presence had to be legitimate. On the door of the inner palace the guard presented arms. She smiled at him in turn, and stepped into the hall, waiting for a moment to allow her eyes to become accustomed to the gloom, then went towards the staircase, but checked as a door on her right opened. She turned and gazed at Chalyapov.

Alarm bells jangled in her brain, but she smiled at him as well. 'Why, Ewfim, how good to see you, and looking so well.'

'So are you, Anna, even if in your case it will be a temporary condition. You are under arrest.'

Anna heard movement behind her. Other doors had opened, and when she turned her head she discovered six men, all looking extremely apprehensive, but all considerably larger than herself. She had once destroyed three Gestapo agents sent to arrest her. But they had been carrying guns, and they had made the mistake of coming too close. These men were unarmed, and they were waiting for her to move.

'It would be very unwise of you to attempt to resist,' Chalyapov said. 'We know all about you. About your skills. But I doubt even you could cope with my people. And I do know that my men would love to get their hands on your body.'

Anna's nostrils flared as she inhaled. But for the moment she was helpless. And one of her greatest assets was patience. 'Aren't they going to do that anyway?' she asked, her voice low and controlled.

'Not if you behave yourself. Give me your handbag and place your arms behind your back.'

Anna obeyed. 'May I ask why you are doing this? What am I being arrested for?'

'You will find out.'

Anna felt the touch of steel, and listened to the click of the handcuffs. She was helpless, and at the mercy of these men – of Chalyapov, whose arm she had once dislocated. She had to protest. 'I think you need to remember that I am a German citizen, and an employee of the German Embassy. I have diplomatic immunity.'

'I do not think your Embassy is any longer interested in you, Anna.'

She stared at him, and resisted the sudden panic that was threatening to cloud her judgement. 'I think Count von Schulenberg may disagree with you. I demand the right to telephone him.'

'You have no rights, comrade.' He came close to her. 'I think this is how I like you best, Anna. I have been informed that you are not carrying weapons on this assignment. But you never know.'

Once again bells jangled in Anna's brain, so violently that she hardly felt his hands sliding over her dress, squeezing her breasts, and then raising her skirt to look between her legs. If this was the worst that was going to happen to her she had nothing to worry about.

She was shrouded in stale cigarette breath, but he was stepping away. 'I am going to see a lot more of you in the near future, Anna,' he promised. 'And hear a lot more from you, as well.' He nodded at his men. 'Take her away. Remember your instructions.'

'Yes, Comrade Commissar,' one of them said. 'You will come with us, comrade.'

Anna looked at Chalyapov. 'I assume you will be informing Marshal Stalin that I will not be joining him for tea. And why.'

Chalyapov merely smiled. 'He already knows.'

Anna was marched into the yard where a car waited. The back door was opened and she was pushed into the interior, not violently, but without the use of her hands to steady herself she stumbled, landed on her knees, and would have fallen had her shoulders not been grasped.

'We do not wish to mark that so beautiful face, do we, comrade?'

Anna got her breathing under control as she was pulled up, turned round, and made to sit, her hands crushed against the back of the seat. She was moving into an unknown situation, but one which could carry a death sentence. But the risk of death was supposed to come *after* she had killed Stalin; up till that moment she had committed no crime. She knew, of course, that the Russians believed in pre-emptive action, that one merely had to be suspected of something to be arrested and put away. But there was nothing for her even to be suspected of. What she had been about to do was known only to herself and Heydrich. And presumably to Heydrich's superiors – certainly Himmler. There was no reason for any of them to betray her; it made no sense. Yet Chalyapov had seemed to know. As, apparently, did Stalin. Indeed, Chalyapov appeared to know a great deal about her secret background.

She had not been looking where they were going, but now they swung through a gateway set in the high wall of a fortress-like building, into a courtyard, to stop before an open door. Around her were more high walls, although these contained innumerable windows.

The car door was opened, and her arms were grasped to pull her out. She stumbled, and one shoe came off. One of the men picked it up, but left her to limp lopsidedly into the hall. There were several people waiting for her, men and women, but only one seemed to matter. This was a slender young woman, trim in a green uniform; with her short black hair and crisp features she would have been attractive but for the glacial coldness of her eyes and her expression. 'You have her file?'

she inquired.

The man carrying Anna's shoe was also carrying both her handbag and a briefcase. These he now offered. The woman's nose wrinkled, but she took all three items. 'Along there,' she said.

Anna debated kicking off the other shoe to restore a little dignity to her movements, but decided against it; she did not feel this was a woman to be antagonised while her arms were bound behind her back. She limped along the hall. 'To the left,' her captor instructed.

Anna turned down the indicated corridor, and came to a door. The woman reached past her, and opened it. 'Go in.'

Anna entered the room, and waited. Behind a desk sat another woman, who also wore a green uniform. But there any resemblance to the young woman ended. This woman was middle-aged, and extremely large. Her face was broad and chubby, and was remarkably good-humoured; at this moment it was wreathed in smiles. Anna felt a surge of relief.

'The Countess von Widerstand, Comrade Colonel,' the young woman said.

'Countess!' the colonel cried. 'This is such a pleasure. Do you know how long it has been since I entertained a countess? Twenty years! I was young then, oh, so young. But you ... you are as beautiful as they said. Welcome. Oh, welcome to Lubianka!'

Ten

Knights Without Armour

'But where are my manners?' the colonel said. 'Sit down, Your Excellency, sit down. Are those handcuffs really necessary, Olga?'

'I was told that you should read the file before making a judgement on that, comrade.'

'Hmm. We are surrounded by paranoia. But sit down anyway, Your Excellency.'

Anna sank on to the chair. Olga took up a position behind her.

'My name is Ludmilla,' the colonel said. 'And while you are here, I am your friend. Remember this.'

'I will,' Anna said.

Ludmilla smiled at her. 'But you must only speak when you are asked a question. It is a rule, you understand.'

'Yes, comrade. Oh!'

A sharp pain had entered her shoulder and raced down her arm. She twisted her head and gazed at Olga's cold face, and at the small, wand-like cattle prod she carried; she had not noticed it before.

'The rule,' Ludmilla reminded her. 'Now let

us see.' She opened the briefcase and took out a file, then spread this in front of her. 'Your name is Anna. What a pretty name. May I call you Anna?'

This was definitely a question. 'Yes, comrade.' Anna's voice was low; her arm and shoulder still ached.

'And you are twenty-one years old. Oh, to be twenty-one again.' She frowned. 'This says you are highly dangerous and are to be kept under the strictest confinement.' She raised her head. 'You are twenty-one years old and you are highly dangerous? How can that be?'

A question. 'I do not know, comrade. I do not know who compiled that file.'

'It says here that in Prague last year you shot two men dead and crippled another with a single blow, all in ten seconds.'

'My God!' Anna snapped, involuntarily, as the penny dropped. Only one person in Russia, other than herself, knew the truth of what had happened in Prague.

Even as she spoke, she tensed her muscles for the electric shock, but there was none: Ludmilla had raised a finger. 'Why did you exclaim like that? Because it is true?'

Anna bit her lip.

'Twenty-one years old,' Ludmilla mused. 'And now you have tried to assassinate our glorious leader.'

'There is no proof...' Again Anna bit her lip, but too late. 'Ooh!' Another streak of agony raced through her body.

'You understand,' Ludmilla said, ignoring

the interruption, 'that there will have to be a trial. It will be a public trial.'

Hopefully that was a question. 'Will I be allowed to defend myself?'

'Of course. It will all be done according to law. But before the trial you have to sign a confession. This must name the people who sent you here, and who have assisted you in this dreadful plan.'

'But if I make a confession, what is the point in having a trial?' Anna asked the question without thinking, and again braced herself for the coming shock, but Ludmilla had again signalled Olga to leave her alone for the time being.

'If you do *not* make a confession, how is the judge supposed to determine your guilt?' the colonel inquired. She might have been speaking to a small child. Had Anna's wrists not been secured she would have scratched her head. 'Of course, whether you make a confession of your own free will is entirely up to you, and will make no difference to the procedure we have to follow. You must be interrogated to ensure that you tell us the truth. You do understand this?'

I am in a madhouse, Anna thought, surrounded by lunatics. But she nodded. 'Yes, comrade.'

'I am so glad,' Ludmilla said. 'It makes life easier for everyone. Now do remember, Anna, that I wish to be your friend. Olga wishes to be your friend.'

Again Anna started to turn her head, and

again changed her mind.

'All we require is your cooperation. Now, returning to this matter of your being dangerous, it is not my business to question the judgements of my superiors. But it also says here that you have a very high IQ. You should therefore understand that both Olga and I are highly trained in unarmed combat. No doubt you are even more highly trained. But for you to attempt to beat us up and fight your way out of here would be *very* counter-productive. For two reasons. One is that if you look up at the top of that wall you will observe a little box. That is a camera that is filming your every moment in here. The moment you attempt to misbehave this room will become filled with men. They will not harm you seriously, because you have to be absolutely fit when you appear in court, but in addition to their combat skills they are also trained to hurt people severely, in places that will not show. I'm sure you would not wish that.'

Anna swallowed. 'No, comrade.'

'And the other reason, of course, is that if you attacked Olga and me, you would make us your enemies instead of your friends. And we so want to be your friends. Don't you want us to be your friends, Anna?'

'Yes, comrade.'

'That makes me so happy. Well, Olga, as the Countess understands the situation, I think you can take off the handcuffs.'

The key clicked, and the handcuffs were removed. Anna rubbed her hands together;

the returning circulation was painful.

'Now,' Ludmilla said. 'I would like you to take off your clothes.' Anna's head jerked, and Ludmilla smiled at her. 'I want to look at you. I do like looking at pretty things, and you are exceptional.'

Anna could not stop herself looking up at the cameras.

'Oh, they like looking at pretty things too,' Ludmilla agreed. 'Poor dears, they get such few pleasures.'

Anna sighed, stood up, and removed her dress, then hesitated.

'Oh, everything,' Ludmilla said.

She could have been Dr Cleiner's sister. Anna removed her cami-knickers and then her stockings; she had already kicked off her remaining shoe.

'Exquisite,' Ludmilla agreed. 'Now, I wish you to go to that table over there, get on to it, and lie down. On your back to begin with, with your legs pulled up. I am going to search you,' she explained, pulling on a pair of thin rubber gloves.

Oh, my God, Anna thought. Not even Cleiner had wanted to do *that*. 'What am I supposed to be concealing?'

'I very much doubt that you are concealing anything. But it is part of the procedure, you see. And I do so enjoy putting my fingers into pretty little girls. They squeal so. But you,' she added regretfully, 'are not going to squeal, are you?'

Anna looked up at the camera, which was

314

moving to follow her as she went to the table. 'No, comrade. I am not going to squeal.'

'There,' Ludmilla said, stripping off the gloves and throwing them into the waste basket. 'That wasn't too bad, was it?'

Anna had to concede that she was right, apart from the humiliation. 'No, comrade. May I get up?'

'Of course you must get up. We must move on.'

Anna had been lying on her stomach. Now she brought her legs together and rose to her knees. Olga, standing beside her, held her breasts as if she wanted to fluff them out; Anna stared at her and she stepped away. The wand hanging from her wrist swung to and fro as if anxious to be used again, but Ludmilla had apparently forbidden this for the time being.

'You will find,' Ludmilla said chattily, 'that the procedure we follow is not on the whole very painful, although it can be, if you prove unnecessarily recalcitrant. It is far better than in the old days.'

Anna swung her legs to the floor and stood up.

'In the old days,' Ludmilla continued, 'the way to make an inmate suffer without it showing in court – apart from beating, of course – was to stuff finely broken glass up his or her ass. This was usually very effective, of course. But it was extremely painful, so much so that in some cases the victim went out of his or her mind. This was counter-productive, as you are required to be lucid when you appear before the judges. And, naturally, it did permanent damage.'

Anna felt like lying down again. 'But this method is no longer used?' she suggested optimistically.

'No, no. We are far less primitive nowadays. Come along.'

She opened a door at the rear of the room, and stepped into a corridor. Anna glanced at Olga, received a quick nod, and followed. A short walk brought them to another door, which Ludmilla opened, to enter a large, square room, entirely devoid of furniture. There was, however, a coiled hose in one corner, beneath a tap protruding from the wall, and a wooden beam extending across the ceiling, from which was suspended a thick leather strap. And in another corner the ubiquitous camera hung from the ceiling, moving slowly to and fro while it focused on Anna. Beneath the camera, set in the wall, there was an electric control box, in which there were several buttons and levers.

'This is the bathroom,' Ludmilla explained. 'You will be spending a lot of time here. Olga.'

Olga pointed to where she wanted Anna to stand, which was exactly beneath the strap, from which she now saw there was suspended a steel hook. Anna assumed the required position, and Olga took the handcuffs from her belt, brought Anna's arms in front of her, and cuffed the wrists together. Then she raised the arms and fitted the links of the cuffs over the hook to hold them there, before going to the wall and pressing a button on the box. Instantly a motor hummed, and the strap receded into the ceiling, just far enough to raise Anna on to her tiptoes.

'There,' Ludmilla said. 'That is not too uncomfortable, is it?'

'No,' Anna muttered. It was actually by no means uncomfortable at the moment, although she knew it would become so if she was forced to endure it for any length of time. She was more concerned by the fact that she was now totally exposed to whatever these two harpies wished to inflict upon her.

She watched Olga cross the room, open a door, and step through. 'It gets very wet in here,' Ludmilla explained. She now picked up the hose by the nozzle. 'The water will be somewhat cold, although not as cold as if it were midwinter, eh? Ha ha.'

'Ha ha,' Anna agreed faintly.

The door opened again and Olga returned, now as naked as Anna herself. She stood against the far wall, next to the control box. 'Now,' Ludmilla said. She still held the nozzle of the hose, and this she directed at Anna. Olga pulled one of the levers halfway down, and the hose began to swell.

Anna took a deep breath, and was then enveloped in a stream of water, playing on her legs, splattering up over her stomach. As the water was in fact not very cold, it was by no means unpleasant. Slowly she allowed her breath out of her lungs.

'Full,' Ludmilla said.

Involuntarily Anna half turned her head, and was struck a tremendous blow between her shoulder blades. The force spun her round and she glimpsed Ludmilla fighting to keep hold of the nozzle. Then water was cascading over her face and hair, and as she was turned again it struck her between her breasts, driving the breath from her lungs. Before she could react the jet was on her face itself, slamming into her mouth and nose and eyes.

I am about to die, she thought. *I am being drowned while standing on my feet.* Then the pressure died, and she was left gasping and spitting; a good deal of the water had got down her throat and she still felt as if she were choking; it was several seconds before she could take even the shallowest of breaths.

She opened her eyes and gazed at Olga, who had come forward and now slapped her on the back, so that she gasped and choked again and vomited.

'That was such *fun*,' Ludmilla said. 'Wasn't that fun, Anna?'

Anna was still gasping too much to speak. In any event, all she wanted to do was curse at her.

'But we cannot just have fun,' Ludmilla said, without regret. 'The hose can be used for a more serious purpose. It can inflict exquisite pain. It can cause damage. It can even kill. We will show you.'

Anna opened her mouth to scream, and then changed her mind. She would not give them that much pleasure. Besides, perversely, she was curious. Olga had switched off the water before coming forward. Now she returned to the panel and lowered the lever again, but only a third of the way. Water flowed, but with none of the earlier power. Ludmilla played the flow over Anna's groin. 'That is very nice, eh? But you see, if I twist the nozzle, so...' She did so, and the jet narrowed. Ludmilla twisted some more, and it became as thin as a pencil, and then as a pencil lead. Now it was quite painful, feeling like a needle jab. 'Try to imagine,' Ludmilla suggested, 'what it would feel like if we were to give it full volume. Do you know, I have cut off a woman's nipple with this jet? And if I were to put it inside you ... an instant hysterectomy.'

Anna had got her breathing back under control, and kept her voice even. 'What happens if I write you out a full confession now, and do not attempt to defend myself?'

'Why, you will be convicted.'

'And sent to prison?'

'For planning to kill Marshal Stalin?' Ludmilla gave a shout of laughter, and even Olga smiled. 'Good heavens, no. You will be shot, Countess.'

'Tell me,' Clive said.

The two men sat at a corner table of a small

café just around the corner from the American Embassy. It was Saturday afternoon and he had only just reached Moscow. He had telephoned immediately on landing, before even calling at his own Embassy, where he would be staying.

Now Andrews poured them each a glass of vodka. 'I think you need to tell me.'

Clive drank. 'I need to know how you became involved. And how involved.'

Andrews considered briefly, then nodded. 'That's reasonable. I met her in the Berlin on Tuesday night, entirely by chance. She told me she was looking for someone. She didn't say who, but I have an idea it was your man Sprague, only he hadn't shown. But she had this large envelope with her, addressed to you, so I'm pretty sure that she wasn't there just for a drink. However, she accepted a drink from me. I could see she was upset about something, so I asked if I could help. She thought about it for a while, then asked if I could send the envelope in our Diplomatic Pouch, and see that it got to you.' He paused to sip his drink.

'And that's all? Doesn't tie in with your telegram, old man.'

Andrews put down his glass. 'I guess not. I'm afraid old habits die hard. I could tell she was on to something big, and frankly I was intrigued. She's a German spy, and you're a British spy-catcher, and here she is sending you a personal letter. So...' He flushed. 'I opened the envelope.'

'I see. And what was in it?'

'I guess some would call it a suicide note. Others might go for a love letter. Either way, it sure was a farewell, from her to you. She had even enclosed some very valuable pieces of jewellery. You didn't give them to her, by any chance?'

'That poor kid! No, I did not give her any jewellery. And on the strength of that letter you made certain deductions. One being that she is actually one of ours.'

'That seemed pretty obvious. I have to congratulate you on that. I wish she were one of *ours*, just for the chance to get close to her.' He sighed. 'I guess you've done that.'

Clive preferred not to answer. 'What about this Friday deadline. Yesterday.'

'The letter was very discreet as to events, but she did say that her orders had to be carried out on Friday. Would those have been your orders?'

'No. She gets her German orders direct from Heydrich.'

'And he had given her orders which could involve her death? Why didn't she just go to your Embassy and get out?'

'Because she can't do that.'

'Would you like to explain that?'

Clive told him the story of Anna's life.

'Holy shit! That poor kid.'

'So what has happened?'

'As far as I know, nothing. There's been no big noise about anything.'

'Nothing from the Kremlin?'

'No. Not that there ever is anything from the Kremlin,' Andrews pointed out. 'You know what the orders were?'

'I have a pretty good idea. She was ordered to enter the Kremlin and assassinate Stalin.'

Andrews stared at him for several seconds. 'If you are as fond of that girl as she seems to think you are, I think it is God damned bad taste to joke about it.'

'One doesn't joke about Anna. You aren't aware of it, but, again on orders from Heydrich, she has wormed her way into a position of being old Joe's favourite woman. They take tea together, in private, every Friday afternoon.'

'Holy shitting cows. And you reckon ... You mean you knew this was going to happen, and you just sat back and did nothing? You actually sacrificed the girl just to cause trouble between Germany and Russia?'

'If we had been prepared to do that, would I be here now? We knew this was on the cards, but didn't know how soon. We've been working on a plan to get her recalled to Germany, but it hasn't worked yet. Now it's too late.'

'Oh, come now. You have to be putting me on. You reckon Heydrich would employ a twenty-one-year-old girl to carry out a high-powered political assassination? And even if he was that crazy, how was it to be done? Not even Stalin's favourite woman gets to see him without being frisked by his bodyguards. So where is she supposed to conceal her tommy-gun, or grenade, or even a small pistol. It's just not practical.'

'Joseph.' Clive spoke earnestly. 'I know you think Anna is the sweetest chick currently walking the face of this earth. And she can be that. But she is also the most deadly woman walking the face of this earth. She was trained, programmed if you like, by the SD. With a gun, she could shoot your eye out at fifty yards. I have seen her at work. But she is even more deadly with her bare hands. I have seen her at work there too.'

Andrews produced a handkerchief and wiped his brow; he could have no doubt that Clive was speaking the truth. 'Her letter gave the impression that you and she were ... had been ... well...'

'Yes,' Clive said. 'We have been lovers, and I sincerely hope we will be lovers again.'

'You mean, knowing what you do about her, you can...?'

'You are starting to sound like my boss. Anna does everything supremely well.'

Andrews digested this while he finished his drink. 'So you reckon Stalin is dead.'

'We have to find that out. And what Anna's present status is. If she wasn't killed outright, she'll be under arrest somewhere. We have to get her out.'

'If she wasn't killed outright, after doing Stalin, she'll be in the Lubianka. Nobody gets out of the Lubianka except to go on trial and then be shot. And by the time that happens, he or she has generally been tortured into a mental state where they cannot tell white

323

from black, and will agree to whatever the prosecutor wants.'

There was a crack, and Clive's glass broke under the pressure of his fingers. But he spoke quietly. 'Then we'll just have to break the mould. I'm asking for your help, Joe.'

'For Anna,' Andrews said thoughtfully. 'Jesus!' He looked up. 'You shall have it, and I hope we both don't live to regret it. I have an acquaintance with Lavrenty Beria. You know him?'

'I know of him. Isn't he the boss of the NKVD?'

'That's right. He's as cold-blooded as they come, but he spends a lot of time brooding on the future, and his part in it. I'm talking about when old Joe dies, even of natural causes. That makes him amenable to suggestion. In any event, he'll know if anything happened in the Kremlin yesterday – and, if anything did, where Anna is now.'

'Then he's our best hope. When can you see him?'

'It'll have to be by appointment. And that can't happen before tomorrow. Good thing the Soviets regard Sunday as a working day.'

'By tomorrow, Anna could have spent two days in the Lubianka.'

'So she could be having a tough time. But if everything you have told me about her is true, don't you think she'll be able to take it? Just remember that the Soviets require their accused to appear in court in apparently perfect health and unmarked.'

'Cheer me up. You do understand that no one can know that Anna is a British operative. What are you going to tell Beria?'

'If life were easy, wouldn't it be a damned bore? But I have some ideas.' He got up. 'I'll be in touch, just as soon as possible.'

'Shit!' Sprague remarked, having listened to what Clive had to say. 'What a fuck-up.'

'The fuck-up is your not being at the Berlin on Tuesday night.'

'For Christ's sake, Clive, she hadn't shown for three months. We had to determine that she wasn't going to play ball any more. Anyway, it was the Ambassador's decision. You know he never was happy about the Berlin set up. It was his decision that it should be terminated.'

'So now we may have lost her. In every way.'

'Well, old man, there does happen to be a war on. People are being done every day. Even beautiful people like your Anna.'

'Listen,' Clive said, 'shut up.'

He had been given a room at the Embassy, and to his surprise slept heavily. But then, he was exhausted, physically from the three days of endless travel, and emotionally by the thought of what might have happened to Anna, or still be happening to her.

When he awoke it was to a familiar sound, but one which belonged to London, not Moscow. He sat up, and his door opened. 'What the hell is an air-raid siren for?'

Sprague was fully dressed. 'The balloon has gone up.'

'Oh, my God! Anna?' Although what she could have to do with an air-raid siren he couldn't imagine.

'She may well have had something to do with it. The Germans have invaded. Planes are supposed to be heading this way now. You reckon they were just waiting for Stalin's death?'

Clive got out of bed and began to dress.

'You realize,' Sprague went on, 'that this puts the kybosh on any hope she may have had of claiming diplomatic immunity.'

Clive was getting his thoughts under control. 'Where is this invasion taking place?'

'Everywhere. Right along every border Russia has with Europe, the whole two thousand miles. Can you imagine the forces that must be involved?'

'But the Soviets have at least as many, haven't they?'

'Maybe. But they seem to have been taken completely by surprise. There appears to be absolute chaos out there. And there is total panic here.'

'What is London doing about it?'

'I imagine London is just waking up to it.'

'Do you think we'll chip in?'

'I doubt it. Winston regards the Soviets as thieves and murderers. He's said so, publicly. Anyway, it makes sense to let them and the Nazis slug it out. Whoever wins, if anyone actually does, will be too exhausted to come back at us for a while.'

'I have to make a phone call,' Clive said. But Andrews was unavailable.

'Mr Andrews,' Lavrenty Beria said. 'I'm afraid I can only spare you five minutes. I am sure you understand the situation.' He was a very tall man, who wore a pince-nez on the bridge of his big nose. The nose and the glasses were the only notable features in the large, bland face and the entirely bald head. But unlike all the members of staff Andrews had encountered on his way up to this office, he seemed to be entirely calm.

'I do,' Andrews said. 'Those bastards. Have they given any reason?'

'I understand Count von Schulenberg called on Comrade Molotov just before dawn this morning, and presented him with a long list of so-called Soviet outrages and broken promises, accompanied by a declaration of war.'

'What did Molotov do?'

'I believe he was as polite as diplomacy requires.'

'And the German Embassy?'

'The staff are receiving their passports now, and will be out of Russia this afternoon.'

'You are very civilised.'

Beria gave a brief smile. 'Not really. We wish the return of our Embassy staff from Berlin. Now, what did you want to see me about?'

'There are two matters, actually. Have you drawn any conclusions regarding the link between this German invasion and the assassination of Marshal Stalin on Friday afternoon?'

Beria's brows drew together, a formidable sight 'How do you know about that? No one knows about that.'

'It is my business to know about everything.'

'Well, you were misinformed. Marshal Stalin is alive and well and preparing to take command of our armed forces.'

'There's a relief,' Andrews said, not entirely truthfully. 'But there was an attempt on his life?'

'I really must discover the identity of your informant,' Beria remarked. 'Yes, Mr Andrews. There was an attempt. Fortunately, we were forewarned, and were able to prevent the assassin from gaining access to the marshal.'

'I congratulate you. What happened to the assassin?'

'She is now in the Lubianka, where she will remain until she is tried and executed. In our present circumstances, this may take a little while. However, it will be worth it, as what she will say in public will reveal the depths of perfidy to which the Hitlerite gangsters are prepared to go.'

'Absolutely. You mean she has made a full confession?'

'At the moment she is being a little stubborn. We have not even found out her true identity. She persists in calling herself by that ridiculous title, the Countess of Resistance. However, I am sure we will be able to persuade her to cooperate.' Another brief smile. 'We are good at that.'

'Oh, quite.'

'Besides, we have been provided with a dossier on her. It is not complete, and frankly, much of what it contains is simply unbelievable. Still, it is something to use in tripping her up when she starts to talk.'

'Would you like me to fill in the blanks?'

'You?'

'Her real name is Anna Fehrbach, and she is an Austrian by birth. For the past three years she has been employed by the Germans as an assassin. She has considerable skills. We know of at least seven murders she has carried out for the SD. And there have been others.'

'My God! That is what our informant claims. But I could not believe it. She is only a young girl.'

'Well, let's see. I believe that Queen Joanna I of Naples was only a teenager when she did her first husband. Not that she stopped there.'

'How do you know all this? About Fehrbach, I mean.'

'We also have a dossier on her. Far more complete than yours.'

'Why?'

'This is confidential. Just over a year ago she attempted to assassinate President Roosevelt.'

'I have never heard of this.'

'Is anyone going to hear about the attempt on Marshal Stalin, until you are ready to make it public? Fehrbach failed, but she did kill two of the President's bodyguards. She is top of the FBI's most-wanted list. But she got out of the country before she could be arrested, and disappeared. I have been tracking her for two years. We are actually in the process of preparing papers for a possible extradition. But now this has happened. We want her, Commissar Beria.'

'So do we, Mr Andrews. And we have her.'

'Her attempt on Roosevelt was before her attempt on Stalin. Don't you think we have a prior claim?'

'In a case like this, Mr Andrews, it is finders keepers. But thank you for your information. I am sure it will be most useful.'

'And that is your last word?'

'I am afraid so.'

'Is that because you are afraid of upsetting Comrade Chalyapov?'

Beria raised his eyebrows. 'Comrade Chalyapov has problems of his own. It is not overlooked by Marshal Stalin that he was responsible for introducing this woman into the Kremlin in the first place. So one could say that without a full confession from the Countess, he could well wind up in the Lubianka himself. But as I say, I regard that as his problem.'

'I have an idea that you do not like Comrade Chalyapov, Comrade Commissar.'

It was impossible to make out Beria's eyes behind the glasses, but his smile was bland. 'You are a perceptive man, Mr Andrews. But that has nothing to do with my decision to bring the Countess to trial. It is my business to uphold the law, and demonstrate the perfidy of the Nazi regime.'

'Ah, well. You win some, you lose some.' Andrews got up. 'Thanks for your time, anyway. And good luck with this war you've accumulated. Do you reckon you can win it?'

'We will defend our sacred motherland to the last drop of our blood.'

'I'm sure you will. And my information is that it may come to that. In modern wars, oil and machinery counts more than blood. Isn't it true that your air force, all nine thousand planes, is antiquated and no match for the Luftwaffe? And isn't it true that while you have a huge army you are very short of modern equipment, and especially transport?'

'This is not something I wish to discuss.'

'Pity. Ambassador Davies said to me this morning, when he heard I was seeing you this afternoon, "make it plain to Mr Beria that we want to help his country in any way we can, especially as regards materiel." Still '

'Mr Davies said that? You mean America would be prepared to help us? As she has been helping Britain for the past year?'

'Well, of course.' Andrews took a deep breath. 'I happen to know that there is a top-level delegation leaving the States today to come here and find out what you need. Mind you, there's going to be opposition. A lot of people over there hate your guts. But if the President were able to convince Congress that you were really prepared to accept our help in the spirit in which it is intended, and that in small matters of protocol you would be prepared to play ball, you know, the odd quid pro quo ... As for illustrating the perfidy of Nazi Germany, I don't think anyone can have any doubts about that, after this un- provoked attack.'

Beria studied him for several seconds. Then he said, 'I think that my people could prob- ably learn a lot from yours about the art of blackmail, Mr Andrews. I feel like a school- boy.' He picked up his telephone.

The young officer saluted. 'You are Mr An- drews.'

'Correct. And you are Captain Skorzy.'

'Yes, comrade. You have something for me?' Andrews held out the sheet of paper, and Skorzy studied it. 'You are to take possession of a prisoner in the female block.'

'Right first time.'

'This is very unusual.'

'The order is signed by Comrade Beria.'

'I am not disputing that, sir.' He pressed a bell. 'If you will come with me.'

Andrews followed him from the office into the hall. He had never liked prisons, and this was the most forbidding prison he had ever entered. They came to a door where an armed guard stood to attention, clicking his heels at the sight of the officer. Skorzy opened the door. 'This is the Women's Section,' he explained. 'Ah, Olga!' He greeted the slender, attractive, dark-haired young woman who was waiting for them.

'Comrade Captain!' Olga's eyes were hostile as she looked at Andrews.

'We have come for the woman Widerstand.'

Olga frowned. 'Come for her? You wish to take her?'

'That is correct.'

'There must be some mistake.'

'Explain.'

'You will have to see Colonel Tserchenka.'

'Then take us to her.'

Olga hesitated, then led them along a corridor. The odour was mainly disinfectant; the sounds were all feminine, if muted. Olga paused before a closed door, and knocked. 'Captain Skorzy to see you, Comrade Colonel. And...?' She glanced at Andrews.

'My name is Andrews, and I am from the United States Embassy.'

'Comrade Captain!' Ludmilla beamed at Skorzy. 'Isn't the news terrible? Those swine.' She looked at Andrews.

'They say they have come for the Countess,' Olga explained.

'What?' The good humour faded from Ludmilla's expression.

Skorzy presented the paper. 'The woman is to be released into the custody of Mr Andrews.'

333

Now Ludmilla scowled. 'Are you making a joke with me? This woman is a German spy and assassin. She is guilty of attempting to assassinate Premier Stalin.'

'Has she confessed to this?' Andrews asked.

'That is not relevant. She is not to leave this prison. I have the orders of Comrade Chalyapov himself.'

'This order is signed by Commissar Beria,' Skorzy pointed out.

'Give me that!' Ludmilla snatched the paper. 'This has to be a mistake.'

'You must take that up with Commissar Beria,' Andrews said. 'If you will look at the paper, it says "immediately".'

'I will have to telephone for confirmation.'

'Immediately,' Andrews repeated, getting a sliver of steel into his voice. 'I will see the Countess now.'

Ludmilla hesitated, looked at the paper again, then jerked her head. Olga stood by the door and the two men stepped into the corridor, following her.

'Who would you suppose has the higher authority?' Andrews asked.

'Commissar Beria commands the NKVD,' Skorzy said reverently.

'Those words are manna to my ears.'

Skorzy glanced at him, obviously not understanding what he meant.

Olga stopped before one of the several doors they had passed. 'Do you wish to look first? She is very pretty.'

'I wish the door opened,' Andrews said.

334

Olga shrugged and unlocked the door. It swung in, and Andrews gazed at Anna, who gazed at him. She had heard the sound and risen from the bare floor on which she had been sitting. She was naked, and for a moment he was quite entranced, but when she opened her mouth in consternation, he gave a quick shake of his head, and she closed it again.

'Countess,' he said. 'The end of a long road. These people have been good enough to find you for me.' He spoke Russian, and went closer to gaze at her. Her marvellous hair was damp as if recently washed, and despite the fact that it was a warm day she was shivering. He could see no bruises.

'What do you want?' she asked, her voice low.

'Why, you, my dear Countess. You have a date with a Federal Court.'

Anna looked at Skorzy, and then Olga, unable to believe what was happening.

'Where are her clothes?' Andrews demanded.

'We have them,' Olga said.

'Then take us to them.'

Olga bit her lip. 'It is along here.'

'Come along, Countess,' Andrews said.

Anna stepped past him and followed Olga, the two men behind.

'She is quite a beauty,' Skorzy remarked. 'Those legs ... what will you do to her?'

'Fill her full of electricity.'

'Ah. That would be better than a firing

335

squad.'

'Is there a difference?'

'Of course. Bullets would tear her body open. Perhaps even mark her face. Your way, her beauty will remain after death.'

'I guess you haven't seen too many people after they've been electrocuted,' Andrews suggested.

Olga opened another door and showed them into a room filled with clothes, some on hangers, some lying on tables.

'You mean everyone in this place is naked?' Andrews asked.

'It is good for prisoners to be naked,' Olga said, apparently making a serious comment. 'It places them at a psychological disadvantage, makes them less likely to rebel.'

'Interesting point.'

Olga began sifting through clothes. 'Do you remember what you were wearing, Countess?'

'Yes.' Anna's voice remained low. 'Those.'

'Oh, yes, of course. A pretty dress. And these.' She held up the cami-knickers. 'I have never seen underwear like this before. But there are no shoes.'

'We will manage without shoes,' Andrews said. 'Get dressed, Countess.'

Anna dressed herself, while Skorzy moved restlessly as he watched; it occurred to Andrews that it was actually more evocative to watch a woman dressing than undressing. 'Now,' he said. 'If you will take us out of this place, Captain, I have a car waiting.'

He looked at his watch; he had been here more than half an hour, and he had a distinct, if illogical, feeling that he and Anna were living on borrowed time. And there was Ludmilla, standing in the corridor outside the door of her office, like some latter-day Brunhilde ready for combat. 'I am instructed,' she announced, 'that you must not leave until after Comrade Chalyapov has come.' She had obviously been on the telephone.

'And we are instructed, by Commissar Beria, to leave immediately.'

'You will stay,' Ludmilla insisted, and drew her pistol.

Anna drew a sharp breath.

'Are you mad, comrade?' Skorzy asked. 'Would you defy Commissar Beria?'

'There is treachery here,' Ludmilla declared. 'Comrade Chalyapov will know what to do.'

Anna looked at Andrews, but he was looking at Skorzy, apparently having determined that the captain was the key to the situation. But Skorzy was looking totally uncertain as to what to do next. She herself had no clear idea of what was happening, or how it was happening. She was in fact only just recovering from the shock of seeing Andrews, so unexpectedly, and of being offered her freedom, equally unexpectedly. Her emotions were in a jumble, but of one thing she was quite certain: she was not going back into that cell to suffer the water torture again.

The outer door opened to admit Chalyapov, and then closed again with a clang. 'What is happening?' Chalyapov demanded.

'I told you on the phone, comrade,' Ludmilla said. 'These people are trying to take Widerstand away.'

Chalyapov looked at Andrews, who had arranged his features in a smile. 'Well, hello, comrade. Nice of you to drop by.'

Chalyapov looked at Skorzy, who had come to attention. 'I am acting on the orders of Commissar Beria, comrade.'

Chalyapov snorted, and pointed. 'This man is an American spy!'

'Is that an accusation, or a compliment?' Andrews asked.

'And clearly,' Chalyapov went on, 'he is acting for the Germans in attempting to regain possession of this bitch. Arrest him.'

'Commissar Beria...'

'I am in command here. Olga, take the Countess back to her cell. Ludmilla, if anyone attempts to prevent this order being carried out, shoot him.'

Andrews and Skorzy both stared at him in consternation. Olga touched Anna's arm. 'Come along, comrade.'

Anna acted with all the speed and pent-up fury that always hovered on the edge of her subconscious. Olga's hand was still on her arm. She half turned, seized Olga's arm in turn, exerting all her strength and exceptional timing, and threw the girl forward. Olga gave a shriek as she was propelled through the confined space to cannon into Chalyapov and

338

knock him against the wall. Ludmilla brought up her pistol, but Anna had not checked her movement, and as she released Olga's arm swung her left hand into Ludmilla's neck with bone-crunching force.

Ludmilla uttered no sound as she in turn fell against the wall, and slid down it to the floor. Skorzy had regained his nerve and was drawing his own pistol, but Chalyapov was quicker, producing a gun from inside his jacket and firing in the same instant. Skorzy gave a cry and went down. Chalyapov turned his gun on Andrews, his lips drawn back in a snarl, but Anna had now taken Ludmilla's gun from her inert fingers and fired in the same movement. The bullet struck Chalyapov in the middle of the chest, and he went down with a gasp.

'Holy Jesus Christ!' Andrews shouted.

Anna stood above Chalyapov. Blood was pouring from his chest, but he was still breathing, and stared at her. 'You...' He gasped. 'You are...'

'You can wait for me in hell,' Anna told him, and fired again.

'Holy Jesus Christ!' Andrews repeated.

Anna looked at Olga, who was trying to push herself along the wall, still sitting. 'Please ... I did not...'

Anna lowered the gun. 'You have a file on me,' she said. 'Fetch it.'

Olga licked her lips, then pushed herself up and went to the office. Anna followed her, still pointing the pistol.

Andrews knelt beside Ludmilla. 'My God! She's dead!'

'It will happen,' Anna said over her shoulder, watching Olga sifting through the filing cabinet.

Skorzy groaned, and Andrews knelt beside him in turn. 'How is it?'

Skorzy's hand was red where it was pressed to his tunic. 'I am hit.'

'Yeah. But you're lucky you're on our side. You'll live. Listen, these people were going to kill you, and they would have done had not the Countess intervened. Remember to tell Commissar Beria exactly what happened.' He stood up as Anna returned, the file tucked under her arm, Olga in front of her. 'We will leave now, comrade. See what you can do about the captain. Give us five minutes, and then call for help. Remember that what we have done is a result of direct orders from Commissar Beria.'

Olga looked at Anna, who smiled. 'Your life,' she said. 'My gift to Russia.'

They went outside. The wing was sound-proofed, and no one appeared to have heard the shots. The guards saluted. They went to the courtyard, where the car was waiting.

'The Embassy,' Andrews said, and sat beside Anna. His hands were shaking. He knew he was suffering from a certain amount of shock at the startling and uninhibited violence he had just witnessed, his feelings accentuated by his glimpse of the naked body of this utterly beautiful creature seated beside him, who now presented the picture of a docile and innocent, if slightly dishevelled, young woman.

But she was not entirely as cold as ice. 'Will they not send behind us?' she asked. Her voice was low, and the fingers holding the file were perfectly steady.

It was time to match her calm. 'No. For two reasons. One is that Beria, and I suspect Stalin himself, will not be sorry to see the back of Comrade Chalyapov. The other is that the last thing the Russians want to do right now is fall out with us. That file ... is it very important?'

'It is to me,' Anna said.

The marine sentry presented arms as Clive entered the Embassy. In the hall a male secretary was waiting for him. 'Mr Andrews is expecting you, Mr Bartley. First floor, door five.'

'Thank you.' Clive took the steps two at a time, was out of breath when he opened the door. Andrews stood before his desk. 'Where the hell have you been? I've been trying to get in touch with you for the last twelve hours.'

'I've been busy. I believe you know the Countess von Widerstand?'

Clive turned, his jaw dropping. Anna had been seated on a settee against the far wall, but was now standing. She wore a dressing gown, and her feet were bare. Her hair was loose, and unusually untidy. 'My God! How did you do it?'

'I used a method recommended by, if I remember correctly, Napoleon Bonaparte, who said, "the bigger the lie, the more chance there is of it being believed". Although I am going to have to do my damndest to make sure that at least part of it turns out to be true. I imagine you two would like to be alone for a few minutes.' He went to the door. 'Oh, please don't get agitated about her appearance. She is merely waiting for some clothes to be prepared for her. Her own were rather past their best.'

He closed the door, and Anna came forward. 'He is quite a man.'

Clive took her into his arms and kissed her. 'Are you all right?'

'Yes. Although it will be a long time before I feel like taking a cold shower again.'

'My God, to have you back But what's this about a few minutes?'

'They have to get me out of the country immediately.'

'I'll get you out of the country.'

Anna shook her head. 'They can arrange for me to get back to Germany. You cannot.'

'But Anna, you can't go back to Germany.'

'I must. You know I must.'

'You have not carried out Heydrich's command.' He frowned. 'You didn't assassinate Stalin, did you?'

'I never got near Stalin, Clive.'

'He won't believe that. Or he'll believe that you deliberately got yourself arrested so you wouldn't have to complete the assignment.'

342

'He will believe what I tell him, because I will prove that it is the truth.'

'I will never see you again.'

She kissed him. 'We will be together when this is over. Until then, there is always Antoinette's Boutique. But listen ... I would like my jewellery back.'

'How do I do that?'

'You give it to Joe. He will have it sent to his embassy in Berlin, and I can pick it up from there.'

'Hmm. This fellow Joe...'

'He saved my life, Clive. He is doing that now.' She gave a little gurgle of laughter. 'And you are jealous. He has never touched me. But listen, as it may be a little while before we can get together again, and we have fifteen minutes ... It has been so long.'

Andrews knocked and opened the door. 'The dressmaker is ready for you, Countess ... Oh! Ah!'

Anna rolled off Clive and the settee at the same moment, stood up, and put on her dressing gown.

'I sure am sorry,' Andrews said. 'I didn't mean to interrupt...'

'Your timing was perfection,' Anna told him, and went to the door.

'It's the next room,' Andrews said.

She nodded, and the door closed.

Clive was still panting. Andrews sat behind his desk. 'Do you know,' he remarked, 'only a few hours ago I saw that girl kill two people,

343

just like that.' He snapped his fingers.

Clive got up and began to dress. 'So now you know all her secrets.'

'Does anyone know *all* her secrets?'

'Good point. But you're still going to help her?'

'God, yes. Not helping Anna, not preserving Anna, is unthinkable. Just so long as she's on our side. You're sure about that?'

Clive knotted his tie. 'I'm sure. Just remember, old boy, that you are in possession of an especially important secret. It has to remain that way. At least until the war is over.'

'And you guys have won it. You sure about *that*?'

Clive grinned. 'Aren't you?' He held out his hand. 'You take good care of my little girl.'

'I'll contact you when the delivery has been made.' It was Andrews' turn to grin. 'If I'm still alive.'

'Anna?' Reinhard Heydrich got up and came round his desk.

'Heil Hitler!'

'Heil! They told me you had been arrested by the NKVD.'

'That is correct, sir.'

Heydrich embraced her 'My dear girl. My dear, dear girl. But how are you here?'

'I was freed by the intervention of an officer in the American Embassy in Moscow.'

'An American got you out of the Lubianka? But how? And why? Sit down.' Anna sat before the desk, and he returned behind it.

'So?'

'He was my lover, sir.'

'Chalyapov was supposed to be your lover.'

'Yes sir. He was. But this was a genuine attachment. I did not let it interfere with my mission.'

'I see. You are not supposed to form genuine attachments. Would this be the man you were meeting clandestinely in the Hotel Berlin?'

'You knew of that, sir?'

'Groener suspected it. He had some information which he did not specify. I dismissed it as speculation. Now it seems I owe him an apology. So, you had an illegal affair with an itinerant American...'

'I am sorry, sir. I have my passions. And if I had not had that affair, I would not be here now.'

'But you failed in your mission. There has been no indication that Marshal Stalin is dead.'

'No, sir. Marshal Stalin is alive. I was prevented from completing my mission.'

'Is that not the excuse of every failure? Oh, I do not suppose it is a vital matter. This war with Russia was planned six months ago. The date had to be postponed because of that Balkan imbroglio, but it was going to happen whether or not you succeeded. On the other hand, the decision that Stalin should be eliminated immediately before the commencement of hostilities was taken at the highest level. I am going to have to report your failure to the Fuehrer, and I cannot say what his reaction will be.'

He paused to stare at her, but Anna's face remained as calm as her voice. 'I can prove that I was betrayed, Herr General. And by whom.'

'Then you had better do so.'

'Yes sir.' Anna opened her handbag and laid the dossier on his desk. 'This I secured from the files of the Lubianka Prison before leaving. The information was supplied to them by Chalyapov, after he had received it from the Gestapo office in our Moscow Embassy.'

Heydrich regarded her for several moments, then looked at the sheets of paper. 'It seems to outline your intentions, and your background, very convincingly. But to say it came from the Gestapo Office ... there is no proof of that.'

'If you will read it again, Herr General, you will see that it seeks to prove that I am an assassin by relating the facts of that incident in Prague last year. As you will recall, sir, only four people know those facts: yourself, Herr Feutlanger, myself ... and Herr Meissenbach. At your command, the business was hushed up as regards anyone else.'

Heydrich read the paper again, then raised his head. 'You are accusing both Groener and Meissenbach of betraying you? Betraying the Reich? That is incredible. Why should they do something like that?'

'Herr Groener, because he hated and distrusted me from the moment I arrived in

Moscow. Herr Meissenbach, because he wished to be my lover and became very angry when I rejected him. As you will see there, the traitor, or traitors, outlined exactly what my instructions were, and these were known only to you and me. They must have opened your last letter to me.'

Heydrich stroked his chin. 'This is a very serious matter. To think that two such men would betray the Reich to avenge themselves on a woman ... I will report the entire incident to General Himmler.'

'And what will happen then, sir?'

'They will be tried, and on the evidence you have provided, they will be executed.'

'Ah, with respect, sir...'

'Don't you want them to be executed?'

Anna smiled. 'I would prefer them to be sent to a concentration camp, Herr General. That way, with your permission, I can go and visit them, from time to time.'

Epilogue

'And were they imprisoned?' I asked.

'Oh, yes,' the Countess said.

'Did you visit them?'

'Once. I did not know anything about concentration camps, then. I don't think many people in Germany did, whatever the rumours and the suspicions. It was safer not to speak of it. But I found that visit nauseating. I certainly had no desire to repeat it.'

'What happened to Greta?'

'She went to Ravensbruek. In the Nazi philosophy, the wife of a traitor was, by definition, a traitor herself.'

'Did you feel guilty about that? I mean, she never actually harmed you.'

'I felt guilty when I heard that she had been arrested. But under questioning she admitted that her husband had told her what he was going to do, and she was all in favour of it. That is no way to make friends,' Anna said, somewhat ingenuously. 'However, unfortunately, she did not stay in prison long. She had money, and she had friends in high places.'

'Don't tell me you met her again?'

'I met her again.'

I waited, but she did not elaborate. 'And so you

348

were back in the clutches of Heydrich.'

'Yes. But not for very long. Within a year of my return from Moscow, Heydrich was dead.'

'My God, yes! I'd forgotten about that. I don't suppose you had anything to do with that?'

Anna Fehrbach stared at me, and I could feel the heat in my cheeks. 'I should have known better than to ask. Will you tell me about it?'

'As I am telling you about everything else.'

'But before then, Washington. Did you ever meet Joe again?'

'Joe was my reason for going to America, Christopher.' She smiled enchantingly. 'I think you could say that I got to know him rather well. After all, did he not save my life?'